Perfect Revenge

JANE BLYTHE

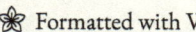

Acknowledgments

I'd like to thank everyone who played a part in bringing this story to life. Particularly my mom who is always there to share her thoughts and opinions with me. My wonderful cover designer Letitia who did an amazing job with this stunning cover. My fabulous editor Lisa for all the hard work she puts into polishing my work. My awesome team, Sophie, Robyn, and Clayr, without your help I'd never be able to run my street team. And my fantastic street team members who help share my books with every share, comment, and like!

And of course a big thank you to all of you, my readers! Without you I wouldn't be living my dreams of sharing the stories in my head with the world!

CHAPTER

One

December 24th
1:03 A.M.

This was the first mission he would go out on where he wasn't the good guy.

He was the villain of this story.

An unsanctioned op that proved to all of them that they had indeed become the monsters they'd long feared they were.

Yet as Steel led his team down a quiet suburban street, he knew there were no forces on earth strong enough to stop him.

While he did not enjoy being placed in this position, he was responsible for his men. He was the one who had led them like lambs to the slaughter, without doing his due diligence to ensure that what sounded too good to be true wasn't just a hoax.

It was because of him that the five men who followed him with such trust had been changed in ways they never would have expected. Therefore, Steel knew he would do whatever it took to right his wrongs and see if there was a way to save his team, the men he considered his brothers, his family.

Even crossing a line there would be no coming back from.

Shouldering the blame for what they were about to do was something he would never complain about. His men deserved a chance to try to reclaim somewhat normal lives, and if this was what he had to do to achieve that for them, he would do it with a clear conscience.

Mostly clear conscience.

Because deep down inside, he didn't have a single doubt that this was wrong. It could probably even be considered evil.

But desperate times called for desperate measures.

Like the well-oiled machine that they were, there was no need to communicate out loud for them to know they were on the same page. Some people considered their ability to almost read one another's minds to be extraordinary.

They wouldn't be wrong.

It wasn't like he heard the voices of his teammates in his mind, it was more that his intuition had been so deeply honed that he somehow knew what they were going to say or do before they did it.

Definitely a skill that came in handy for ops that were delicate in nature. Like the one he and his team would be enacting in just a couple of minutes.

Thunder brought the van to a stop outside an ordinary-looking house. It was a two-story, colonial-style, with a simple but neat garden. In the summer, Steel was sure there would be a riot of color in the garden beds that lined the front of the house, and the two large trees in the yard would look stunning in all their autumnal glory.

Now a blanket of snow covered the ground, smothering all that beauty. Or rather replacing it with something harsher, but in his mind still carrying a beauty of its own.

Unlike every other house on the block, there was not a single Christmas light strung up around the porch, no wreath hanging on the front door, and no decorations filling up the yard. It was like this house existed in another universe, one stripped of the joy and peace people were supposed to feel at this time of year.

The barren emptiness the quiet house showed left him with a twinge of guilt in a place deep inside of him. As though he were about to break something that was already broken.

For some reason, that felt ... wrong somehow.

Outside of his team, Steel didn't allow himself to feel anything for anyone.

Couldn't feel anything anymore.

At least not in the normal way most people experienced emotions.

As part of Prey Security's Delta Team, he respected the hell out of his boss Eagle Oswald. The man had given them a chance to rebuild their lives, and Steel knew the other man would be both disappointed and furious with what they were doing tonight. Prey was a family, and Delta Team would do anything to protect any member of that family in any way they could. However, the only one of them he truly felt any sense of love toward was Beth Lindon. That woman had been through hell, and Steel and any one of his men would move heaven and earth for her.

The van rolled to a stop, and they all paused.

Dragon, Blade, and Lion used their enhanced senses, and when the three men nodded to give him the all-clear, he slid the door open and climbed out into the night.

Steel had no doubt that what they were about to do would be captured on any number of video doorbells, which was exactly why they'd brought a handy little device along with them. It would jam all Wi-Fi signals the area around the direct perimeter of the house they were targeting, allowing them to complete their mission unseen.

Handling the device was Thunder's job, and he felt no need to micromanage the man. His team was as good as they were because they all acted with autonomy. While he was the team leader, he trusted his men implicitly, which couldn't be explained to anyone outside of them.

When you were dragged kicking and screaming into hell, you learned to trust those who suffered alongside you.

Without making a sound, the six of them crossed the small brick path leading to the porch. The lack of twinkling fairy lights or anything else Christmassy, and the gloominess of the comparison between this house and the others surrounding it, added to the darkness that lived inside him.

Led to a familiarity he couldn't afford.

Picking the lock was much easier than it should be, and he felt a small pang of pity for the naïve person inside who believed they were keeping bad guys out.

Inside the house was as undecorated for Christmas as the outside. It was obvious that the occupant did not feel the Christmas spirit that everybody else seemed to rave about as soon as Thanksgiving dinner was eaten. The house was, however, a riot of color screaming at him from every direction. Bright pink and purple walls, vivid blue floorboards, splashes of yellows, reds, and greens dotted about in throw pillows, blankets, and an eclectic mix of armchairs and chairs sitting around a dining room table.

It was like stepping inside a rainbow.

The open concept of the house's ground floor made clearing it easy, and when Dragon, Blade, and Lion once again nodded to tell him every-thing was as they'd expected, Steel headed for the stairs.

This was going to be easy.

Almost too easy.

Maybe he'd feel a little better about this if their target had even a chance to fight back a little.

But there was no way anyone could take on the six of them and win. Not even the five of them, because Thunder would be remaining down-stairs, ready to move the van if anything changed and they needed to take another route out. Not that Steel was expecting it.

Upstairs, four doors were grouped around an open foyer. Three were open, indicating a bathroom and two guest bedrooms, but the fourth was closed.

It was behind that closed door that lay the answer to all their problems.

All their revenge.

Fair or not, they were getting justice for what had been done to them, no matter how they had to do it.

Creeping down the hall, Steel eased open the door in case the person inside the room was a light sleeper, but he may as well have not bothered.

Sprawled in the center of a king-size canopy bed, wearing a pair of bright pink unicorn pajamas, and partially covered by a dove gray sheet, and snoring softly, was their target.

Like taking candy from a baby, Steel crossed the room to stand on one side of the bed, Voodoo on the other, and Blade at the end of the bed, while Dragon and Lion waited by the door. None of them were expecting any problems, but better safe than sorry.

Waiting until Voodoo held up the syringe that would make transporting their captive easier, once he saw it, Steel reached over and brushed a lock of dark red hair off the sleeping woman's face.

Creamy soft skin dotted with freckles, red lashes fanned out, a small smile on her cherub lips, the last smile Rose Gardner would ever give. However this played out, the woman would have little to smile about in the coming days and weeks.

Closing his fingers around her slim neck, he felt fear flooding her system as his touch roused her from sleep before her eyes snapped open in terror.

Forest green eyes stared up at him, cloaked in sleep for a moment longer before reality sank in and she began to thrash in his hold. For a tiny thing who couldn't be more than five-foot-two, over a foot shorter than his six-foot-four frame, she fought like a wildcat, and he gave her a molecule of respect for it.

Pinning her arms easily, he nodded at Voodoo, who leaned in and pierced the bare skin on the woman's bicep, injecting her with the sedatives.

"Lights out, little ladybug," he murmured as the woman put up a valiant fight against the drugs flooding her system.

In the end, it did no good.

Unconsciousness stole her away, and Steel gathered her into his arms, a tiny flicker of guilt lighting in his chest at the knowledge that he had become this woman's bogeyman.

Not enough to stop him, though.

He carried her down the stairs and out into the cold, binding her wrists and ankles once he had her in the van. Regret had no place on this mission. And as Thunder started the engine and they took off down the street, he knew that for their captive, hope would have no place where they were taking her either.

~

December 24th
   7:54 P.M.

The soft clink of a lock nudged her awake.

For a second, Rose thought she was a child again. Locked in that hole in the ground that was supposed to build character.

Build character?

Yeah, right.

All it built was major distrust in every person in existence, a whole lot of trauma, and a deep-seated rebellion that no number of beatings could ever dislodge.

Somewhat fearfully, she cracked open her eyes to be met with only darkness, when she'd been so sure she was going to find the tightly packed dirt walls of the old well surrounding her on all sides, and the sticky, muddy bottom rank with urine and feces.

Both words she'd known despite being six years old the first time she'd been put in there to, quote, "build character". Poo and pee weren't acceptable words in her family. Too babyish, and God forbid anyone be allowed to be a child when they were quite literally a child.

Today, however, there was no mud, no stench. If anything, the room she was in actually smelled too clean. Like it had very recently been bleached from top to bottom.

Why would someone bleach a room from top to bottom?

There was no additional fragrance mixed with the bleach, so she wasn't in a bathroom someone had recently cleaned. Not that she could think up a logical reason why she would be in a bathroom.

Not that she could think up a logical reason why she should be anywhere that wasn't her bed.

Gasping, Rose jerked up.

The man.

Standing beside her bed.

She'd been kidnapped.

It was a clear indication that she was messed up inside because her first reaction wasn't terror, it was anger. After how long she'd spent fighting to get away from her family's clutches and forge her own path in life, she sure as hell was not going to let anyone mess with that.

If the Bedroom Man thought he'd captured himself a wilting little flower, then he was about to find out he was sorely mistaken. She was a rose, and she came with thorns. Thorns she wouldn't hesitate to use any way she could to make him sorry he'd ever chosen her house to break into.

Fear did hum in the background, though, particularly as she looked down her body to check if she was still wearing clothing.

Thank goodness she was.

Despite the room she was in being one step away from pitch black, Rose could feel the soft flannelette material brushing against her skin as she moved. Her favorite pair of bright pink unicorn pajamas was still in place. So she likely hadn't been raped.

Relief made her lightheaded for a moment, or maybe it was whatever drugs she'd been injected with against her will.

Definitely the drugs, she decided as she placed her palms on the ground, knowing she needed to check out her surroundings to gather as much intel as she could if she wanted a chance at surviving whatever fresh hell Mr. Bedroom Man had conjured up for her.

Damn. She was so tired of people wanting to hurt her.

Why couldn't she just be left alone to live out her life in the way she chose?

And why the hell did bad stuff always happen to her at Christmastime? It was no wonder she despised the holiday. Joy and peace? Nah, pain and suffering, that was her experience with Christmas. It was why she refused to celebrate the overly commercialized holiday. She'd even been known to issue the famous Charles Dickens quote when someone wished her a merry Christmas.

Bah humbug.

Beneath her palms was something hard and rough. Concrete. As her eyes adjusted slightly to the oppressive dark, she could just make out four walls and a door in the wall furthest from where she'd been put.

It must have been the door locking that roused her from unconsciousness.

For a moment, Rose almost wanted to laugh. If leaving her in a concrete cell without any light and no furniture was the best her abductor could do, he was going to have a hard time breaking her.

Torture was as natural a part of her childhood as cartoons were to most kids.

Not that anyone in her family would ever call it torture. Nope, to them it was merely character building. Or at least trying to mold her character into what they thought it should be.

The joke was on them because she'd spent her life doing the opposite of what was wanted of her.

Same thing she'd do now.

Pushing herself up, Rose hated that she had to throw out a hand to catch the wall so she didn't crumble right back down again. Damn drugs were making her woozy, and she hated that feeling. Medication was not permitted when she was a child. Pain was to be toughed out as a character-building exercise, and unless you were close to dying, antibiotics were also prohibited. There was no cough syrup if she caught a cold, just a cocktail of vitamins that were supposed to help her develop into the best version of herself she could be.

Sorry, Mr. Bedroom Man, but if you think I'm going to sob and cower at your feet, you took the wrong girl.

Knowing her determination to do the opposite of what anyone expected of her—something that had been finely honed throughout her twenty-three years on this earth—was going to drive her captor crazy, made her smile as she started her search of her new home. If she was given some light later, she'd do a more thorough one, but the best time to start collecting intel was now.

Waiting could get her killed.

Or hurt.

While she could endure any amount of pain, practice definitely made perfect with that particular skill, Rose had spent her life craving the opposite.

Tenderness, affection, warmth, care ... love.

Everything she wanted and everything she'd never had.

Although she craved every one of those things, she did her best to avoid them. Allowing anyone to get close enough to feel anything for her was just asking to get hurt. Having someone love her and then yank that love away, that would leave real scars behind.

Real scars?

An almost hysterical laugh burst out of her at her stupid thoughts.

What do you call the massive physical and psychological scars you already have? They're not real enough for you? You need more?

Shaking her head at her internal dialogue, Rose shoved away any thought from her mind that wasn't pertinent to her mission. Trying to find any weaknesses that could be exploited to get her the hell out of this windowless basement cell and back to her life. It was lonely, but it was hers. Even if she wasn't doing anything she truly loved, she was making her own choices and that meant everything to her.

So exploration time it was.

Making her way cautiously around the room, she almost lost her balance when her foot plunged into a hole in the ground. Her toilet, she quickly deduced. Another almost hysterical laugh fell from her lips. If they thought having to do her business in a hole in the ground was going to break her, she'd love to tell them how she had to stand in her own waste at six years old in what was supposed to be a lesson to teach her that she controlled her mind, it didn't control her.

Ditto the dark. That couldn't break her. Darkness had been her friend as a kid because at least when she was locked in the dark, whether it be in a well, a closet, or her bedroom, it meant she was alone and nobody was going to hurt her.

The concrete floor would be her bed, but since she'd grown up sleeping on a hard wooden bed with no mattress and no pillow, just a thin blanket for warmth, she could sleep absolutely anywhere. That childhood room had contained just her bed and a dresser for her clothes, but no toys because she was supposed to be honing her mind, not wasting time playing silly games.

It was a good thing she was content to sit in the dark and enjoy the peace and quiet.

Sucks to be you, Mr. Bedroom Man, because none of this is going to break me.

Rose was vaguely aware she was sounding more than a little psycho herself, but she didn't care. Just because she'd fought hard to break away from her psycho family didn't mean that a little of their insanity hadn't rubbed off on her.

It was nothing to be ashamed of.

As her fingers found the smooth steel of the door, she noticed something else. Something she would have missed if she weren't trying to be as thorough as the dark allowed her to be.

Up in the corner was a tiny red dot.

A camera.

He was watching her. Bet he'd been expecting sobbing and screaming, begging and pleading. It filled her with immense joy to know she hadn't provided that for him, and she wiggled her fingers at the camera, hoping it would capture her wave.

Welcome to my particular brand of crazy, Mr. Bedroom Man. I hope I ruin every single one of your plans for me.

CHAPTER

Two

December 24th
8:13 P.M.

"What the hell? Did she just wave at us?" Steel demanded as he and the rest of his team watched the little ladybug explore her new home.

The journey back to their mansion was uneventful. The little ladybug slept peacefully throughout it, and since she was unconscious, he hadn't bothered keeping her bound once they got her on the plane. Instead, he'd buckled her into the seat beside him, put in some earbuds, and gotten some sleep.

Well, that was what he was claiming anyway.

What he would swear to if anyone asked.

But in reality, he was frozen in place because the unconscious woman's body had listed sideways slightly to rest against him. While he knew it was nothing more than his imagination, he would have sworn she'd sighed contentedly as her head nestled against his shoulder.

When they got back to their remote Gothic estate, he'd quickly taken the young woman down to the cells they had in the basement. Briefly, he'd considered stripping her of her clothing, but the sudden need to get away from her had him simply setting her down on the hard concrete floor and leaving.

According to the guys who were gathered around the kitchen table watching the feed from the camera in Rose Gardner's cell on a tablet, she regained consciousness as soon as he closed and locked the door behind him.

By the time he made it upstairs to join them, the little ladybug had been pushing to her feet. He'd expected to see hysterics. To hear her sob as terror overwhelmed her, begging and pleading for mercy, to be set free, the word why to be screamed into the empty cell.

Instead, the redhead had done none of that.

She had merely proceeded to make her way around her cell in a manner more methodical than he would have given her credit for if he hadn't seen it with his own two eyes. She hadn't even seemed fazed when one of her feet fell into the hole in the ground that would serve as her toilet.

Craziest thing was, she'd actually giggled a couple of times as though this whole thing amused her in some sick sort of way.

"Looks like she did," Voodoo replied in an almost amused tone, and Steel threw him a glare.

There was nothing funny about this.

What good was a prisoner if they weren't afraid? How were they supposed to work with that?

"She'll break soon," he said confidently, his hands gripping his coffee mug a little too tightly, and he reined it in. The last thing he needed was to crack the mug and have to clean up the mess.

"Yeah?" Thunder asked, somewhat doubtfully as they all watched the woman make her way to one of the corners of the room, carefully sit herself down, cross her ankles, and then fold her hands in her lap as she tilted her head back to rest against the wall.

"Did we kidnap a psychopath?" Blade asked.

"She's not a psychopath. If she were, our intel would have indicated it. She edits romance novels for a living," he added as though that were the deciding factor. There was no way the woman could spend her days reading about happy ever afters and couples in love having sex if she were some sort of psychopath.

"You know who her family is," Dragon reminded them all.

They did know who her family was, and unfortunately for Rose Gardner, it was why she was currently sitting in one of their prison cells, apparently taking a nap.

"So what are we going to do with her now that we have her?" Lion asked.

Of all of them, Lion had been the most against this plan. Or at least the most reluctant, since they all knew this could be their one and only way to get to the person responsible for what had been done to them.

Although he knew that, understood it, Lion was the only one of them who had been forced to leave someone behind after their lives were forever changed. The rest of them had families, sure. But not the kind of families whose hearts would be broken when contact was cut off.

For all intents and purposes, the men of Delta Team were dead.

There were no death certificates lying around, no fake graves sitting empty with their names on the tombstones, but when they joined Prey and moved out to this house, they had dropped off the face of the earth as far as anyone outside of Prey was concerned.

It was the way it had to be, and they all accepted that.

All except Lion, who still longed for the impossible, to find a way to claim the life he'd left behind.

A glance at Dragon, whose lips were pulled into a tight line, told him that wasn't exactly true. A favor for a friend, well six of them, the Charleston Holloway brothers of Charlie Team, had changed something in Dragon.

It had also cost him something.

Something the man wasn't likely to get back.

"We're going to do what we planned to do," Steel said firmly. As the team leader, it was his job to keep his men focused on their goals. Life might not be fair for Rose Gardner, she was going to pay for sins she'd likely never committed, but if they wanted their revenge, he didn't see another way.

"Even if she looks bored rather than scared right now?" Blade asked.

"Then we figure out what it takes to make her scared," he answered simply.

They weren't complete monsters. He intended to do whatever it took to make the woman break ... within reason. The little ladybug wasn't who they were after, she was merely a means to an end, a connection they would use to get to the man they wanted. They were all ninety percent sure Rose had nothing to do with what had been done to them, she was too young for a start, only twenty-three, which would have made her still a minor back when their lives were forever altered.

Treating her like they would any other prisoner was off the table, he wouldn't slice her open, wouldn't cut off body parts, wouldn't send electrical currents flowing through her body until she passed out from the agony.

But he would break her.

Would find a crack and exploit it.

His men were counting on him, and he wasn't going to let them down.

Never again.

"Everyone is afraid of something," he reminded his men. The little ladybug wasn't infallible, even if that was the impression she was giving off right now. Scrutinizing the tablet as closely as he could, he noted that her muscles did actually appear to be relaxed. She wasn't faking because she knew she was being watched.

What the hell did that mean?

Steel hated that they hadn't been able to dig up more intel on the Gardner family despite all the resources at their fingertips. Other than a birth certificate telling him Rose was born on October 30th, twenty-three years ago, there were no other records on her until she popped back up on her eighteenth birthday. Homeschooled, living with her family on a small farm deep in the Appalachian Mountains, there was no way to ascertain what her life had been like for the first eighteen years, and he didn't like that.

When she resurfaced five years ago, she started an editing business, and despite her young age, she had clients lining up to use her services and a stellar five-star reputation. Tracking her online movements told them she rarely left her house other than to go for her daily runs, she worked, she watched Netflix, she did all her shopping online and never posted anything remotely personal on her social media accounts, they were one hundred percent business-related.

What makes you tick, little ladybug?

"We talked about limits before we did this, but we also assumed she was going to wake up terrified out of her mind," Thunder said. "What exactly is your plan to find out what she's afraid of?"

"I need to go in there," he said slowly. "It's one thing for her to put on a façade when she's alone, not scared of what we're going to do to her. It'll be another for her to keep up that charade when she's face-to-face with me."

At least Steel hoped that was the case.

Because if it wasn't, they wouldn't get what they wanted out of this, and instead, would have just dragged another person down into their own personal hell.

"We'll give her a couple of hours to stew, then I'll flip on the lights and go in. Chances are, a couple of minutes with her will have her the sobbing, hysterical mess we anticipated picking up. Don't worry, the little ladybug will soon be screaming for us, and then we'll use her exactly the way we intended."

Despite his talk of façades and charades, as Steel pushed away from the table and set about cooking some dinner, he couldn't help but feel like he was the one pretending. What the hell had they gotten themselves into?

~

December 24th
    11:26 P.M.

Because she just might be a little more psycho than she'd ever realized, Rose had actually fallen asleep sitting on the cold concrete, waking only when she heard the snick of the door as it closed.

Years of knowing that being caught asleep left you vulnerable to attack, she slept with a hair-trigger alertness. The slightest sound usually had her snapping awake, which was why it was so irritating that Mr. Bedroom Man had gotten into her room without her waking.

She'd gotten complacent. Felt safe there. Hadn't thought she needed to be on high alert.

Now she knew better.

After spending so many years believing she had escaped her hellish family without being warped by their insanity, well major trust issues aside anyway, it seemed she had been sorely mistaken. They had managed to paint her with their crazy brush, because along with the icy cold anger, was curiosity, a desire to solve a puzzle that had been presented to her.

Well, there was a small undercurrent of fear too, but it mostly stemmed from the fact that she had no idea what this man wanted from her, if he had targeted her specifically, or if he'd picked a house at random and she had been unlucky enough to be inside it. Without answers, she didn't know what to expect, but once she understood the ground rules, she would know how best to work with this situation.

There was no doubt in her mind that Mr. Bedroom Man was currently in her little cell, but he hadn't said anything yet and had made no move to touch her or hurt her. If he tried touching her, she would do her best to defend herself. It wouldn't work, of course, it never did, but she was no wilting little flower. She was a rose, and he was about to see how sharp her thorns could be.

Opening her eyes, she saw the shadowy figure standing by the door. She'd chosen one of the two corners furthest away from the door on purpose, it gave her a couple of extra seconds and sometimes that made all the difference.

Since she'd gotten the barest glimpse of the man in her bedroom when he abducted her before he was holding her down and she was injected with something, she was surprised to see his size. He wasn't just bigger than her, he was huge. Looked like he had at least a foot of height on her, and he had to outweigh her by at least a hundred pounds. Damn her genes which made it difficult to bulk up no matter what she ate. It had always been something she liked because it helped with her gymnastics, but now she wished she had another hundred pounds to even things out.

As though seeing, or maybe sensing her eyes on him, his head nodded.

At first, Rose thought that was directed at her, an acknowledgment that he knew she was awake. But as soon as he nodded, the room was suddenly flooded with light.

It had been a while since she'd been forced to play this game. Ensconced in darkness only to have her sadistic family suddenly switch on the light because they knew it sent shafts of pain shooting right through your eyes.

"Very amateurish," she murmured, feeling the man's surprise since she couldn't see him as she'd been forced to scrunch her eyelids closed to protect her vision. As well as using what she would consider to be baby tactics, he'd also tipped his hand. Now she knew he wasn't alone, there was at least one other man—or woman—here, because Mr. Bedroom Man hadn't turned on the lights.

A hint of a memory tickled the back of her mind, but she didn't have time to hold onto it right now.

"What the hell is up with you?" the man muttered, she assumed more to himself than to her, but nonetheless she heard him and chuckled.

"Trust me, a question I've asked myself many times over the years," she assured him. She had never realized how messed up her family had left her. Oh well, seemed their personal brand of crazy was only going to help her now.

Easing open her eyes, she found Mr. Bedroom Man still standing by the door. Since he hadn't moved and was watching her like she was some kind of newly discovered specimen, she took the time to study him back.

Dressed in black from head to foot, black boots, black jean-clad tree trunk-like legs, a black long-sleeve T-shirt that stretched across a broad chest, black gloves, and a black balaclava that allowed her to see nothing more than his eyes. If he was trying to look like the bogeyman, he was doing a pretty good job of it.

For anyone else at least.

Anyone normal.

"I thought the bogeyman wore blue coveralls and a white Halloween mask," she told him. "Oh, and he's kind of addicted to his knife."

"What the hell are you talking about?" the man before her growled.

"Not a horror movie fan then? Michael Myers, you know, from the Halloween franchise. He was the bogeyman. I presume that's the vibe you're going for. Just thought you should know you didn't get it quite right. Maybe you'll do better next time."

A growl was his response, and she offered him a smile. This was not what he'd expected when he came in. Too bad for him, if you played with toys that were already broken, you didn't get the fun of breaking them yourself.

"Are we going to do introductions, explanations maybe?" she prompted. Rose had no time for this silliness. The man had to get to the point and tell her what he wanted from her. Once she knew, she could start figuring out a way to try to get herself out of here or die trying.

"You're not what I was expecting," he grumbled.

"Yeah, well suck it up, because you weren't how I was expecting my day to go either."

Another growl, and he took what Rose assumed was supposed to be an intimidating step toward her. If she hadn't spent her entire life being intimidated, it would probably work too. Not only was he huge, but he had an air of danger about him that she was just too experienced to worry about.

This man could torture her, but it wouldn't be anything she hadn't survived before. He could kill her if he wanted, but at least then there would be no chance anyone else could ever hurt her, so she couldn't be too angry about that.

"You have something that I want," the man snarled. There was a tiny tremor in his voice as he said that, and she knew whatever he was after was personal to him.

"I really doubt that. I don't get out much, and my job is as a romance book editor." She actually laughed because he was beating around the bush, like this was some sort of game when it was clear it was anything but. Men. They were dramatic, and they had the gall to claim that women were the more emotional sex.

Her laughter set him off, and he moved quicker than she'd been expecting.

His hand clamped around her neck, dragging her to her feet and shoving her up against the wall so her toes barely touched the floor. The grip was tight enough to make it difficult to breathe, but not enough to cut off her air supply. She was guessing he also wouldn't like it if she told him she knew he was holding back, taking care to not actually hurt her.

Sweet.

"Think this is funny, little ladybug?"

"Actually no, not at all. I do, however, think that nickname is ridiculous."

Rose would have sworn he smirked beneath the mask. "You're as close as we're going to get to your brother, the only chance we have of drawing him out when he learns baby sister is in danger."

If his hand hadn't been around her neck, that definitely would have made her laugh. This man was dreaming if he thought that Ridge cared about anyone but himself.

"You're going to stay here until you crack, and then you're going to bring your brother right to my doorstep." Mr. Bedroom Man lifted a hand, trailed a gloved finger down her cheek, then his thumb pressed bruisingly against her bottom lip.

It was definitely a bad sign that the rough touch had a spark of arousal lighting inside her.

Yep, they totally messed you up, Rose.

Broke you in ways you didn't even know.

Now is not the time to be getting the hots for Mr. Bedroom Man, you know you're going to kill him if given half a chance.

"Your brother has a penchant for playing God, destroying lives."

Tell me about it, Mr. Bedroom Man, tell me about it.

"You, little ladybug, are going to pay the price for your brother's sins."

Story of my life.

"You think you'll still be laughing by the time I'm done with you, little girl?" Mr. Bedroom Man gave a derisive chuckle. "You don't know the first thing about what I'm capable of, or what it's like to pray for the sweet relief of a death that never comes."

I really wish that were true.

Problem for you, Mr. Bedroom Man, is I already know I can survive anything you throw at me. I've been surviving since I was in diapers.

CHAPTER
Three

December 25th
12:38 P.M.

So much for Christmas lunch.

It wasn't like Steel had expected his team, his family, to be chirpy and chatty, full of laughter and the joy of the season, they never were, not even on Christmas Day. But he hadn't expected the mood to be this somber.

They had all agreed that once they finally managed to procure the name of the person at the head of the program they had unwittingly signed up for, they would do whatever it took to get to them.

When that intel led them to a lone family member, once again, they had all agreed that they would use that family member, a much younger sister, to lure out the man who was the very definition of crazy scientist.

Ridge Gardner wanted to advance human physiology and create a new race. Stronger, faster, smarter, and better senses than the old one. He wanted to be the king of that new race, to rule over it with an iron fist.

Delusions of grandeur aside, the man had gotten his dreams off the ground. He and the five men sitting around the table with him were living, breathing proof of that.

Superior strength, superior sense of smell, hearing, and vision, superior speed, and an unnatural ability to heal.

Those were the skills he and his teammates had been given.

The experimental program they had signed up for when they were newly minted special forces operatives, drafted to form a new team spanning different branches of the military, turned out to be nothing like they had been told it would be.

What they thought were some injections that would improve their abilities in the field turned into something that altered their DNA in a way that could never be reversed. Along with their improved skills came a deadening of their emotions, a difficulty in forming attachments outside the men they had bonded with through a rigorous training regime that could only be described as torture.

Rage lived inside every single one of them like a living, breathing being.

They had been turned into lethal killing machines, and Steel knew without having to ask any of his men that the reason they were all particularly quiet today was because of their visitor holed up downstairs.

Despite them believing the little ladybug was the bait they needed to finally get their hands on the man who had turned them into monsters, the fact that she was nothing like they had been expecting had them all on edge.

For three years, Steel and his team had been kept in a secure facility, locked in a bulletproof glass-encased room. They were watched every second of the day, forced into submission, had tests performed on them at all hours, and were only allowed out when their king needed his specially modified soldiers for a mission.

Escaping was a pure stroke of luck, and they'd left a pile of dead bodies in their wake.

Spending a year moving from location to location, being constantly hunted, it wasn't until they learned of a former decorated billionaire SEAL who had used his resources to start the world-renowned Prey Security that they made a decision.

From everything they could gather on him, it had seemed like Eagle

Oswald was a good man, one who could be trusted, and they'd all put their lives on the line to contact him, brutally aware of what would happen if the medically retired SEAL turned them in.

But Eagle hadn't turned them in.

In fact, the man had gone above and beyond to protect them. Eagle had found this old, abandoned Gothic mansion, hidden deep on a remote mountain. He gave them jobs, a purpose, he'd provided a steady presence in their lives while also giving them the autonomy to live alone as they chose.

Eagle had been nothing but good to them and had used Prey resources and every contact he had to try to find the name of the man responsible for the secret project. Those resources had eventually paid off, and Eagle had promised to help them get to the man who seemed to have disappeared off the face of the earth.

Yet they had betrayed Eagle.

Going after Ridge Gardner's little sister hadn't been sanctioned by Eagle and Prey. They'd gone rogue, and if he found out they had an innocent woman currently being tortured in the home he'd bought for them, Eagle would be furious. They'd betrayed him, and Steel had no idea what he'd do to them.

If they wanted, between the six of them with their enhanced abilities, they could kill Eagle without blinking an eye. And yet not a single one of them would ever raise a hand to the man who had effectively saved their lives. Eagle was a good man, arrogant and egotistical, definitely, but he worked hard to provide every employee not just with a paycheck but with a family. He went above and beyond. He used his power, influence, and money to save countless lives across the globe and make the world a safer place. He took on a heavy load of responsibility, not just for his wife and two young children, not just for his five younger siblings and their families, but for every single person who worked for his company.

Including Steel and his team.

And they might have thrown that all away on a quest for revenge that hampered their ability to think straight.

"So are we just going to give up on this farce?" Blade asked, tearing Steel out of his mind to see that none of them had done anything more than load their plates up with the Christmas lunch they'd spent hours cooking and push it around those plates.

Their betrayal of their boss, who they all respected the hell out of, and their little, somewhat psycho prisoner, had them all out of sorts. Even for them, men who were never in sorts.

"Yeah." He sighed, shoving his chair back from the table but not standing up.

"It's just another day after all," Lion said bitterly, but it didn't go unnoticed by him, or he suspected the rest of their team, that Lion was compulsively spinning the ring he never took off.

That ring had almost cost them their lives.

When Dr. Gardner realized the injections they'd been given were working, he had effectively abducted them, locking them up in the secure compound that would be their home for the next almost three years. When that happened, they were stripped of everything they owned, literally. They were given tactical gear to wear only when they were sent out, the rest of the time they lived naked side by side.

That day, when the new guy forgot to properly seal them into their glass cage and they escaped, Lion refused to leave without the ring that had been taken from him. The delay in leaving almost got them caught. In the intervening seven years, Steel had never once seen the other man take the ring off.

Despite being family now, the six of them hadn't known one another before they were teamed up, so none of them knew exactly why the ring was so important to their brother. But they didn't need to. They just knew it belonged to someone important who Lion couldn't forget.

Didn't want to forget.

"Just another day," Dragon echoed, and not a single one of them had to guess who the man was thinking about. Cassandra Charleston. Youngest member of the Charleston Holloway family. They'd guarded her for several months while her brothers hunted for the people responsible for setting up their parents as traitors. During that time, Dragon and Cassandra had grown close.

Close enough that when she left because she knew they were planning something they wouldn't come back from, something she refused to be a part of, it broke something in Dragon, a man Steel thought could never be hurt by another person.

In silence, the six of them began to clear away the table, packing up the food and putting it away in the fridge where it would be lucky to last out the day. Just because none of them could pretend long enough to have a Christmas meal together didn't mean that they didn't have ravenous appetites.

They'd just eat that food alone, lost in their own thoughts.

Lost to their own demons.

As the kitchen emptied, food packed away, dishes loaded in the dishwasher, counters wiped down, and everything back in its place, Steel found himself drawn to his tablet. A couple of taps with his fingertip was all it took to bring up the feed of the woman ensconced in the basement, currently suffering through a much worse Christmas Day than any of them were.

In her cell, Rose Gardner sat on the floor with her back against one of the walls, naked as the day she was born. Even through the camera, he could see her skin was flushed red and dotted with sweat thanks to the heat he was currently having pumped into the small room.

Steel had never intended to enjoy torturing Dr. Gardner's little sister, she was an innocent after all, but he'd never expected to feel bad about it either.

"I'm sorry it had to come to this, little ladybug, but I need you broken if I'm going to reel your brother in," he murmured, surprised to find that under all the rage that fueled him, he still had a heart.

෴

December 25th
2:19 P.M.

Beads of sweat rolled down her body in a near constant stream.

If there was even a breath of air in there, then it would probably help to cool it down. Then again, the point was to make her so uncomfortably hot she would break.

Rose almost wished she were capable of cracking so they could just move on with this farce and get it over with.

Farce was exactly what this was.

Because if Mr. Bedroom Man and his friend honestly thought that her brother cared one iota about her, they were stupid as well as amateurish.

Despite the strength she felt emanating from her captor, he actually hadn't hurt her when he'd dragged her up off the floor earlier. And after issuing his threat, he'd merely dropped her back onto the floor and stalked out of the room.

Almost immediately, the heat started pumping into the room, and she'd actually laughed when she realized he thought being hot was going to bother her.

It was unpleasant, of course, it had to be well over one hundred degrees in the small room, hot enough for the concrete to heat and feel like it was burning her skin when she touched it, which of course she had to because there was nothing else to climb on to get off it. But she'd quickly stripped out of her pajamas, since the flannelette was only going to take her to heat stroke quicker, totally uncaring of the fact that she was now naked in front of these men.

Sick freaks were probably watching her, but she didn't care enough about that to let it bother her. If they wanted to get themselves off to the sight of her naked body suffering through their torture, then she'd rather that than them touching her.

What they failed to understand, because they hadn't bothered to ask, was that whatever gripe they had against her brother was totally overshadowed by her own.

No one had more reason to hate Ridge than she did.

Ridge was her parents' treasured progeny.

River and Rock Gardner—and those were actually her parents' birth names—were the very definition of crazy scientists. At least from the few memories she had of them and the stories she'd heard from Ridge, who had raised her after their deaths.

They lived in a small cabin that didn't run on anything that wasn't designed and built by them. Off-grid but still with all the modern conveniences that everyone else had. They had planned to have only one child, who they would mold into their image, and together the three of them would ...

Well, she never knew exactly what they had planned, but chemistry and biology were the center of their lives. The cabin had a lab, and it didn't matter to them that Ridge had been a child, he worked from sunup to sundown, every single day of the year.

Their mind games had worked because after their deaths, Ridge raised her the same way.

Rose was the unplanned pregnancy none of them wanted. River and Rock wanted a sole heir, one they could pour all their time and energy into. She was the accident that got in the way of that. Especially since she wasn't like them.

Glancing down at her naked body, and then at the camera, Rose amended that to not completely like them.

Apparently, she had caught a little of their psycho because she honestly didn't care what Mr. Bedroom Man and his buddy were doing right now.

Her brother hated being saddled with her, but after an explosion almost killed them both and took out their parents and both sets of grandparents, there was no other choice. He'd hoped to mold her just like their parents had molded him, but it had never stuck.

She didn't care about science.

Didn't want to learn chemistry and biology. Although she understood both branches of science just fine, when she'd caught on to how badly her brother wanted her to master them, she'd realized the best way to get out from under his thumb was to pretend she couldn't grasp what he was trying to teach her. Something she'd managed to do the second she turned eighteen.

Thankfully, Ridge had been happy to be freed from the burden of responsibility for her, believing she was no use to him, and he'd left her alone these last five years. There was no way he was going to care that she'd been caught. The only thing he'd care about with her captors torturing her was that he didn't get to be the one to do it himself.

Only four when her parents died, she didn't know if they were sick and demented like Ridge, but given they'd raised him in their image, she had to assume they were. Rose did know for a fact that her brother got off on other people's suffering.

Making her do farm chores in the snow, wearing nothing more than jeans and a light shirt.

Locking her in the attic on sweltering summer days.

Refusing to let her sleep as she ran laps around the yard in the middle of the night.

Forcing her to stand for hours in the rain.

Caning her for any infraction or act of disobedience.

And all of that was just the lighter end of the spectrum of abuse and torture she'd suffered at the hands of her brother, starting when she was just four and ending only when she left at eighteen.

According to Ridge, it all built character, strengthened her, toughened her up, but in reality, she knew he just loved it when his torturous games caught up with her

These men could talk about making her crack all they wanted, but if she hadn't broken at four, she wasn't going to break now with almost twenty years of experience under her belt.

Sucks to be you, Mr. Bedroom Man.

As though he could somehow read her mind, the overbearing heat suddenly seemed to drain out of the room. For a moment, Rose thought she was getting a reprieve. She had no idea how long she'd been there, because she was unconscious when they took her from her bed, and when they brought her into this cell. There were no windows, and no way for her to judge the passing of time. But she did know that she hadn't been given anything to eat or drink, and there was no way in hell that the heat they'd been pumping into the room hadn't badly dehydrated her.

Whatever short-lived reprieve she got was quickly wiped away as Rose realized what her captors were doing.

They weren't just turning the temperature inside her cell down, they were trying to shock her system into a meltdown by going the other way.

Freezing air began to fill her cell, and she got maybe a handful of minutes to enjoy no longer feeling like she was being boiled alive before her body shook as the cold seeped inside her.

With another laugh, she stood proudly, looking directly at the camera, refusing to cower in shame at being naked before them. These men wanted to break her, she was in a fight for her life, and there was no time or energy to be wasted on modesty.

"Hot then cold?" she asked, hoping that the camera picked up sound. "That's the best you've got? It's going to take a whole lot more than that to break me, Mr. Bedroom Man, and however many friends you have with you."

Rolling her eyes, although she wasn't sure that would be picked up by the camera, Rose reached for her discarded pajamas and slipped them on, then she sat back down.

Her body was already protesting the hard concrete, but it and her clothing had been warmed by the heat, and for the next little while, they helped to keep the worst of the cold at bay.

Still, if it came down to it, she'd pick cold over heat any day.

Heat reminded her of the explosion.

Memories of that day were hazy at best. She'd been only four years old, but she remembered that for once they were having a huge feast. It was Christmas Day, and while she hadn't been given any presents like most other little girls across the globe would have been, she'd been excited about the piles of food covering the kitchen counters.

When her mother had set a plate stacked with more food than she'd ever been given before in her little life, she'd actually giggled. Something that was usually frowned upon, but that day her mother had merely given her an indulgent smile and ruffled her red locks.

No sooner had Rose taken that first bite than the loudest sound she'd ever heard, and a wall of heat encompassed the room.

She would have sworn someone shoved her onto the ground a second before it happened, but maybe she was remembering things wrong. All she knew was that the next thing she could recall, she was under the table, and the broken remains of the cabin lay in piles around her.

Of the eight people in that cabin on the day of the explosion, only she and her brother survived.

With no one else to take her in, Ridge had no choice but to take on responsibility for her. Raising her as he continued with whatever crazy plans he and their parents had cooked up. There had been no more Christmas Day feasts after that, no more anything that wasn't hours of grueling schoolwork and farm work, and one torturous punishment after another.

Was it any wonder she now loathed Christmas?

Even more so now that she had once again had her life blown up on the holiday that was supposed to be about love, joy, and peace.

Silent tears rolled down her cheeks, although Rose didn't make a sound or any move to stop them. She wasn't crying for her situation now, but for the little girl who had died that day even though she continued to breathe.

CHAPTER

Four

December 25th
3:02 P.M.

Something visceral twisted in his chest as small teardrops trailed silvery lines down the little ladybug's cheeks.

Steel was overcome by a sudden need to break something.

Preferably, whatever had Rose Gardner crying, but since that was him and the rest of his team, he settled for crushing the tablet he was still watching in his hands.

The device was no match for his enhanced strength, and it easily cracked and bent. It still wasn't enough, so he picked up the broken pieces and hurled them across the room. They connected with the wall, shattering into a dozen smaller pieces. The wall also cracked, with a large hole where the tablet had hit it, and the sight of the crumbled pieces of drywall lying among the remains of the tablet went a small way toward easing the sudden tightness in his chest.

Normally, tears would mean nothing to him. The drugs Ridge Gardner had injected him with had messed with his biology in more ways than just making him ten times stronger than the average man his size.

They had quite literally changed his brain chemistry, and his ability to process emotions was forever tainted. It was like there was a gap there. He could recognize the emotions he used to feel in others, but he was unable to connect that to any empathy within himself. While he didn't wish pain on people, he was no longer able to feel anything when it came to other people's suffering.

Without the ability for empathy, he was little more than a monster.

So why were the little ladybug's tears affecting him?

Bringing her here was supposed to be a quick and easy way to lure out Dr. Gardner. They had all assumed that as soon as the young woman woke up, she'd be panicked and hysterical. They'd let her stew for a few hours, then send the crazy scientist a little Jack Skellington-worthy Christmas gift.

Easy.

Only their little prisoner hadn't woken up panicked and hysterical. Instead, she'd been completely unimpressed with their behavior. The crazy woman hadn't even hesitated to strip naked to make the heat they'd been pumping into the room a little more bearable.

Not once had she shown a single crack, maybe that was why her tears bothered him.

Or maybe it was the way she was crying. Steel didn't get the feeling that it had anything to do with him and his team abducting her. They weren't messy or loud tears. They just rolled silently down her cheeks as she sat there, staring at nothing.

Was she staring at nothing?

It seemed more like she was staring straight into whatever darkness lived inside her head.

Maybe that was why he was having a hard time with ... all of this.

Darkness lived inside that woman's mind, there was no doubt about it, and that made her a kindred spirit of sorts.

What did that say about him that he still intended to do exactly what he'd planned?

Breaking the little ladybug wasn't personal, but it was necessary. How else were they supposed to draw out Dr. Gardner?

Ever since Steel and his team managed to escape their prison, the man had gone deep underground. While as far as they could ascertain the doctor was no longer involved in the trial that active military could sign up to be part of, none of them doubted he was still out there, playing his sick games, toying with people's lives, trying to be God by creating a new species.

Stopping the man was for the world's benefit, but the torture they'd deliver before they finally stole his life would be their own personal revenge.

Unless Rose knew where her brother was hiding, breaking her and delivering proof to Ridge was their only chance to get to the doctor. If they tried to film a video for Ridge now, he had no doubt that Rose would try to communicate something to him that would alert her brother that it was a trap.

Broken.

That's what he needed.

And yet as Steel stormed across the kitchen where he'd remained, glued to his tablet while the rest of his team did whatever they were up to right now, he had to fight against a need to go down to the basement.

What he'd say to the woman, he had no idea. Try to explain to her why he needed her to crack? That wouldn't serve any purpose, after all, he'd already told her he needed her broken to get to her brother. But maybe if she understood why he and his team needed to destroy Ridge, then she wouldn't be sitting down there cold and alone, crying.

Somehow, he managed to rein in the compulsion to head to the basement. Instead, he took the stairs three at a time, both sets, up to the fourth floor where he and his team had their rooms. In his room, there was another tablet. Going down to the basement wasn't possible, but he needed to maintain some kind of connection to the little ladybug.

It made him feel like she wasn't alone, even though she had no idea he was watching over her.

Made him feel like he wasn't alone, even though he'd never cared about that before.

So long as his team was there, he was never truly alone. They understood what each other felt, they'd all lived through the same thing. Eagle kept a check on them, and they interacted with anyone else on an as-needed basis only.

Yet the little ladybug was messing with his head.

"Stop doing it," he ordered, though she couldn't hear his words with four floors between them.

Pulling up the camera feed for the basement cell as soon as he had the tablet in his hands, Steel was surprised to find that Rose was no longer silent. She wasn't sobbing or crying, although tears continued to tumble, seemingly unnoticed, down her pale cheeks.

She was singing.

Softly and sweetly.

Almost unaware she was doing it, if the vacant look in her eyes was anything to go by.

If it were anyone else, he would have thought they were hovering on the edge of a breakdown, almost ready to crack and break.

But this wasn't anyone else.

It was the little ladybug.

A woman who just minutes before she started to weep silent tears had rolled her eyes at the camera and told him that it would take more than hot and cold to break her.

Mr. Bedroom Man.

That's what she'd called him. Hearing her say it had made him snicker, the small sound surprising him, because Steel couldn't remember the last time he'd laughed. There hadn't been anything to laugh about when Dr. Gardner trashed his life so he could play at being a god.

Other than her lips moving, and the odd tremor rocking her body as it responded to the freezing air now being pumped into her cell, Rose was still. Her eyes stared at nothing, and her singing was audible only because he had the volume turned up high.

What are you thinking about, little ladybug?

Why are you so confident that we won't be able to break you?

When they'd made the decision to go after Ridge Gardner's sister, they'd never stopped to consider anything more than the basics. She was a law-abiding citizen, with no criminal history, no drug or alcohol-related charges. She had a job, paid her taxes, and mostly kept to herself. They hadn't thought they needed to know more about her than that.

Now he realized they'd made a possibly critical mistake.

It was more than obvious that Rose was no stranger to torture. Given that there was no boyfriend in her life, and no friends either, although she was active online in book-related communities, she hadn't become acquainted with it in the last couple of years.

Which meant it was more than likely something she'd experienced for a long time.

Possibly most of her life.

According to their research, her parents had died when she was young and she'd been raised by her brother, which was why they thought she would be the best possible bait they could find.

Had her brother abused her?

The two had lived off-grid, as had the family when the siblings' parents were still alive. A small farm, they grew their own food, and provided for all their own needs, similar in fact to the way Eagle Oswald and his siblings had grown up, before their parents were murdered.

As Steel stood there, clutching the tablet, listening to the little ladybug sing softly to herself, he became more convinced that he and his team had made a mistake going rogue with this one. If they'd spoken with Eagle about their plans to go after Ridge's sister, he knew the man would have insisted on sending someone to speak with her first.

Maybe the crazy little ladybug would have been willing to help them.

Too late for that now, though.

They'd started down this path, and there was no going back, no do-overs.

So he was going to have to find a way to crush Rose's spirit, break it down to nothing, and then pray that once he and his team had what they needed, it wouldn't be too late for her to rebuild herself, putting her broken pieces back together.

～

December 26th

9:25 A.M.

The cold was making her sleepy.

Rose was lying in a corner of her cell, curled up in a ball in the best attempt she could make to ward off as much of the cold air as possible. Her body had been shivering for hours, to the point where every one of her muscles ached.

Between the heat and then the cold, she hadn't had a chance to sleep, and still hadn't been given anything to eat or drink. While the cramping in her stomach from hunger pangs was annoying, she'd grown up being deprived of food if she didn't perform her schoolwork up to the desired standard, so she was more than used to that.

However, the lack of water was hurting.

It made her body feel heavy and lethargic. Made it harder for her to form any sort of coherent plan, and even if she could, it made it less likely that her body could do what she needed it to do to even stand a chance at escaping.

Right as she was about to drift off into a hypothermia-induced slumber, one she actually hoped she might not wake from, the air in the room began to shift. It was warm air, but not as hot as it had been earlier.

Immediately, she was pulled back from the edge as her body began to shake in earnest in an attempt to generate enough warmth. Whoever was watching her must have realized that if they didn't tone down the temperature torture, they would push things too far and lose the only leverage they believed they had.

They didn't want her dead, she knew that. A dead sister was no way to lure out her brother.

Then again, a live sister wasn't either.

If Mr. Bedroom Man and his friend had done even the most rudimentary of searches into her and Ridge's relationship, they would have seen that they didn't have one. She was glad to be out from under his thumb, and since she hadn't lived up to his expectations, he was glad to be done with her so he could go about his crazy plans, whatever they were.

Apparently, they included hurting people.

Well, she was assuming that anyway, since it was clear that the man hated her brother.

Slowly, the shaking in her limbs began to taper off, and Rose felt exhaustion weighing heavily upon her. There was no time for her body to get the rest it needed to recover, because she knew whatever these men had planned for her next would come swiftly.

It turned out to be even quicker than she'd thought.

The soft thunk of someone undoing the lock on the door to her cell told her the men were coming before the door opened.

Not bothering to move, she watched as Mr. Bedroom Man entered the room along with five other men. She knew which one he was, even though they were all dressed in the same black outfit. They looked like some campy, stereotypical version of bad guys with balaclavas and gloves. Enough so that she giggled as they stalked into the room.

All six of them were around the same height, and they were all bulked up like they spent most of their time in the gym. There was an air of danger that clung to them like a soft mist, but honestly, she'd spent so much of her life in the dark that a little more of it didn't scare her like it probably should.

"Morning," she drawled. "Or afternoon, or evening. You know you guys aren't very gracious hosts." A giant yawn felt like it split her face in two, and her eyes were heavy. What she wouldn't give to have spent her day in bed like she had originally intended to spend her Christmas.

"You think this is amusing, little ladybug?" Mr. Bedroom Man growled as he closed the distance between them.

"I can tell you what I don't find amusing, and that is that nickname," she informed him, tilting her head back a little so she could look up at him as he towered above her. "How do I in any way resemble a ladybug?"

"The red hair, for one." Mr. Bedroom Man crouched before her. One of his hands reached toward her, stopped, hovered where it was for a moment, before the gloved pad of a fingertip ghosted over one of her cheeks. "The freckles for another. Especially when your cheeks were red from my hand around your neck."

Without another word, that hand that had so gently brushed across her skin snapped out to lock around both of her wrists, and he dragged her up and off the floor. The movement made her head spin, and by the time it had stilled enough that she could think, he already had her thrown over his shoulder and was marching out of the room with her.

The other men hovered around them, but no one else moved to touch her as they walked down a dark corridor with closed doors just like the one that had trapped her in that concrete hell of a room. At the end of the short hallway was a larger open space. A large hook hung in the center of the room, above a drain, and she didn't need to have a vivid imagination to figure out what this space was.

It was a torture chamber.

Glancing around, Rose noted multiple tools hanging on the walls to the left and right of the entrance. The back wall was empty, but two metal chairs were sitting there.

One of the other men stepped up to her, grabbed her hands, and bound her wrists with a heavy-duty plastic zip tie. Because they apparently hated her just because of the DNA that ran through her veins, the man pulled it tight enough that it dug into her skin.

As he did, another of the men reached for the hook and pulled it lower. Mr. Bedroom Man carried her over to it and lifted her now bound hands, hooking them over the sharp metal.

"I'm not the only one making up nicknames am I, little ladybug?" he asked as one of the other men began to do something that lifted the hook she was attached to. While her feet were flat on the floor at first, it kept going until she was balanced on her tiptoes, barely able to balance. Didn't help that her body was weak and exhausted. "Mr. Bedroom Man, was it?"

Despite the pain already pulling through her shoulders, Rose chuckled, shrugging as best she could at the awkward angle. "You never introduced yourself, and a girl's got to have something to call the man who so rudely interrupted her Christmas plans to spend the day in bed reading and eating way too much chocolate."

None of the men spoke, but she would have sworn she felt amusement buzz between them. Too bad it didn't stop them from hoisting her up higher until she was left swinging from her bound hands. The plastic cut easily through her skin, and she could already feel wet, sticky blood dribbling down her forearms.

Good thing she wasn't squeamish.

Part of Ridge's training had been learning first aid skills. Not just the regular kind, like bandaging and CPR, but more detailed skills like suturing. On herself. Ridge wasn't going to cut himself to have her practice, and there was no one else around to do it on. While her brother regularly left their cabin, she was never permitted to.

So she'd learned how to stitch up her own wounds, ones Ridge also made her inflict on herself.

If she could do that when she was eight years old, she could handle whatever they had planned for her. They wanted to hurt her, okay, they could have at it. They wanted to make her bleed, okay, she'd bleed a river for them. In the end, it wasn't going to get them what they wanted.

As though to disorient her, the men moved around the room. They clunked things, she knew to try to make her on edge, to confuse her, and to amp up her fear about what was going to happen next.

But Rose kept her attention focused on only one thing.

Mr. Bedroom Man.

For some reason, he was her anchor in this crazy place he'd brought her to. She didn't like him, he'd brought her here to hurt her, but she felt some connection to him that transcended understanding.

Darkness lived inside his head, and she was only now realizing how dark her own mind had become without even realizing it. There was no trust between them, but the darkness bonded them in some sick and twisted kind of way.

For that reason alone, she didn't break her gaze away from his.

Not even when one of the men slipped up close behind her and tugged her pajama bottoms down enough to bare her backside to the room, and she sent up a silent plea that it was physical pain they intended to inflict on her and not sexual.

CHAPTER Five

December 26th
9:40 A.M.

They were really doing this.

The acceptance in Rose's eyes almost had Steel backing out.

There was no judgment there, she hated him, but she had made her peace with her fate, and she wasn't going to beg him not to hurt her, plead with him for her safety, or even her life. She was going to take whatever hell he and his team dished up without complaint.

Then he wouldn't put it past her to kill him if given half an opportunity and not lose sleep over it.

Unfortunately, the time to back out and choose a different path had passed. He and his team were committed, the opportunity of turning Rose Gardner into an ally was lost to them forever. It was continue with this plan or lose what could be their only chance at getting their hands on the man who had so carelessly and callously played God with their lives.

If it were only him, he might back out, sedate Rose, and take her back to her home, leave her in her bed with the safety of knowing that she had never seen his face and had no way of identifying him when she went to the cops.

But it wasn't just him.

Already once before he'd led his men into a situation that had changed their lives forever. Steel had failed them that day, and he couldn't fail them again. Couldn't take this chance away from them, even though he knew not a single one of the men dressed all in black surrounding the small woman with the dark red hair and defiant eyes, felt entirely comfortable being in this room with her.

She was an innocent.

They'd sworn an oath to protect the innocent.

Not only was the little ladybug innocent, but she was like them. She'd been warped and twisted into something she didn't want to be, but didn't know how to escape. Darkness lived inside her soul, making her a kindred spirit.

Perhaps that was why Steel didn't move a muscle as Rose locked her gaze onto his.

Neither of them flinched as Dragon moved in behind her and tugged down her pajama bottoms enough to bare her backside to the camera Blade was holding.

The ridiculous pink unicorn pajamas were perhaps the saddest part of all of this.

They were so incongruous with the room and its purpose that it almost made him laugh.

Not a laugh of joy or amusement, though, a pained laugh because in doing this, he and his team were crossing a line from which they would never come back. They were now the monsters that Dr. Gardner had tried to create. They were giving in to the darkness that the man had placed inside them, allowing their lack of empathy to destroy whatever human parts of them still existed.

This had better be worth it.

The thought passed through his mind a second before the whip Thunder had pressed into Dragon's hand whizzed through the air, connecting with a sickening crack against Rose's bared backside.

Of the seven of them in the room, Steel was pretty sure the only one of them who didn't flinch was the one who had just been struck. He knew she felt the pain because he saw it flare in the gorgeous forest green eyes that seemed locked on his, but other than that, she didn't show any outward sign that she'd just been whipped.

Without breaking eye contact, Steel began to speak. The words were for the camera, for the recording that would be sent to her brother, but it felt like he was speaking to Rose, explaining in some small way why he had to do this, almost as though that could lessen the sting of what he was inflicting upon her.

Not that he could really do that. Nothing could lessen the sting. Rose would wear the marks on her skin and in her soul.

"We have something of yours, Dr. Gardner," Steel spoke, his voice low and rough, his heart beating harder than it should be, and he half wished that Rose would scream and thrash, beg and plead. "Something we're going to have fun playing with. Destroying."

Although, as he said the word at the same time Dragon delivered another blow to the little ladybug's delicate skin, Steel realized that destroying this woman would not be possible. Nor did he really want to.

Carrying through with this charade was inevitable, the wheels were already in motion and there was no stopping them. But even if they couldn't lure in the psychotic scientist, he would ensure the woman was delivered back to her home and her life. Rose Gardner didn't deserve to pay for her brother's sins any more than she already had.

Again, Rose didn't make a sound despite the pain he knew she felt.

Nor did she cry out as Dragon struck her again, and again.

Despite her lack of sound, Steel could feel the tension in the room mounting. None of his men liked treating a woman like this, especially an innocent one. But they felt trapped, they'd been searching for Ridge Gardner for almost a decade, and they hadn't even had his full name or any details on his family until recently. They couldn't wait another decade to get one step closer to the crazed doctor.

But this was wrong, and they all knew it.

"You want her back while there's still some pieces left to put back together, then you better follow our instructions," he said, ready to end this. Steel wasn't sure he could take another second of the little lady-bug's stoic silence, and he could tell Voodoo in particular was about to break, even if Rose wasn't. Voodoo was a healer, and he'd been the most vocal about his desire to keep this as clean as possible, use other ways to break Dr. Gardner's sister without inflicting physical pain.

Why couldn't you have just been the hysterical woman we expected you to be?

Why did you have to be so strong?

Why couldn't you just crack so we could get this over with and get you back home?

Dragon delivered one last blow, and other than that flare in her eyes, Rose showed no other sign she felt the pain they'd just wrought on her body.

Blade lowered the camera, nodded to let him know they were done, and quickly eased up the material of Rose's pajamas to cover her, give her some modicum of modesty back. The video would be processed through their programs to ensure it didn't include anything that would tip off their location to Dr. Gardner, and then it would be sent to the doctor's old military email address in the hopes he still monitored it, along with instructions for making contact.

"We need to put antiseptic cream on the welts," Voodoo said, and Steel knew the man was desperate to ease the pain they'd just inflicted on their strong little captive.

"No," Rose said, her voice rough, but firm as her gaze finally shifted to the man who had stepped up behind him.

Steel wanted to growl at her and order her to return it to him. He and he alone deserved the privilege of holding her gaze, shouldering whatever small amount of her pain he could.

"They could get infected," Voodoo lectured, like she wasn't already aware of that.

"It will help with the pain as well, numb them a little," Lion piped up.

That earned them all an eyeroll. "Yes, I'm sure you're all very concerned about my pain. Totally believable since you were the ones who kidnapped me, tortured me, strung me up, and whipped me."

Unfortunately for them, they did care.

Which made them the world's worst abductors.

They knew what they'd done, and it would be a well-deserved smear on all of their souls. They were desperate, but that didn't give them the right to hurt others, which was exactly what they'd done.

Now Steel knew he wasn't the only one desperate to make amends in some small manner. Not that their little captive would ever believe that.

"You get the cream," Steel growled. Flicking his gaze up to the dribbles of blood streaking her arms from where the plastic zip ties were cutting into her skin, he clenched his teeth as he tried to drag in a calming breath. "For your wrists as well."

"Fine," Rose huffed like she found them all to be interminably irritating. "But I'll do it myself."

"You won't be able to reach the wounds on your ... ah ... butt," Voodoo finished lamely, his gaze refusing to land on Rose, who actually chuckled.

"I manage well enough, no need to worry about me," she told him. Something in the way she said the words made it clear without her having to say it, that she was well used to caring for herself and didn't expect that anyone would ever worry about her.

Only Steel was finding that he did.

This was supposed to be an easy way to get to the man they all craved revenge on. Rose was supposed to be just a tool to use along the way and then throw away when they were finished with her.

But it wasn't.

It had become a whole lot more complicated, and he had no idea how he was supposed to deal with that.

December 26th
  9:59 A.M.

"You're not tending to your own wounds," Mr. Bedroom Man growled at her like the idea was offensive to him.

Which was crazy.

After all, he'd abducted her and planned this all out. She was his prisoner, and he'd used her like he always intended to.

"You are aware that they're wounds *you* inflicted," she reminded him. Probably not her smartest idea, but then again, Rose had always regretted never standing up to her brother.

Sure, she'd done things her way, refused to cry when she knew it was what he wanted, bitten down on screams that wanted to escape because she knew he craved them, and been purposefully obtuse at chemistry and biology since she knew it was what he wanted her to study. All of that had infuriated her brother, but she'd never actually told him to go to hell, and she'd always wished she'd done it.

Now was her chance not to be the silent little victim.

They didn't care about her, they were just more people who wanted to use her. Story of her life, and she wanted to be the author of that story and not a passenger along for the ride.

Mr. Bedroom Man's mouth tightened into a line, and there was a flash of pain in his eyes. Which again made absolutely no sense. This was what he wanted.

Was there any chance he was having second thoughts?

Could she use that to her advantage?

"We fix what we break," he snapped, then nodded at one of the other men dressed all in black. It was the one who had been concerned that she wouldn't be able to reach the wounds from the whip they'd inflicted on her skin.

Unfortunately, it wasn't the first time she'd been whipped, and she knew she was in for a sucky time for the next couple of days. The placement of the wounds along her backside would make any attempt at sitting or lying down hellish. Hopefully, they weren't like Ridge and didn't get some sort of sick pleasure from tearing up the skin on her butt, then forcing her to sit on it.

Agony.

There was no other way to describe it.

Only the impression she got from these huge men that surrounded her was that they were deriving no pleasure from this entire ordeal.

It was clear Mr. Bedroom Man was the boss because at his nod, the other man moved, disappearing from her view for a moment before returning with two small pills in his hand.

If they thought she was going to swallow them, they were crazy.

"You're going to be a brat about this, aren't you?" Mr. Bedroom Man asked, sounding as close to amused as she could guess he ever sounded.

"I don't think it can be classified as being a brat not to take drugs from the people currently holding you captive," Rose said primly. No way was she going to allow them to give her anything.

The best-case scenario was that they were sedatives that would knock her out and make her completely vulnerable before them. Just because they hadn't raped her so far didn't mean that they wouldn't.

Worst-case scenario, the pills were something like cyanide that would kill her, and she wasn't going down without a fight.

"Take the pills, don't make us do this the hard way." Mr. Bedroom Man grunted.

"No thank you. I have no intention of letting you give me something that could kill me."

"Wouldn't kill you that way, little ladybug." Mr. Bedroom Man sounded insulted by the idea. "No way to kill a worthy opponent."

There was most definitely something wrong with her that those words reassured her.

"Open wide, little one," the other man instructed as he clamped a hand around the back of her neck.

Nope.

No way she was doing that.

The words were reassuring, but she was still in survival mode. Which meant not taking anything from a stranger. Multiple strangers. Multiple strangers who had abducted her, hurt her, and likely planned on killing her. Though according to them, not with pills.

"Brat." As he muttered the word, Mr. Bedroom Man pinched her nose, effectively cutting off her air supply since opening her mouth meant they could give her the pills.

While she held out as long as she could, far too soon Rose was forced to open her mouth to draw in a sharp breath. The second she did so, the pills were popped on her tongue, and the man who had given them to her looked at her with apologetic eyes as he clamped his large hand over her mouth, sealing it and preventing her from spitting out the pills.

Exactly what she would have done.

With the pills now where he wanted them, Mr. Bedroom Man released his grip on her nose, and instead, his hand circled her neck. It didn't squeeze, and his touch was almost tender as he began to massage her throat to get her to swallow.

"Stop making this harder than it has to be," he murmured, locking his gaze onto hers the same way she'd done to him when his friend was whipping her.

Then his steady gaze had grounded her, given her something to hold onto, and sick and twisted as it was, given he had all the power and was deliberately inflicting pain on her, it had also offered her comfort.

There was definitely something wrong with her.

Because as Rose found herself unable to blink away from this man's gaze, his hand stroking her neck, making her swallow the pills, she found that same comfort. Who knew you could develop some sort of Stockholm Syndrome this quickly?

"Good girl," he rumbled as the pills he'd given her began to take effect and she started to get sleepy.

His hand never left her neck until the world faded to black around her.

When she next blinked open her eyes, Rose found herself back in the cell. Other than the time jump, there was no gap in her memory. What had happened in the torture room was painted vividly in her mind, another horror story to add to the collection that made up her life.

A glance down at her body showed that not only was she still dressed in her bright pink unicorn pajamas, but she'd been covered with a gray woolen blanket. Her head rested on something soft, a pillow she saw as she looked down, and she'd been laid out on her side, presumably so she wasn't resting against the raw wounds on her backside.

One of her hands was pillowed beneath her cheek, and she could see that her wrist was wrapped in a crisp white bandage. With a sigh, she had to assume that they did indeed take their *we fix what we break* motto seriously, and her butt had also been cleaned and treated. Since she wasn't hurting too badly and she knew from experience she should be in more pain, Rose also had to assume that one of those pills had been a pain reliever.

As she shifted slightly, realizing she needed to pee, she also noted that the temperature in the room had been modified to a comfortable level. Were they trying to mess with her head now? Confuse her by hurting her and then offering her small kindnesses?

It would be a more effective way of breaking her than inflicting pain was ever going to be.

Rose had grown up on a steady diet of pain and suffering, her kryptonite was love and affection.

Not that she could let them figure that out.

If they thought that hurting her, then tending to her would mess with her head, that's exactly what they would do.

Worse, it might even work.

Ignoring the fact that the men were probably watching her every move, she kept her head held high as she walked over to the hole in the ground where she would have to do her business. Wincing as the material of her pants brushed across her poor, injured bottom, she placed a hand on the wall to balance herself as she squatted over the hole.

There was a tiny wound in the back of her hand, about the size a needle would make if they'd inserted a cannula. Was the reason she had to pee so badly because they'd replenished the fluids she'd lost in their game of roast the captive alive?

Since there was no toilet paper, Rose stayed squatted above the hole until any lingering drips had stopped, then pushed herself back into a standing position so she could carefully ease her pajama pants back up.

Her backside protested the movement, and she limped back over to the blanket and pillow. There was every chance she was being watched, and she knew she had to take advantage of this opportunity while it presented itself.

One thing she knew for certain was that Ridge didn't care enough about her to be interested in these men abducting her. When they realized that, they would up their torture game. Just because they'd patched her up this time didn't mean they would next time, so this could be her only chance to be clear-headed enough to try to find a way out.

Like always, if she waited for someone else to save her, it was never going to happen.

Good thing Rose had plenty of practice being the hero of her own story.

CHAPTER
Six

December 27th
    11:22 A.M.

While Steel couldn't argue the fact that he was confused as hell about this entire situation he and his men had gotten themselves into, there was one thing he was certain about.

They couldn't go on like this.

All the things they thought they'd be able to achieve by having Ridge Gardner's little sister in their possession were now clearly not going to happen.

Yesterday, after they'd forced Rose to take the drugs, one a painkiller the other a sedative, he and Voodoo had spent a couple of hours in the basement cell with the little ladybug, cleaning her wounds, putting antibiotic cream on them, bandaging the ones on her wrists, and rehydrating her. As they were doing that, the others were getting the video ready to send.

It had now been twenty-four hours since the video had hit the doctor's email.

The video had been watched, they knew that thanks to the tracking virus they'd hidden in it. Unfortunately, they hadn't been able to get a read on the doctor's location, though. Wherever the man was hiding, he was using protections so he couldn't be found.

If the crazed scientist had watched a video of his sister being tortured and yet made no attempts to reach out to them despite their threats that they would escalate things, then nothing was going to work.

Personally, Steel didn't see how a man could watch a woman he was related to strung up, bleeding, and being struck with a whip, and not want to tear off the heads of the people doing it.

He had been the one overseeing the torture, and he wanted to rip off his own head and those of his team who were only following his orders.

They had miscalculated the doctor's attachment to his only living family member, and because of that, they'd needlessly inflicted suffering on an innocent woman. One he knew was messing with all of their heads with her crazy behavior, refusal to cower before them, and bratty confidence.

"Still no replies?" Steel asked Dragon, who was monitoring communication for them.

The man shook his head, and as he looked around at the faces of the other men sitting around the kitchen table, he knew it was time for him to make some tough decisions. He'd promised them that he would get them retribution, and made the decision to go after Rose, even though the others had all agreed. He'd insisted on continuing with things even when his gut was nudging him to admit that what he was doing wasn't only wrong but wouldn't get him the desired results.

That they had to change up their plans was a given, but Steel hated letting his men down again. Seemed it was all he managed to do.

"None," Dragon replied, frustration emanating off him in angry waves.

Steel got it, he did, he felt the same way. This was supposed to work, supposed to be a slam dunk. Yet instead, all they had now was guilt over harming an innocent, and confirmation that the soulless killing machines Dr. Gardner wanted to create had finally come into existence despite them fighting against it for a decade.

Spearing his fingers through his hair, Steel prepared himself for what he had to say. Knowing he had no choice didn't make it any easier. "He doesn't care about her," he admitted, a hard admission to make, because really they should have been able to guess that a man who would so easily play God with other people's lives didn't care about anyone but himself.

Angry grunts and growls came from the other men, and he knew they were all having as hard a time understanding that as he was. They had all walked away from their families to protect them. If they found out any one of their parents, siblings, nieces, nephews, grandparents, aunts, or uncles had been harmed, they would move heaven and earth to save them.

Not callously ignore the problem.

"What does that mean for your little ladybug?" Thunder asked.

Shifting uncomfortably at hearing her called his, Steel hated that he had been transparent enough with his ... interest in the woman that the others had picked up on it.

He hated even more that it wasn't just an interest.

Attraction.

Denying it didn't make it any less true. The little ladybug was twelve years younger than him, pretty much still a child, and despite whatever had led her to a place where she could not only tolerate torture but refuse to bow down before them and beg for her freedom, she had dug herself out from under it.

Built a life for herself.

A life they'd torn her away from with no care or consideration for her feelings. They'd viewed her as nothing more than a tool for them to use, and that left him with this unpleasant knot of guilt sitting heavily in his gut.

"We letting her go?" Blade asked.

"We can't," Dragon immediately protested.

"Why?" Voodoo asked.

"Girl has no value to us if her brother doesn't care about her," Lion reminded Dragon. "What else are we going to do with her?"

"Can't keep her locked in the basement forever," Blade said.

"Steel's little ladybug will find a way to gut us eventually," Thunder said with a smirk, amusement dancing in his gray eyes.

"If we let her go, she's going to go running straight to the cops," Dragon protested.

"So what if she does?" Lion asked. "Not like she saw our faces, or knows where we brought her. I don't think the cops are going to have any chance of tracking down Mr. Bedroom Man."

Huffing a small chuckle at Rose's ridiculous name for him, Steel nodded in agreement. "She no longer holds any value to us. We're going to have to look for another way to get to Ridge Gardner."

"Or we do what we told him we'd do," Dragon persisted.

"What? Up our torture game?" Voodoo asked as he shifted in his seat. The man had always been a healer, and now with his almost other-worldly ability to heal others, Voodoo had taken on a heavy burden. He took other people's pain and deaths personally. The first time he'd been unable to save an innocent who got caught up in a black ops raid they'd performed, Steel had worried for his friend's sanity.

Voodoo could handle inflicting pain on someone who deserved it, but they all knew Rose didn't. If Voodoo had struggled with whipping Rose, there was no way he would handle anything more.

Besides, nothing they did to Rose was going to bring out her crazed scientist brother.

"And what exactly do you propose we do to her?" Steel asked, trying to remind himself that Dragon was taking out his frustrations at losing Cassandra Charleston over their plans for Rose, on Rose herself. But it wasn't the little ladybug's fault that she was related to Dr. Gardner, that they'd targeted her because of it, or that she was strong enough to with-stand what they'd done to her so far.

"Whatever it takes to get our revenge," Dragon answered simply.

"You want to cut off body parts? Skin her alive? Electrocute her?" Voodoo demanded, and Steel was glad he wasn't the only one who looked a little queasy at the idea. The last thing he needed was to take out his own anger on Dragon and rip the man's head clean off his body.

"None of that is going to break her," Steel said confidently. While he had no idea just what Rose's life had been like before she started over, it was obvious enough that it had included firsthand experience with torture.

Another reason her brother had to die.

Ridge had raised Rose after their parents' deaths, so if Rose knew all about someone inflicting pain on her for fun, it had to have been her brother who did it.

"I want to do whatever it takes to get us what we want," Dragon growled.

"Torturing Rose isn't going to get us her brother," Lion said.

"And it's not going to break her," Thunder added.

"Besides, I don't think our fearless leader likes the idea of playing with his little ladybug," Blade said, shooting him a smirk that dared him to disagree.

Refusing to play into that and admit he felt anything at all for the fiery woman downstairs, Steel kept his expression impassive. "Just because this didn't work doesn't mean that we won't find something that will. None of us is going to stop until Ridge Gardner rues the day he ever decided to play with other people's DNA."

With an irritated growl, Dragon slammed the lid of the laptop closed and stalked out of the room.

"Follow him," he told Thunder, who nodded and pushed away from the table. "I'll make the little ladybug some food, lace it with sedatives, and we can get her prepped to return her to her house tonight."

"Your little ladybug will be okay, she'll bounce back," Blade told him, clapping him on the back as he headed for the fridge.

Steel prayed that his friend was right, but the problem was that no matter how strong you were, the weight of the world on your shoulders eventually broke your back. Look at them, when their DNA had been altered, their brain chemistry changed so they could be molded into Ridge Gardner's perfect killing machines. They'd vowed to never use their skills to harm an innocent, yet they had one they'd tortured locked in their basement.

～

December 27th
12:00 P.M.

. . .

It was time.

Rose kept her body still, her expression impassive, but inside she was hyper-focused, taking in every single minute detail, because she was going to find a way out of this room.

Even if it killed her.

She was all too aware that she was a whole lot less worried about that possibility than she should be. But after you'd lived your entire life as a series of torturous events one after the other in a never-ending stream, the end didn't seem as terrifying a prospect.

Only she'd found her end. At least it was supposed to be.

Years of enduring punishments as she pretended that her brain just couldn't comprehend the chemistry and biological lessons her brother wanted to teach her were all to convince him that she was useless for whatever plans he had. It had worked, she'd told him she was leaving the day of her eighteenth birthday, and because he believed she was of no use to him, he'd let her go.

Editing romance books wasn't her dream job, but she did enjoy it. She was used to her own company, so she rarely got lonely, but she did worry that she'd lost the ability to interact with other people in any sort of meaningful way. Or maybe she'd never developed the ability at all.

Five years of peace and quiet had all come crashing down around her, and it was all because of her brother. Even if she managed to escape, she was going to have to pack up her entire life and disappear, because these men would keep coming after her.

There was no way she was allowing them to lull her into any sort of false sense of security. None.

Patching her up, rehydrating her body, bringing her food, they were just trying to mess with her head, and it wasn't going to work. Rose had not a single doubt that their little whipping game had done nothing to lure in her brother, which meant next time they would have to up their game, making whatever they did to her that much worse.

While she could endure whatever these men did to her, she didn't want to.

Finally, she knew what she wanted out of her life.

Freedom. True freedom.

For five years, she'd just been surviving, trying to learn to accept the peace she'd created for herself, trying to believe that her life was her own. It was only now, as she sat on the cold, hard concrete floor of a prison cell, using the pain from the welts the whip had left behind, that she realized all she'd really been doing was hiding.

If she made it out of there, she was done with the hiding. She was going to figure out what her dream job actually was, then keep editing to pay her bills while she went back to school. Then she was going to make an effort to make real-world friends, and build herself a community, so that if she ever went missing again, someone would actually notice.

And care.

As it stood right now, nobody truly cared if these men killed her and disposed of her body, and that left her feeling horribly empty inside. She was a human being, and she deserved to have people in her life who cared about her.

Maybe even loved her.

Allowing her fear of someone using love against her to rule her life kept her trapped just as much as Ridge had done the first eighteen years of her life.

No more.

Since there was nothing else to do there but try to think up ways to escape, Rose thought she might have come up with something. Thankfully, Mr. Bedroom Man—and she really wished she knew his name so she could stop calling him that—had delivered her food, which she guessed was a couple of hours after she woke up back in the cell.

Good food, not broth, or bread and water, but what looked to be the reheated remains of a Christmas dinner. Knowing that while she had been locked up down there, being tortured by smothering heat and then overwhelming cold, Mr. Bedroom Man and his band of merry followers were right upstairs enjoying a home-cooked Christmas meal had enraged her.

Not that she'd let on.

Instead, she'd merely accepted the food with a thank you. She wasn't too proud to accept any handouts they were willing to give and had eaten it. There had been no more meals, but that along with the fluids she'd been given, was enough to revitalize her body.

Add in the rage she continued to stoke because she knew she would need its power, and Rose was sure she was ready to make her move.

It was a risky one, especially given that she knew they were likely watching her on the camera feed around the clock. But staying there and doing nothing was even riskier. These men weren't suddenly going to decide to be nice and let her go. Her brother had done something bad enough to them that they were prepared to abduct an innocent woman and torture her just to get to him.

When they realized their plan wouldn't work, she became a liability.

One they wouldn't hesitate to get rid of.

So escape was quite literally her only option.

Growing up, her life consisted almost solely of study and chores, but there was one other thing she'd been allowed to do. Apparently, part of grooming her included keeping her body as strong as their twisted torture games were supposed to make her mind. Little Rose had learned early on that she enjoyed tumbling and climbing things, and after seeing a video of someone performing gymnastics, she'd become hooked.

Thankfully, her parents, and then her brother, had agreed that gymnastics was an appropriate way to tone her body, so she'd started studying every video and tutorial she could find. Hours of practice, any time she had a free moment, she would work on her skills. Adding to her repertoire and perfecting each trick she learned, strengthening her body, one muscle at a time, until she was good enough that if she'd lived a normal life, she would have tried out for an Olympic team.

Now those skills might save her life.

Getting through the door was out of the question. It was reinforced steel, and there was no access to screws to try to undo them and take the door off its hinges, even if she'd had something that would have worked as a screwdriver.

Waiting until the men were there and trying to get past them was also off the table. There was no way she would get past Mr. Bedroom Man even if he was alone, let alone if he was with one or more of the others.

Which left only one other option.

The vent.

Earlier, it had been her nemesis, blasting her with air hot enough to push her system into heat stroke, then enough cold air to make her hypothermic. Now it had become her lifeline.

Never in her life had Rose been so glad that she was small. Her brother had often criticized her for her stature as though she'd decided to only grow to five-foot-two to bother him personally. While strong from hours of working through gymnastics routines, her muscles looked small and insubstantial.

Yet she knew better.

She was small and strong, and hopefully just small enough to fit through the vent.

Where it led, she had no idea, but she would follow it for as long as she could, then find a way out of it, and then out of this house. Failure was not an option.

Getting to the vent, however, was going to be tricky. There was no furniture she could use to get up close to the ceiling, which meant she was going to need every one of her skills.

Her plan was to use the door handle to get her three feet off the ground, then she'd have to launch herself at the vent. She had no idea how sturdy it was or how hard it would be to rip it off, and once she launched at it, there would be no way for her to perch up there and figure out how to remove it.

Which meant she was betting on her body weight being enough to pull it free.

Then all she'd have to do was land safely, then fling herself right back up to the vent and wriggle her way inside it.

A million things could go wrong, but Rose wasn't going to dwell on them.

What was the point?

If she talked herself out of this, she was accepting her fate, and she'd never once accepted the fate anyone else had tried to determine for her.

Being watched was her biggest problem, because if they thought she was up to something they'd be down there in a heartbeat.

So instead of making any attempt at getting to the vent, Rose merely started a warm-up routine and then began to flip and tumble her way across the floor. She'd cleared an entire room in her house so she could do her floor routines, and she'd even toyed with the idea of once again building her own equipment, parallel bars, uneven bars, and a balance beam.

This was her happy place because it was the only thing back in her childhood that she'd had any sort of control over. Now she prayed that if anyone was watching her, they'd quickly get bored, thinking she was just trying to stave off boredom and panic, so that when she made her move, they weren't ready for it.

CHAPTER

Seven

December 27th
12:10 P.M.

"You know there are leftovers in the fridge."

Steel grunted at Voodoo and set the large casserole dish back into the oven. He knew there were leftovers in the fridge he could have heated up for the little ladybug, but still here he was cooking for her.

"We have bread and cheese and stuff too. Could have just made her a sandwich," Voodoo added.

"Pretty sure the least we owe her since he stole her from her bed on Christmas Eve and made her miss the holiday is some real food before we send her packing," he mumbled, even though it had nothing to do with that.

"Pretty sure your little ladybug didn't have plans to celebrate the holidays," Voodoo shot back. "If she did, her house would have been decorated like all the others."

Yet it wasn't.

Like their own home, it had been left bare, as though Christmas didn't even exist.

"You want to know why," Voodoo said.

"Why what?"

Even if he hadn't been facing his friend, he would have known that Voodoo rolled his eyes at that. It was a lame thing to ask because Steel knew he wasn't fooling any of them. For some irritating reason, the little ladybug had gotten under his skin. It wasn't like he cared about her or what happened to her—not exactly anyway—he just felt this pull toward her that was completely unwanted.

"Really? You're going to play at being obtuse. That's insulting, given not only your own high IQ but ours as well."

The fact that they had all been both physically strong and highly intelligent had been the reason they were accepted to the program that Dr. Gardner was running. If only they'd known what exactly it entailed, they never would have signed up for it. Then again, that had been the point, the crazed scientist hadn't wanted anyone to know what he was really trying to do.

"I don't care why Rose doesn't celebrate Christmas," he said, somewhat belligerently. But the problem was he didn't even understand what he was feeling for the little ladybug, or why he was feeling anything at all, since Dr. Gardner had destroyed their ability to love and empathize with other human beings. The last thing he wanted to do was talk to someone else about what he himself couldn't figure out.

"Liar." Voodoo said the word, but there was no heat in it, it was just stated like a fact. "You know we aren't monsters. Not really. Only if we let ourselves become them."

Of all of them, Voodoo was the one who had clung to his humanity the most. They'd always assumed it was just because the man had always been a healer, a saver, so it had been harder for the drugs they'd been given to amputate that part of his humanity.

"Lion has never given up on the woman from his past," Voodoo continued. "He stays away from her, but whoever she is, he still loves her. What they did to us couldn't take that from him. And he watched over Monique while she was here, looked out for her. Dragon fell for Cassandra, we all watched it happen. And none of us can deny that we would burn the world to the ground for Beth. I'm not denying that what they did to us was wrong, or that it didn't have a profound impact.

The rage we all struggled to contain during those first months, the detachment we all feel, and the tight control we keep on our emotions that we only allow out when we have a deserving target before us. We're changed, but we're not monsters."

A part of him wanted to believe that what Voodoo was saying was true, that their humanity hadn't been completely stripped from them.

There was a part of him that wanted to believe it wasn't as well. Ten years was a long time, and they'd long ago accepted that this was who they were now, this was their life.

"All I'm saying is there's nothing wrong with admitting that you feel something for her. Hell, the woman has been a rock star since we brought her here. She wasn't anything like we were expecting. She's strong and brave, tough and sassy. She doesn't back down even when she has to be scared."

"We're broken," Steel reminded his friend. It was true, not only had there been uncontrollable rage inside them when they first underwent the treatments that altered them, but there had been suicidal thoughts as well. In fact, the other team that began treatment at the same time hadn't survived the first three months. Two of the six men killed themselves, then a third killed the other three and then himself. Like the rage over time, they'd learned to control those impulses, but they hadn't completely gone away.

Even if he did feel anything for the little ladybug, where did that leave either one of them?

It wasn't like Rose was going to be tripping over herself to go out on a date with him after he'd abducted and tortured her. He wouldn't even know what to do to plan a date anymore, that part of his life felt so long ago. Delta Team lived out there alone, to protect others and themselves, they battled their anger and suicidal thoughts, they searched for a way to get their vengeance, and they worked for Prey. There was no room for anything or anyone else in their lives.

"Your weird little ladybug is tumbling around the room like she's possessed," Blade announced as he strolled into the kitchen with a tablet in his hand.

"Tumbling?" he repeated, glad to have something else to focus on other than the heavy conversation Voodoo had brought with him. In the end, it didn't matter if he felt a pull toward the little ladybug, after he fed her and she passed out, they were packing her up and returning her to her home.

All the while praying they hadn't damaged her too badly. The little ladybug already seemed to carry a lot of scars, he didn't want to add to her nightmares, even as he knew that they had. For one thing, she'd likely never go to sleep again without fear of waking up with a man dressed all in black standing beside her bed.

Crossing to the table where his tablet lay, he snatched it up, unlocked it, and brought up the camera feed from the basement cell. Sure enough, there Rose was, flipping and spinning backward and forward across the small room. Her form was near perfect, and it was clear that she was a highly trained gymnast.

Watching her was mesmerizing. She reminded him of the wind, moving with grace and a strength that couldn't be measured by normal standards. She didn't stop for breath, moving with a restlessness that he was sure came from the stress of being held in a tiny, windowless room for three days now.

There was no way Rose didn't know someone was watching her, but there was freedom in her movements. She was tumbling without a care in the world, and she was stunning. Each time she flipped her pajama top moved with her, showing glimpses of the underside of the small swell of her breasts, and a growl rumbled from his chest before he even realized it.

Both Voodoo and Blade laughed.

"Okay, we won't keep watching to get another glimpse of your girl's breasts," Blade said with a smirk as he set his tablet down and strolled back out of the kitchen.

"Think about what I said, yeah?" Voodoo added as he too sauntered off, leaving Steel alone with the tablet and the meal he was cooking for the little ladybug.

"I didn't think I'd feel any regret for using you," he whispered to the woman flipping so effortlessly on the screen he held a little too tightly. "You were just a tool, a means to an end. I thought we'd use you, then ship you off home once we killed your brother. I never let myself think about the consequences of using you, how it might break you, how you'd recover, if you even would. But I underestimated you, didn't I, little ladybug? Because you're not breakable."

There was no doubt that Rose was a kindred soul, and he knew that the person responsible for leaving both of them with scars that ran deep enough that neither would ever be considered normal was the same man.

"When I kill him, I'll get in some strikes for you, little ladybug," he assured her. Some of Ridge's screams before he took his last breath should be for Rose, it seemed only right considering she was likely the man's first victim. Ridge might not have played with his sister's DNA, but whatever he'd done to her had forged a strength that didn't flinch in the face of torture.

Just as he was about to set the tablet down and check on the meal he was preparing for his little ladybug, he watched as Rose suddenly flung herself off the ground, using the door handle as a steppingstone as she flew across the air.

For a second she seemed to hang there, and he was already preparing himself to assess how badly she'd injured herself when she came down on the hard concrete floor.

Only she didn't come down.

Her fingers connected with the flimsy covering for the vent.

Swinging her body side to side, when she did hit the ground, it was with the vent cover in hand, and with a graceful landing.

Already moving for the basement stairs, Steel watched as Rose didn't hesitate to perform the same maneuver, this time toward the open vent that was just large enough for her to fit inside.

But when she managed to scramble up inside it, he watched in horror as the ceiling began to sway and dip, not designed to hold a person's weight, not even someone as small as Rose.

As she fell, this time along with the ceiling, Steel knew he could never make it to her in time to save her.

December 27th
    12:26 P.M.

. . .

After tumbling around the room for what she had to guess was close to fifteen minutes, maybe even twenty, it was hard to keep count when she was flipping and spinning backward and forward across the floor, Rose decided anyone watching her was bored now.

Lulled into a false sense of security.

Maybe they thought she had lost her mind, maybe they thought she was trying to do her best to cling to it, it didn't matter.

All that mattered was that they not be prepared for her to make her move.

Dying in this place at the hands of these men wasn't on her bingo card, and if she was going to die, it was going to be at her own hand. Rose was prepared to throw herself off a roof, or slit her own wrists, whatever it took. The only thing she wasn't prepared to do was remain as Mr. Bedroom Man and his friends' plaything.

If they wanted to play, they needed to find a new toy.

Praying this worked, with her next flip, Rose aimed at the door. The handle was small, but thankfully so were her feet, and she only needed to use it as a springboard, nothing more.

Pushing herself higher than she felt she needed to go, she tried to make her aim as accurate as she could and was rewarded a moment later with the feeling of the cool metal under her bare feet.

Using the door handle to launch herself, Rose threw everything she had into the flip and was grateful the room was as small as it was, otherwise, she doubted she'd stand a chance at getting to the vent.

For a moment, it felt like she was flying.

Ever since she could remember, she'd been obsessed with flying. All her childhood dreams had centered around having wings so she could soar across the great expanse of sky and find her way to freedom. It didn't matter what the flying thing was, a plane, a bird, a butterfly, a bee ... a ladybug ... if it had wings of some kind, it captured her attention.

No wings grew from her back, but still it felt as though she was flying as she crossed the room, her arms stretched out, fingers ready to grab hold of the cover blocking the vent.

When they connected, she hissed in a pained breath. Now not only was her backside aching, protesting all the flipping, but she was sure she'd just ripped at least a couple of nails.

Oh well, at least nails grew back, and skin healed, but if she stayed there, her life would be over.

Swinging her body from side to side, creating her own momentum, she was rewarded with a small creak before she fell.

Ha! Take that, Mr. Bedroom Man.

To minimize any damage the fall might cause, Rose tucked her body and rolled with the landing, coming up on her feet.

Because she knew that someone might not have gotten bored watching her tumble, she didn't allow herself even a second to catch her breath. Instead, she lined up with the door once again, and then took off for it.

Repeating the same moves that had gotten her up to the vent before, Rose sailed effortlessly up to the vent, grabbing hold of it, and once again using her body's momentum, only this time to swing her legs up so she could crawl into the vent.

Feeling as though eyes were on her, she turned and looked at the camera, giving a little wave.

Run, run, as fast as you can. You can't catch me I'm the ladybug girl.

If she was being watched, she didn't have long to make this work. Already, Mr. Bedroom Man and his buddies would be figuring out how to catch her, and she had no intention of letting them.

Shifting her weight so she could squeeze through the vent that was barely big enough to fit her body, and thankfully way too small to fit any of her captors, Rose heard an ominous creak.

The ceiling seemed to creak and shift beneath her.

Damn, girl, how do you have the world's worst luck?

That was her last thought before she was once again falling toward the hard concrete ground, only this time she wasn't alone.

An entire concrete ceiling seemed to be coming down with her.

How the hell was she supposed to survive this?

It wasn't the fall that would kill her, break an arm or a leg possibly, but nothing more serious than that, she just wasn't high enough. But the concrete that was plummeting alongside her could easily crush her like the bug Mr. Bedroom Man kept calling her.

Unsure what her best move was, and with only split seconds before she hit the ground, it had to have been some sort of instinct that had her turning so she'd land on her front. That way, she could curl into a ball and try to do her best to protect her head and vital organs from the worst of the fall.

It wasn't likely to change anything.

Especially since the universe seemed to hate her.

But at least it was something.

Pain ricocheted up her wrists and knees as they took the brunt of the fall. There was no time to worry about it, because already the concrete was raining down around her.

In the end, Rose had no idea if she managed to roll up in a ball and try to protect her body, because something connected with her head, and it was lights out for her.

With a groan, she swam back to consciousness sometime later.

Why aren't I dead?

That was her first thought, and she wasn't proud of it, but who could really blame her for wishing for death over being a plaything to a bunch of psycho men who were stupid enough to believe her brother would ever care about anyone but himself?

They'd plucked her from the quiet, safe little life she'd carved out for herself, and thrown her back into a hell she'd barely survived once before.

A hell she didn't want to battle through again.

No one could blame her for that, right? She was so exhausted from fighting every day just to survive, only to end up with nothing to show for it. Nobody was going to miss her, her clients would just be angry, thinking she ghosted them, her community, which she stayed on the fringes of, would brand her a scammer. She wasn't even leaving behind a pet that would mourn her.

Nothing.

Rose wasn't sure if it was the pain swamping her body, the growing sense of claustrophobia, or her own frustration with herself and her choices that had nausea swelling in her stomach.

Bile burned her throat as her stomach determined it must empty itself, and she was eternally grateful that nothing much was in there to come up. Coughing and gagging until her stomach cramped, and tears leaked from the corners of her eyes, when it finally stopped, she tried to turn her head the other way, away from the bile she'd just vomited up, but there was nowhere to go.

She couldn't even turn her head.

Slowly, she became more aware of the pressure against her entire body. The entire ceiling had come down with her, and now it was pinning her in place.

Burying her alive.

Choking on a sob, Rose frantically looked around, but there was nothing to see but complete and utter darkness. She'd been trapped before, locked into small spaces, but she'd always been able to move, at least a little.

Now she couldn't even turn her head.

Completely stuck.

There was no way she could even attempt to dig herself out, and even if Mr. Bedroom Man and his friends did the honors, they weren't going to let her go. They might just kill her outright, or maybe they'd toy with her a little longer, the cat playing with the mouse before it gobbled it up.

Maybe they'd even ship her broken body back to her brother.

As far as she was concerned, she'd rather die at the hands of her captors than her brother. She didn't want to give Ridge the satisfaction of ending her life.

Didn't want to give these men that satisfaction either, but trapped as she was, she couldn't even grab a rock and bash her own skull in. Something she absolutely would have considered if she'd had the use of her arms.

But like always, she was stuck.

Stuck in her childhood, unable to escape.

Stuck in her own head, unable to let go of her childhood.

Stuck in this cell, her childhood coming back to torment her once more.

Always stuck.

Frustration bubbled up inside her, rage that her life had been so unfair, fury that she was partly to blame for her own circumstances because she used her past as a crutch, a reason not to have to step outside her comfort zone.

A bitter laugh escaped, filling the deafening silence. "Maybe if you'd just stop fighting so hard, you could finally get where you want to be."

Peace. That's what she wanted, what she craved. So, dragging in huge mouthfuls of air, she could only hope she used up the remaining oxygen trapped with her as quickly as possible so she could finally get her peace.

CHAPTER
Eight

December 27th
12:32 P.M.

Watching in horror as Rose was buried alive by a pile of concrete, Steel found himself frozen.

The need to get to her, to do something, pulsed through his body, and yet he was unable to move.

"What the hell was that?" Lion asked, appearing out of nowhere.

Shoving the tablet at his friend, Steel wrenched open the door in the kitchen that led to the basement and hurried down the stairs. Before he even reached the bottom of the steps, Thunder was there. Thank goodness for enhanced speed, because he was going to need all of them to even stand a chance at saving Rose before it was too late.

"Was that the ceiling that fell?" Thunder asked.

"Rose." That was all Steel could force out because it felt like his lungs had constricted, making it almost impossible to draw in enough oxygen to function.

Was she already dead?

Surely she had to be, how could a woman barely topping five-foot-two, hardly over one hundred pounds, possibly survive a pile of concrete crushing her?

"Thought she was doing tricks?" Thunder asked.

"She was. Only those tricks were trying to escape," he muttered. "Basement. Now!" he screamed, knowing that Blade, with his superior hearing, would hear him no matter where he was in the mansion and gather the others.

"No way she survived that, man," Lion said gently as they reached the basement and headed for the hidden door that led to another flight of stairs that would take them down to the underground cells.

Those cells weren't there when Eagle originally set them up with this place. The six of them had built them after moving in, although they'd always been intended for Ridge Gardner and the men and women who worked with him. Not someone as small as Rose, so there had never been any consideration that anyone would try to escape through the ventilation system.

The underground cells were deep. It had taken them almost a year to dig out enough space under the building, while ensuring the mansion didn't collapse because of it. If it had occurred to him that Rose wouldn't be safe down there, he would have locked her in a bedroom.

Damn woman probably would have tried to throw herself out a window, though.

"Whoa," Voodoo murmured as the rest of his team joined them at the bottom of the stairs.

Rose's cell had been the one closest to the stairs. There were another eleven down there, then the room down the end. The torture room where they'd strung the little ladybug up and whipped her.

At the bottom of the stairs, a pile of concrete lay where the corridor leading between the two rows of cells should be. There was no way to know how bad things were because the concrete was completely blocking their entry.

"Find her," Steel ordered as he began to grab chunks of concrete and toss them aside. Never in his life had he been as glad for his superior strength as he was in this moment.

At first, after they started the trial with Dr. Gardner, the extra strength had been kind of cool. Until he and his team started becoming consumed with rage and suicidal thoughts, and they learned that enhancing their skills wasn't the only thing Dr. Gardner had done. Then he'd resented the changes because they'd been lied to. If he'd known the extent of what the doctor had planned, he never would have agreed to be a guinea pig.

Now their skills could be the only thing that saved Rose's life.

The little ladybug wasn't dying minutes before he was going to feed her, knock her out, and return her to her home.

"She's got to be dead," Dragon announced, and Steel spun on the man. Dragon was his friend, his brother in every way that mattered, but he was also the only one who had wanted to keep torturing Rose in the hopes that they could lure her brother in.

"You want her dead, don't you?" He snarled as he shoved his friend up against the closest wall. His hands clamped around Dragon's neck, and while the other man was strong, no one was a match for Steel's enhanced strength.

"Don't care one way or the other," Dragon rasped, the words barely able to pass through the tight hold he had on the man's neck. "You shouldn't either."

"And if it was Cassandra in there?" Voodoo asked, and Dragon's dark blue, almost violet-colored eyes all but shot daggers at him.

"That's what I thought. Is Steel falling for Rose Gardner inconvenient? Sure as hell it is. But it is what it is. Deal with it. Not like the woman has done anything wrong. She's only twenty-three, which means she was only thirteen years old when her brother turned us into monsters," Voodoo ranted.

Defiance still danced in Dragon's purple eyes, and Steel was sorely tempted to tighten his grip just a tiny bit more and snap the man's neck.

It was like he was possessed, protective rage consumed him, and he deemed anything that wanted to get in the way of him and his little ladybug as a threat. Even one of his men.

"I hear something," Blade announced, and Steel threw Dragon to the side, pleased when he heard a thump and a grunt of pain.

"What?" he demanded, striding over to where Blade was standing at the top of the small opening Steel had made by throwing chunks of concrete out of the way.

"Breathing," Blade replied.

"She's not dead." Steel wasn't sure if it was a question or a statement, but it was all he needed to push past his friend and begin throwing more concrete out of his path. If Rose was still alive, nothing was going to stop him from getting to her.

The others all began to help. They might not have his strength, but they were still men who worked out hours a day and had the bodies to prove it.

Each second felt like an hour.

Each minute a day.

"There," Lion suddenly called out.

They'd all been clearing away the debris from where Blade had indicated he could hear Rose's breathing, now they hyper-focused on that area.

"You can still hear her?" Steel asked Blade, who nodded. "And you're sure that's where she is?" he asked Lion, who also nodded. When he looked at Dragon, the man huffed, but gave a single, sharp nod.

"Yeah, I can smell her blood, and it's coming from right where they said," Dragon said, although he didn't sound pleased about it.

Steel, on the other hand, found himself more than pleased to see a small amount of blood streaking his friend's face.

In comparison, the thought of Rose's blood ...

He couldn't even think about it.

With renewed efforts, he tossed concrete aside, leaving it to the others to move further out of their way. All he cared about was finding the little ladybug and getting her out. Knowing she was alive but trapped, buried alive, made him feel sick, and he could only imagine how much worse it was for Rose if she was conscious.

Conscious meant a better chance of living, but it also meant she was suffering, and at the way his heart hammered in his chest, Steel realized he wasn't so distorted to not feel empathy as he'd been led to believe.

"Careful, we're close," Blade cautioned, and Steel tried to do as his friend instructed.

When he glimpsed a lock of dusty red hair, he froze. She was there, close enough to touch, but he was worried any move he made was only going to make things worse.

"We got this," Voodoo said softly, and when he glanced up, he saw all five men watching him. They all offered reassuring nods, even Dragon.

Moving more slowly, Steel carefully continued moving concrete until he uncovered Rose's body. She was curled in on herself, in the fetal position, mostly on her side. There were smudges of blood mixed with the dirt from the concrete, and the beginnings of what would be some pretty horrific bruises.

As he shifted away the last chunk of concrete, tossing it effortlessly to the side, he saw wide green eyes looking at him.

"How did you do that?" she croaked, before her eyes rolled back in her head and she passed out.

Guess the cat was out of the bag now.

Although that was a worry for another time.

Gathering her into his arms, Steel growled possessively when Voodoo moved to take possession of the small woman he was cradling close.

"I got her," he snapped, not able to put into words how badly he needed to feel her tiny body in his arms. Then he fixed his friend with a death stare. Never would he have guessed he would threaten one of his brothers, the men he'd relied on for everything this last decade. But never had he uttered words he meant more than the next ones he spoke. "You'd better save her life."

～

December 27th
    1:01 P.M.

Pain.
    Darkness.
    Threatening to pull her under.
    No.
    Can't.
    Helpless.

Vulnerable.

Have to fight.

The words tumbled through Rose's mind as she felt her body floating.

That couldn't be right.

She wasn't doing any tumbling, and she didn't really have wings.

If she did, she would have flown away from her life a long time ago. Found some remote little spot on a mountain somewhere where no one would ever find her. Thanks to her upbringing, she knew how to survive with nothing. Could build her own shelter, dig herself a well or utilize a stream, hunt for food, and grow some of her own. She could even make her own clothes, there was no reason she couldn't live completely self-sufficiently.

That way she'd never have to see another person ever again.

Damn, she hated people. Nothing good ever came from being around people.

Darkness washed over her, taking her away with it into a place that was blissfully free of pain.

Until it wasn't. A moan fell from her lips as she was jostled.

"Don't hurt her," a voice snarled.

Wait. She knew that voice.

It almost sounded like ... Mr. Bedroom Man. Only ...

Why would he care if anyone hurt her? After all, that was the exact reason he and his friends abducted her. They *wanted* to hurt her. They *had* hurt her.

Except afterward, he'd told her that they fixed what they broke, then knocked her out so he could tend to her wounds and rehydrate her.

Rose was getting a headache trying to figure out what was going on.

Or maybe that was because the ceiling had collapsed on her.

"Don't touch her," Mr. Bedroom Man growled, and someone else gave an annoyed huff.

"How exactly do you expect me to help her if you won't let me touch her?"

She knew that voice, too. It was the man who had given her the pills in the basement that made her pass out. Was he some sort of doctor? Weren't you supposed to take some kind of oath to do no harm when you became a doctor? You know, because you wanted to save lives not take them.

Mr. Bedroom Man grunted, but she felt herself move again, and she couldn't help another moan escaping.

Damn, she hurt all over.

"Would you stop looking at me like that. I heard your threat loud and clear. She dies, I die," the other man said, and Rose had no idea what that could possibly mean.

No one cared if she died.

Certainly not enough to kill someone else because of it, which, if she was reading the words correctly, a threat had been delivered from Mr. Bedroom Man to Doctor Man involving her and whether she lived or died.

Too bad for them that the idea of dying didn't seem so bad right now.

Set down on something soft, Rose would have assumed it was a bed, but why would they put her on a bed? There were no beds in her cell, and they'd put her back in her cell after whipping her, so she doubted they would upgrade her accommodation just because she had managed to pull the roof down on herself.

Then again, Mr. Bedroom Man was sounding awfully possessive all of a sudden.

Hands began to skim her body, and she didn't need to open her eyes, something which it seemed she couldn't do anyway, to know that Mr. Bedroom Man was shooting death glares at Doctor Man.

What the hell was up with him?

Why was he worried about her dying when he planned to kill her anyway? Her brother wasn't going to care about her and give them what they wanted, so the only logical next step was for them to kill her.

Yet it seemed he was trying to fix her instead.

Something sharp pricked the inside of her elbow, but honestly, she was hurting so badly all over that it barely even registered on the pain scale.

When hands brushed across her arm, Rose screamed and jerked off whatever she'd been set down on. That didn't just hurt, it broke the pain scale.

"Hold her down," Doctor Man instructed.

"Give her something," Mr. Bedroom Man countered, sounding almost panicked.

"Can't, don't know how badly she's hurt. From the way she's breathing, I know there are cracked ribs at least, but if I give her too many drugs without properly assessing her, I could kill her. That what you want?"

The responding growl was answer enough.

"Thought so. Hold her down, I have to fix this break in her arm."

Rose would have sworn the hands that covered her shoulders and eased her back to lie against what she would have sworn was a mattress were shaking. But then again, maybe it was she who was shaking so badly that it felt like Mr. Bedroom Man was shaking along with her.

The most pathetic whimper came from her as Mr. Bedroom Man held her down, and Doctor Man gently circled her wrist and elbow. She knew what was coming, but there was no way to prepare herself for the onslaught of pain that assaulted her when her broken arm was snapped back into place.

At least the pain did something helpful and shoved her into unconsciousness.

That was where she hovered.

In the dark, surfacing briefly for snippets of time. Sometimes the room was quiet, sometimes hushed voices spoke, always Mr. Bedroom Man sat beside her, his low voice murmuring soothing words whenever the pain got too bad and she became restless.

"What are we going to do with her?"

"She knows about us."

"Can't let her go now."

"She'll tell."

"Her brother will try to use her to find us."

"Never should have done this."

"Eagle is going to kill us."

"We should kill her and be done with it."

After those words, she would have sworn she heard the sounds of flesh hitting flesh, and a grunt of pain.

Pain. Her own threatened to steal all her strength from her, and

Rose whimpered and licked her dry lips. "Yes," she croaked, liking the idea of no longer being forced to suffer very much. "Kill me."

"No," Mr. Bedroom Man snarled, and she saw, or maybe felt, him move so he was standing over her. A large hand—his she assumed—brushed across her forehead in a gentle caress that made her whimper again. Not in pain this time, but because she craved touches like that more than she craved her next painful breath. "You have to live, little ladybug."

"Don't want to anymore, too tired," she murmured before the darkness came for her again, sweeping her away into the sea of nothingness.

There were more whispered words around her, but no more talk about killing her, and she almost regretted her words. Maybe if she'd kept quiet, they would have done it.

Time passed slowly. Or maybe it was quickly. Bright sunlight hurt her eyes, then there was darkness, then sunlight once again.

Next time she woke, Rose felt a little more with it. The pain was still there, but she was able to find some strength to shove it into a box. Blinking open her eyes, she found herself in a bedroom. It was gorgeously decorated, the walls were covered in a deep burgundy wallpaper with a small gold flower pattern, she was lying on a huge four-poster bed, the dark wooden posts carved with flowers, an actual chandelier hung from the ceiling in the center of the room, drapes that matched the wallpaper covered what she assumed was a window. The rest of the room's furniture, two nightstands, a dresser, a wardrobe that could have come right out of The Lion, The Witch, and The Wardrobe, was all in a dark wood stain, and a chaise lounge that was upholstered with the same pattern as the wallpaper and curtains was pulled close to the bed.

"You're awake." Mr. Bedroom Man stood as he spoke, towering over her, and the hint of a memory trickled into her mind.

Buried under the rubble, Rose had been positive she was going to die. Not only had her body been burning with pain, but there wasn't much oxygen left around her. Just surviving the initial fall and the concrete debris piling up around her was a miracle, but she'd been certain that she would never make it out alive.

How could she? There was no way six men could remove that much concrete quickly enough, even if they wanted to save her, which they didn't. At least she'd thought they hadn't, now she wasn't so sure.

But she remembered watching as Mr. Bedroom Man literally lifted a chunk of concrete that had to be half the size of her like it was nothing more than a pebble.

Eyes widening, she stared up at the man looming above her. He was no longer wearing a balaclava, so she could finally see all of his face and not just his eyes and mouth. It was an annoyingly handsome face given the reasons why had to look at it, strong jaw, high cheekbones, perfectly shaped lips. Some distant part of her mind recognized that it couldn't be a good thing that she now knew what he looked like, that it meant he didn't intend to let her walk away alive. But right now there was a more pressing issue she had to address. "Who are you, and how did you lift concrete like it was nothing?"

CHAPTER Nine

December 28th
8:46 P.M.

There was no fear in Rose's eyes as she looked up at him. Just curiosity and pain he wished he could eradicate as easily as he had picked up that concrete and tossed it aside.

Answering her question wasn't possible, though.

Rose was alive and relatively in one piece, thanks to Voodoo and his almost magical ability to heal, but that didn't mean she was safe. Not only did Dragon want to kill her so she couldn't go back and tell anyone about them, but they'd planted cameras in Rose's home in case her brother went there, and someone had broken in last night and trashed the place. What they were looking for, he didn't know and didn't care, but their pulling Rose into their game of revenge had placed a target on her back from her brother as well.

No one was laying a hand on his little ladybug. Dragon knew what would happen if he went rogue, and if Steel truly believed the man was a threat to Rose, then Dragon would already be dead.

But for now, the man was banned from Rose's room. Dragon

needed to find another way to work through his anger at losing Cassandra, taking it out on the little ladybug was not an option.

"I don't know what you mean," he said evenly, keeping his expression neutral.

Rose rolled her eyes at him and then winced as it obviously caused her pain, making him want to break something.

Knowing she was hurting and being unable to fix it left him feeling like a nest of wasps had made their home under his skin. The fiery burn wasn't something he was used to. Worrying about someone who wasn't a member of his team wasn't anything he'd thought he would ever do again.

But there he was.

Worrying about the little ladybug.

"Liar," she muttered, shifting and wincing again.

"Stop doing that," he snarled.

"Doing what?" she asked, genuinely confused.

"Moving."

Her look conveyed more than any words could. It was clear she thought he was being weird, which he was, no arguments there.

"I'm uncomfortable," she said slowly as though she were talking to an idiot. And the thing was, when he was around her, that was exactly what Steel felt like he was.

"What are you doing to me?" he murmured, more to himself than the woman looking at him like he'd grown two heads.

"Umm ... nothing?"

"Stay still," he ordered, when she continued to shift in the bed.

"Ugh, I wish I'd stayed unconscious," she grumbled, but thankfully, she stilled so he didn't have to watch her cause herself more pain.

Steel was glad she'd woken up, even if Rose wasn't.

It had been a hellish thirty-two hours with her hovering in and out of consciousness, not having the tools they needed to treat her, relying only on Voodoo, who had somehow managed to do what he always did and deal with the worst of Rose's wounds. There were cracked ribs, the broken arm, a concussion, but thankfully no internal bleeding. How the hell she'd survived with relatively minor injuries, Steel had no idea, but he did know that without Voodoo, there would have been no way to tell if she had internal bleeding or not, and if she did no way to treat it.

"Is our little patient awake?" Voodoo asked as he came strolling into the room.

"Why do you have a black eye?" Rose asked, her brow scrunching adorably before she lifted a hand and rubbed at her temple.

"What did I say about staying still?" he growled, reaching out a hand and banding it around her wrist. Beneath his fingers, her bones were so delicate, so easily snapped, it had been a long time since he'd been so very aware of his enhanced strength and how different it made him from everybody else.

"Relax," she told him, like she had no awareness of how easily he could break her. Maybe she didn't. She'd seen what he could do, but she was weak and woozy from her injuries, and he doubted it had fully sunk in yet.

"I would if you would stop causing yourself undue pain. Do I need to tie you to the bed, little ladybug?"

Although he'd meant the words as a threat, arousal flared in Rose's forest green eyes, and she squirmed on the bed. Huh. Seemed the little ladybug had a kinky side, although by the confusion warring with desire in her gaze, he assumed it might be one she was unaware of.

"No tying up my patient," Voodoo said, watching their exchange with amusement.

"Thank you, Doctor Man," Rose said, her gaze locked on where his hand still circled her wrist.

"Doctor Man?" Voodoo repeated.

Rose shrugged. "Don't know your real name."

"Stop moving, little ladybug, or I will absolutely tie you to this bed and not feel an ounce of remorse for it," he warned.

"Idiot," she mumbled, but turned her attention to Voodoo. "How did you get the black eye?" Concern overtook her features. "Were you in the basement when the ceiling fell down?"

How the hell could the little ladybug care whether her actions had hurt one of the people who were holding her captive? She was all sorts of surprising, and Steel found he almost enjoyed unraveling another of her layers.

"Mr. Bedroom Man here didn't like me touching you," Voodoo explained with a smirk.

"Touching me? I'm so confused. Why am I even here? You want to hurt me, that's why you kidnapped me. My brother won't play your games, so you're going to have to kill me anyway. Why didn't you just leave me to die? Why am I in a bed? Why do I have an IV? Why is there a cast on my arm? I remember someone saying you should kill me, but then I remember you saying I have to live. I don't get it," she finished, an almost helpless look on her face that he wanted to wipe away, but she moved again and winced, and he was growling before he even realized what he was doing.

"Ropes!" he yelled so Blade would hear him.

"You're not really going to tie me to the bed, are you?" Rose asked uncertainly.

"No, he's not, he's just being a little caveman because he hates seeing you in pain. I have you on pain meds and antibiotics along with the fluids. You have several cuts from the concrete, and while they look okay now, and we cleaned you up as best as we could, I didn't want to risk infection," Voodoo explained.

Glancing at the bag hanging from the post of the bed, Rose shook her head, then immediately shot him a worried glance, like she still wasn't sure if she was going to find herself bound to the bed. "You're putting fluids in me, but I don't have to pee. I'm so confused," she wailed.

"Catheter," Voodoo told her, then pointed to the black eye. "Your caveman didn't like me putting it in, but since I was the only one who knew how to do it, he didn't have a choice."

"But he gave you a black eye for doing it?" Rose asked, her gaze bouncing between the two of them.

Voodoo grinned at him, but Steel just grunted. Thankfully, he was saved from having to think up a reply when he wasn't sure how to explain the extent to which he hated anyone touching her for any reason, because Thunder appeared in the doorway with rope in his hands.

"Do we still need this?" Thunder asked, obviously having caught the end of the conversation.

"No," Voodoo and Rose said in unison.

"Yes," Steel replied at the same time.

"Okay. How about I just set these down here?" Thunder said slowly as he put the ropes on the nightstand, his amusement evident, and Steel couldn't think of a time he'd seen any of his men in such good moods as they'd been watching him tie himself in knots over the little ladybug.

"How about someone tell me what's going on?" Rose said. "You were lifting concrete," she said, looking to him. "You came up here with rope really quickly," she added, looking to Thunder. "And you were supposed to save my life, but I get the feeling that has nothing to do with you being a doctor," she said to Voodoo.

"Actually, I'm not a doctor," he told her with a cheerfulness that reminded Steel of the old Voodoo, the one before the experiments.

"Well then, what am I supposed to call you?" Rose snapped.

"Sorry, little ladybug, no names," Steel informed her. Since they would have to return her to her home at some point, once she was healed enough, it was better that she stick to her silly made-up names for them.

"What does it matter if you're going to kill me anyway?" she demanded.

Uncurling his fingers one at a time, which were still wrapped around her wrist, he lowered his hand until it circled her neck, squeezing just tight enough to get her attention but not to cause her any pain. "Thought I already told you that you have to live."

"But I don't understand." She huffed in annoyance.

Giving her a one-sided smile, Steel nodded. "I know. Don't make me regret not putting these on," he said with a nod at the ropes, then indicated to Voodoo and Thunder that they should follow him from the room.

As he closed the door behind them, he could hear Rose muttering and grumbling to herself, and the other side of his lips curled up into a real smile. The little ladybug was wild, but she was certainly breathing fresh air into their stale lives.

∼

December 28th
  9:10 P.M.

How dare he just walk out of there without telling her anything.

Rose was fuming, and a childish part of her wanted to scream after him, to rant and rave, to make sure he knew how much she hated him for shattering her illusion of freedom.

However, a bigger part of her cared more about self-preservation.

For however long they'd been keeping her there she'd been in that basement, no access to the outside world, but now she was sitting in a bed, in a real room, with a window and a regular door. The last thing she needed was to get his attention and make him come back in and tie her to the bed.

Mr. Bedroom Man would do it too. He'd seemed genuinely concerned about her being in pain. That made zero sense to her. That was exactly why he'd brought her here, to hurt her, so why was it driving him crazy if she shifted slightly on the bed and aggravated her wounds?

The man was crazy, no doubt about it.

Although she was one to talk.

Something that felt worryingly close to arousal had flooded her system when he mentioned tying her to the bed. And she'd reacted to his hand around her throat several times now. What the hell was wrong with her? Rose never felt sexual urges, ever, not for anyone. She'd never even had sex, and she didn't feel as though she was missing out on anything, she was just built differently.

Shrugging off the crazy thoughts, she could worry about why her captor's threats made her feel all needy, with a most inconvenient throbbing between her legs, but now was the time for action.

Waiting a few moments to make sure Mr. Bedroom Man, Doctor Man, and the other guy weren't going to come right back, because she wouldn't put it past them to try to trick her so they had another excuse to hurt her, when the door didn't open again, she began to move.

Pain pulsed through her body with each breath she took, but it wasn't so bad that she couldn't function. Mainly in part due to the IV that was delivering pain meds. Unfortunately, she was going to have to do away with it.

Grateful for about the thousandth time since she'd been abducted for her childhood and what it taught her about survival, Rose made quick work of removing the IV port from the inside of her elbow. If she hadn't been forced to learn to deal with anything life threw at her, no matter how terrifying or painful, she would be a sobbing, hysterical mess right now, still locked up in a basement cell.

This was her chance of escaping, and she couldn't waste it.

It didn't matter that she didn't understand why they had looked for her under the rubble, or brought her to a bed, or treated her injuries. It didn't even matter that Mr. Bedroom Man had some kind of super strength. It was the only way to explain how she'd seen him lifting concrete as though it weighed nothing. The man who'd brought the ropes had to have some sort of super speed because he'd been up way too quickly, unless he'd been standing right outside the door with them?

No, that didn't make sense, because if Mr. Bedroom Man knew he wanted the ropes, he would have brought them with him.

Doctor Man, who apparently wasn't a doctor after all, had some sort of healing skills. It was a guess, but one she was basing on the desperation she'd heard in Mr. Bedroom Man's voice when he ordered Doctor Man to save her.

As much as she wanted to know who these men were and how they could do what they did, she wanted to get out of there more.

Sitting up wasn't fun. Her stomach revolted at the idea, threatening to throw up something if there had been anything left in there to come out. Her head also wasn't fond of the move, and the room did one of those sickening spins around her.

Clenching her eyes closed, Rose waited until the dizziness and nausea faded a little before opening them again. Looking down at her body, she could see that not only was she naked, but she was literally covered in bruises. There was hardly a spot that wasn't some shade of black, blue, or purple.

The tubing between her legs caught her attention, and her cheeks flamed with embarrassment at knowing someone had touched her there, even if it was inserting a catheter and nothing sexual. She didn't care about these men seeing her naked body, but touching it was different.

Maybe she wasn't so upset about Doctor Man getting a black eye, even as she understood he'd only been doing what he had to do to tend to her.

As she did a visual sweep of the room, she spotted her pajamas sitting neatly folded on one of the nightstands, the one without the ropes.

Steadfastly ignoring the ropes and everything they represented, from prolonged captivity to her previously latent sexual desires awakening, she removed the catheter then swung her legs over the side of the mattress and stood. Her legs felt as shaky as a newborn calf's, but she had no choice but to make them work.

If she hobbled a little as she rounded the bed and grabbed her clothing, it didn't matter, she was up and moving, and that was all that counted. Making quick work of pulling them on, Rose gritted her teeth at the shooting pain in her arm as she used it, and cursed the cracked or broken ribs that were making every breath feel like she was inhaling shards of glass.

How the hell was she supposed to escape when she could barely function?

Stop complaining.

Complain later. Once you're safe.

Creeping over to the window, she edged the drapes open just enough to peek out. It was pitch black outside, but she could make out the shadowy shapes of trees. The fact that there wasn't a single light in sight meant that wherever she'd been brought was remote.

Damn.

Of course, the universe would make this as hard as it could be for her.

While she had no idea how long she'd been kept there, she knew it couldn't really be more than a handful of days, possibly a week or so. Certainly not long enough for winter to have morphed into spring.

Which meant there was probably snow outside. If there wasn't, the ground would still be icy cold and the air temperatures would match it.

The chances of her being able to make it anywhere were slim to none, but she still had to try.

Staying there was a death sentence. At least out there she stood a chance, however small.

Of course, the lack of shoes worried her, and the fact that she was wearing nothing more than flannelette pajamas, no coat, no gloves, no scarf, no earmuffs, meant she had nothing to offer any real protection from the cold.

"The universe really does hate me," Rose muttered as she crossed the room to the door.

Pressing her ear up against it, she tried to listen carefully to figure out if anyone was out there. Unfortunately, all she could hear was her own rasped breathing and the pounding of her pulse.

Since she was pretty sure nothing was going to make her situation worse than it was, not even being caught trying to escape, because really, they should expect her to try, Rose eased open the door enough to peek out.

Empty.

The hall outside was blissfully empty, and because she knew she was living on borrowed time, she slipped out and began to walk as fast as she could manage. Other heavy wooden doors lined the corridor, but she didn't stop to check what was behind them. Even if there were other prisoners, injured as she was, she couldn't do much to help them. Her best bet was to get out and then bring the cops back.

Each step felt like stepping on a potential landmine.

At any second, she could be caught.

The stress had her stomach cramping painfully.

But she kept going.

Step after step, until she reached a staircase. It was grand, and the balustrades were intricately carved. If she weren't held captive, she could definitely appreciate the grandeur of the house.

Praying there were no squeaky steps, Rose made her way down, almost sagging in relief when she spotted what looked like a front door across a large foyer at the bottom of the staircase.

If she could just get to it, her odds would increase dramatically.

The fear of being caught was almost overwhelming, but she didn't let it slow her down. She kept moving because she knew her life depended on it.

When her hand closed around the knob and it turned, Rose almost sobbed in relief. She'd half expected it to be locked because the universe would love letting her think she'd made it only to mess with her at the last second.

Wrenching it open, she yanked it closed behind her and took off at a dead run to the line of trees that ringed the house.

She didn't make it even halfway when she heard a voice call out.

"Running is pointless, little ladybug. When I catch you, I'm going to spank that pretty backside of yours until it's bright red and you remember your punishment every time you sit. I told you what would happen if you kept causing yourself pain."

Mr. Bedroom Man's words spurred her on. She blocked out the way the throbbing between her legs started up at the mention of a spanking, because now was not the time to worry about the fact that she apparently had some bedroom kinks, and focused only on what would happen if she was caught.

She'd wind up tied to the bed and helpless all over again.

CHAPTER

Ten

December 28th
9:29 P.M.

"Your little ladybug is flying away," Blade announced as he stepped into the kitchen.

"Of course she is," Steel said with a sigh. Why would he think the crazy woman would actually listen to him and give her body the rest it needed to begin healing? "Little brat," he muttered as he shoved back his chair and stood, stretching out his back.

There was no way he wasn't watching over Rose while she slept, so he'd spent the thirty or so hours she'd drifted in and out of consciousness in a chair beside her bed. While he couldn't put a name on what he felt for the little ladybug, it was useless to pretend he felt nothing, so he'd given up trying to hide it from the guys.

Other than Dragon, they all found it amusing, and other than teasing him any chance they got, they were slowly attempting to make their peace with the idea that Rose wasn't going anywhere.

Returning her to her old life was too dangerous now that they knew someone had trashed her house, likely looking for any clues he and his team may have left behind. As if they would be stupid enough to do that.

But if dropping her back off at her house left her vulnerable, they might have to keep her there with them. Something the little ladybug was not going to accept easily. She'd fight them every step of the way, and there was no chance he was putting her back in the basement even once they got it fixed. Locking her in a room likely meant she'd just try to jump out of a window, even if he moved her up to the fourth floor.

Which didn't give them many other options. They might have to read her in on the truth.

But first, he had to catch her.

Lucky for her—or unlucky depending on how you looked at it—Steel loved a good hunt.

"Need help?" Thunder asked, sticking his head into the kitchen.

The man's extraordinary speed would make this quicker, but Steel found he looked forward to playing with his little ladybug. "Nope, I got it. Not like she's going to get far. She had no shoes and nothing but a pair of pajamas, and it's snowing out there. Add in her cracked ribs, bruises, and broken arm, and she's not going anywhere."

Striding to the front door, he stepped out onto the porch, immediately catching sight of Rose not even to the trees yet.

"Running is pointless, little ladybug. When I catch you, I'm going to spank that pretty backside of yours until it's bright red and you remember your punishment every time you sit. I told you what would happen if you kept causing yourself pain," he called out.

Chances were, he could probably be persuaded not to tie her to the bed, and he wasn't going to spank her when she was already hurting and in pain. When he did, and he was starting to feel as though that were an inevitability at this point, he wanted her to beg for it, wanted her to enjoy it as much as he would, wanted her screaming his name as pleasure tore through her system.

Rose didn't falter at his words, and he had to give her credit for determination. The little ladybug was nothing like he'd expected her to be when they'd broken into her home less than five days ago. He'd expected a weak woman who would easily break and give them what they needed to get her brother to fall into their trap. Instead, he'd gotten a woman who fought them at every turn, who was strong and confident, who took anything life threw at her.

A survivor who hid her pain and trauma behind a shield.

A woman more like him and his team than he ever could have imagined.

Now she was running from him and his primal side, which had been enhanced by Dr. Gardner as his humanity was washed away, found it didn't like that very much.

Damn, did he want to claim the woman? Mark her as his?

That wasn't going to work, but still something inside him urged him to chase, to catch, to claim.

Because he wanted this to be fun, instead of running right after Rose, he instead headed off at a ninety-degree angle from the route she was taking. The little ladybug really should have assumed that the front door would be alarmed and they would be alerted to her leaving.

Actually, they'd known the second she opened the door to her bedroom and heard her creep around. Too bad she didn't completely understand who she was dealing with, beyond knowing there was some-thing weird about their abilities. If she'd known Blade had heard her door opening, then she likely would have stayed in her bed where he'd left her.

Dressed more appropriately for the weather than Rose was, Steel at least had on shoes, jeans, and a long-sleeve shirt. His body was better able to cope with extreme temperatures, whether they be hot or cold, another side effect of Dr. Gardner's psychotic games.

The man had managed to create the super soldiers he'd wanted, but he'd underestimated his creations. He'd thought they would develop blind loyalty to him, accept him as their leader. Now the man would do anything to get them back, but he wasn't stupid enough to walk into a trap unless they found something he cared about more than himself.

That wasn't his sister, and Steel doubted there was anything. Which meant they'd have to find another way to locate where the cowardly scientist had hidden himself away.

For now, though, he wanted to enjoy the hunt.

His legs ate up the distance to the trees, and he'd learned in his regular military training how to move without making a sound, keeping each footfall light. His enhanced skills had only added to that, and Rose wasn't going to know he was there until he grabbed her.

It had been years since he'd actually had fun. He and his team worked for Prey, and they searched for Dr. Gardner, they hung around the house, passing the time, but they didn't have fun.

While he knew how to move quietly, he hadn't expected Rose to be as silent as she was. Although he paused every so often and listened, it took him longer than he would have anticipated to pinpoint her location.

The only thing that gave her away was her ragged breathing, caused by overexerting her injured and weak body, exacerbated by her cracked ribs. Seemed she, too, had learned how to run without making a lot of sound, and he hated that it was likely her brother who had taught her that.

What hell had she lived through as a child?

Had she suffered more at the hands of Ridge Gardner than he and his team had?

"Don't worry, little ladybug, I won't stop hunting your brother until I get him, and I won't end his life until his screams soothe the pain inside you," he vowed softly.

Tracking Rose was easy enough, and although she was constantly trying to alter her path to make herself harder to follow, he quickly noticed the patterns in her movements and circled past her so that she'd run right into him.

Leaning up against a tree trunk, he crossed his ankles and waited.

"I'm coming for you, little ladybug. There's nowhere to hide," he called out, throwing his voice so it sounded like it was coming from behind her rather than in front.

From her sharp gasp, he knew she was close, and he couldn't wait to catch a glimpse of her. With her skin flushed red from the cold, her long red locks billowing behind her, and defiance burning brightly in her forest green eyes, she would be a vision, the perfect prey, because even though she hated him, she was as affected by him as he was by her.

Fate played the cruelest of games, taunting him with something he could never have.

Or could he?

Rose couldn't go home, it wasn't safe for her. Keeping her there was the only logical thing, because calling in Prey meant Eagle learning that they'd gone rogue. Where else would the little ladybug go? She hated him now, but maybe if he told her everything, she'd understand. After all, who better to grasp what a psychopath her brother was than Rose herself?

She'd slowed down, nearing the point of exhaustion and no doubt in all sorts of pain. If she wanted, she could paint him as the bad guy for this, but he would ensure she gave her body the rest it needed to begin healing.

Even if he had to tie her to the bed to do it.

Her pain ... it affected him. He felt it in every way he wasn't supposed to anymore, in ways he'd thought had been stripped from him.

Maybe Dr. Gardner wasn't as good at creating soulless killing machines as he'd thought he was.

"There you are," he said with a grin as his little ladybug stumbled through the trees toward him. "Are you ready to take your punishment like a good girl?"

~

December 28th
9:42 P.M.

Argh.

Why did she like hearing him call her a good girl?

What the hell was wrong with her?

Her body couldn't seem to get it together and get in sync with her brain.

No one messed her up like this. She'd learned through necessity, basically from birth, to go with the flow, take whatever life gave you, deal with it, work through it, and survive.

Survive.

That was all she should be focusing on right now.

Mr. Bedroom Man was going to kill her. Rose didn't care that he'd denied it and told her that he wanted her to live. She wasn't naïve enough or stupid enough to believe that.

Why would he abduct her and then not kill her when his plans failed?

There was no way she was going down without doing everything she could to save herself, so instead of responding to his ridiculous threat and her body's reaction to it, Rose turned and darted back the way she'd just come.

Behind her, he sighed and moved with way more speed than her body had in it right now, grabbing hold of her wrists with one of his hands and lifting her up, draping her over his shoulder. The position sent pain searing through her worn-out body, and even though she hated to show even the tiniest amount of weakness in front of her kidnapper, a small moan managed to escape.

Stilling, she felt the tension in Mr. Bedroom Man's body, and without warning, his hand came down with a dull thud on her backside. Immediately, he began to soothe the slight sting before she even had time to register it.

"Didn't want to do that yet, little ladybug," he muttered. "Not while those welts haven't healed. Not when you're covered in bruises. Can't seem to control myself around you. Knowing you're hurting ..."

When he trailed off and didn't finish his sentence, Rose felt tears prick in the backs of her eyes. He sounded sincere, like her pain really did bother him, but she wasn't going to believe anything this man said to her. Especially when he denied her any answers to her questions or a meaningful explanation of why they brought her here to punish her brother.

"You don't care if I'm in pain," she said defiantly, with as much dignity as she could muster while hanging upside down with a much too close for her liking view of his perfectly toned butt.

The answering growl he gave was more animal than human, and he flipped her around quicker than she could process, so she was now cradled in his arms like a bride about to be carried over the threshold. Without any warning, his lips crashed down on hers, his tongue demanding entrance, and Rose found herself powerless to resist as he ravished her mouth with her very first kiss.

"Almost wish I didn't care, little ladybug," he said as he walked back toward the house.

Crazy thing was, she believed that.

Didn't mean she doubted he would crush her like a bug the second he changed his mind.

Beginning to struggle in his hold, desperate to get away from him, away from this house, away from the unwanted feelings he stirred up inside her, Rose didn't even care that it was pointless. She hated this man almost as much as she hated her brother. He'd abducted her, tortured her, kissed her without her permission, and yet she sensed his genuine confusion and attraction to her.

There was also something about his dominance that made her wildly independent nature want to submit.

That thought alone was enough to have a few of those tears she'd tried so hard to keep buried trickling free. They felt like tiny icicles rolling down her cheeks, and it wasn't until this moment that her body seemed to remember it was freezing outside and she was in no way dressed to be out in the snow.

Mr. Bedroom Man cursed, tightening his hold on her, as she began to shiver. "Do you have to be so stubborn all the damn time? Even when I'm trying to help you?"

"Yes," she snapped, making him laugh. The sound was beautiful, albeit a little rusty, and even in the near darkness, she could see that the hard lines of his face softened when he relaxed like that.

Why did she have to like it so much?

Why did he have to look more human when she needed to remember he was nothing more than a demon who had abducted her?

Okay, not a real demon, but he may as well be. What else would you call your captor who had grand plans of abusing you and then ... not wanting you to die?

Rose knew fighting was utterly pointless so gave up, she had to do whatever it took to regain what strength she could. Another opportunity would present itself, and she had to be ready to take advantage of it when that happened.

Still a sense of desolation blanketed her as the house came into view. She wanted to be back in her colorful little home, surrounded by the things she loved that had meaning to her. It was a sad and lonely little life according to most people's standards, but it was hers, and she'd fought hard for it.

When Mr. Bedroom Man stepped inside, the sudden warmth on her frozen skin made it feel like a thousand small, sharp knives stabbing into her, and she began to shiver harder, until her teeth chattered loudly enough that everyone could hear.

"How's your little ladybug?" one of her captors asked with a smirk as Mr. Bedroom Man carried her into a large living room.

"Would you stop calling me his?" Rose snapped, annoyed with the whole situation, but mostly herself for not being stronger, smarter. "I don't belong to him. I don't belong to anyone but myself."

"Not entirely true, is it, little ladybug," Mr. Bedroom Man said, his voice low and husky, and when he set her down on one of the couches, her next shiver had nothing to do with her wacked out body temperature. "Right now, you belong to us. You're completely at our mercy."

Since she was at least ninety percent sure they weren't going to gang rape her, Rose rolled her eyes at him, making him chuckle as he took the blanket someone passed him and tucked it around her.

One by one, the men trailed into the room, and she hated not having any names to put to their faces. Sure, she could make up names, but them knowing hers when she didn't know theirs was just one more way they had an advantage over her.

Enough.

She was done with that.

They had her where they wanted her. Mr. Bedroom Man was right, she was completely at their mercy. Even if they didn't have some sort of superhuman skills, they were six big, muscled men, and she was one small woman. Yes, she had training, she could throw knives and shoot with perfect accuracy, but unless she got her hands on some weapons, she didn't stand a chance of getting out of there.

"I want answers. Now," she added, her voice firm even though there were still little frozen tear tracks staining her cheeks, and she looked a wreck. She didn't have any power, but she was no pushover. A little crazy maybe, but not a pushover.

Glances were exchanged, and instead of anyone offering her any sort of response, Doctor Man, who wasn't really a doctor, strode over to kneel beside the couch.

"Running was stupid when you're in so much pain," he told her, his tone rebuking, like he was talking to a recalcitrant child.

"Oh, I'm so sorry, I guess I should be a better hostage," she said, injecting as much sarcasm as was humanly possible into her tone.

Five of the six men laughed, the other just shot her glares, and Rose decided then and there that he was her favorite. Maybe he looked at her like he'd prefer to snap her neck and be done with it, but at least he was honest about it. He wasn't playing with her emotions like the others seemed intent on doing, and she appreciated that.

"That would be helpful, little ladybug," Mr. Bedroom Man told her as he lifted her legs and sat on the other side of the couch, resting her calves on his massive thighs and tucking the blanket around her.

The damn man was going to give her whiplash. And it drove her crazy not to have a name. Knowing she should be paying more attention to Doctor Man, who had picked up her arm and was setting up an IV, more than likely to kill her and finally put an end to this bizarre charade, she glared at Mr. Bedroom Man.

"If you don't tell me your name right now, I'm going to—"

"What?" he asked, interrupting her and smirking at her like her life was one great big joke to him. Which only infuriated her more. "What are you going to do, little ladybug."

"This." With a smirk of her own, she lifted one of her legs and slammed her heel down into his crotch. His grunt of pain was pure music to her ears, and she sweetened her smile.

Even the grouchy one managed a small smile as the other guys all laughed. Despite being pleased she'd got in a single strike, Rose felt all kinds of out of sorts. Not enough sleep, not enough food, the torture, the roof collapsing, the run through the woods, it was all too much, and it was all catching up with her at once.

She needed something to hold onto before her world spiraled so far out of control she could never rein it back in.

"Steel," Mr. Bedroom Man muttered, wisely slipping one of his hands under the blanket to cup his family jewels so she couldn't get in another kick.

"Huh?"

"My name."

"You playing more games with me?" she snapped. Nobody named their child Steel.

"No," he said simply. "Steel is what everybody calls me. It's not my birth name, but it is my name."

"Why do I get the feeling my brother is the cause of that?"

CHAPTER

Eleven

December 28th
9:55 P.M.

His little ladybug was spiraling, and Steel couldn't handle watching her fall apart.

Rose was too strong for that, and if she needed something to hold onto, he could give it to her.

Glances at his team told him they were okay with him providing information. They'd taken Rose for a reason, and while that initial plan wasn't going to work out the way they'd hoped, it didn't mean they couldn't still use her in a different way.

Besides, if what Steel thought was true, then maybe Rose would be more than willing to voluntarily help them bring her brother down.

From the arch of her brow, it was obvious she still wasn't convinced that Steel was his name, but what he'd told her was true. It might not be the name he was given by his parents at birth, but it absolutely was his name now. It was who he was. There was no going backward to who he'd been before Dr. Gardner's experiments, and he no longer thought of himself as that man.

He was Steel.

When his teammates all moved to take seats, he took that as their final permission to not hold back and share everything with Rose. Even Dragon looked resigned to this. More than that, there was a grudging flicker of respect in his unusual violet eyes.

It seemed that Rose had managed to win all six of them over. No easy feat, but as he met her gaze and held it, he almost regretted his earlier comment that she belonged to all of them, that she was at their mercy. Steel had said the words to taunt her, but the truth was, he didn't want anyone else ruining her but him.

Even Voodoo's touch, professional though it was, had him itching to do something about it. Something he could see his friend was aware of by the smirk on Voodoo's face as he finished checking Rose's vitals and moved to sit in the armchair by the fire.

"So ..." Rose drew out the word. "We're all just going to sit here in silence now? Tell me what the hell is going on. Why am I here? How do you know my brother? What is with the superhuman skills you seem to have? Why did you save me from the roof collapse and then tell me I wasn't going to die?" That last question was asked with a hint of desperation, and he couldn't not smile knowing that was what was bothering her the most.

"Guy you gave the black eye to is Voodoo. Guy with the longer on to hair is Lion. Guy with the nose that looks like it was broken at some point and healed a little wrong is Thunder."

"You saying I'm ugly, dude?" Thunder piped up with a smirk.

"You said it not me," Steel shot back. "Guy playing with the knife is Blade."

"Very appropriate," Rose muttered.

"And the guy with the unusual eyes is—"

"The one who wants me dead," Rose finished for him, making him chuckle.

"He doesn't want you dead. And he's Dragon."

"I'd say the violet eyes were cool, but since you do in fact look like you want to kill me I'll go with unusual instead." Rose's small smile faded, and she grew frustrated again. "So you all have weird names that I'm assuming none of you were born with," she said with a huff, but he noticed she sank back against the pillows Voodoo had piled up behind her, relaxing slightly now she had some intel to focus on.

"You're assuming correctly, little ladybug."

That earned him an eyeroll. "Just because you guys all like nicknames does not mean I'm in the market for one. And if I were, it certainly wouldn't be ladybug."

"It's pretty cute as far as nicknames go," Voodoo teased her.

"Exactly. And cute is the last thing I am."

As far as he was concerned, that was up for debate. Rose was adorable with her bottom lip stuck out in a pout, waves of red hair tumbling around her shoulders, and a smattering of freckles just visible beneath the bruises marring her perfect skin. She was more than cute, though, she was sexy enough that it was all he could do to control himself from throwing her down, ripping off her clothes, and thrusting inside her.

Much as he'd love to do that, consequences be damned, it would only make Rose hate him more than she already did, and that left an uncomfortable tightness in his chest that made breathing difficult.

"Strong is what you are," he murmured as his hands began to absently massage her feet. From the way she squirmed, he knew the skin there must be tender, not just from running but from the cold. It was lucky she hadn't gotten frostbite. If she'd been out there much longer, she likely would have. If she'd spent even the night outside, she'd have been dead from hypothermia by sunrise.

Something softened in her gaze, and her tone was less defensive when she spoke. "I want to know what Ridge did."

With a sigh, Steel kept working on her feet, needing something to do to keep him from stripping her off and dragging her into his arms, even if it was just to hold her. "We're all former military," he began. Not only was he the team leader, but he was the one finding himself obsessed with her. It was only right that he had to be the one to try to make her understand why they needed her help. Why they'd felt they had no choice but to take her to use as bait.

Maybe then she'd stop hating him.

Anger he could handle, even enjoy, but he didn't want her to hate him.

"Ridge isn't in the military," Rose said. "He has PhDs in chemistry and biology. How did you meet him?"

"Seems your brother was working with the military under the guise of running an experimental program," he explained.

"Your special skills," she said, a statement, not a question.

"We were all right out of special forces training, chosen specifically because we were the best of the best. When we were approached by our various branches about joining a special task force, we all said yes. We trained together, worked together for a year before we were approached about participating in a medical trial. It was supposed to be something that would enhance the skills we already had, such as strength and speed. It was supposed to give us better stamina to survive heat and cold, and to need less sleep. It sounded too good to be true."

"Nothing with Ridge is ever as simple as it seems," Rose said softly.

"Things got worse pretty quickly. Hours after the first shots, we all started getting this anger we struggled to control. Dr. Gardner insisted it was normal, just our bodies adjusting to the drugs. That the anger would pass. We talked about pulling out. Something felt off, but we all liked the idea of being bigger, stronger, better than everyone else. We were egotistical young men, and he used that against us."

"Ridge always uses your weaknesses against you." There was so much understanding in her words that Steel wanted to force her to tell him everything her brother had done to her so he could make sure Ridge suffered sufficiently before they killed him.

"We decided to persist, but within days, we were all but consumed with rage, and battling suicidal thoughts. Dr. Gardner insisted that we come in so he could monitor us more closely, adjust the dosages, and determine why we were having these negative reactions. Instead, he lured us into a remote facility and locked us up in a reinforced glass cell. We were kept there for three years before we managed to escape. Throughout that time, your brother kept us naked and locked up twenty-four hours a day unless he was performing tests or using us as his own personal super soldiers. If he sent us out, it was with shock collars that even I couldn't break, locked around our necks. We were watched constantly, our cell had gym equipment, metal beds with no bedding, a table and chairs, a single toilet, and a showerhead embedded in the ceiling. We survived only because we had each other."

"You formed a family, and it made you stronger than what my brother tried to do," Rose said.

"When we escaped, we spent a year constantly on the move. We knew there was no way your brother was going to let us go, not after he'd put all that time and money into making us what we are. You know I have enhanced strength. Blade has enhanced hearing, Dragon enhanced smell, Lion enhanced vision, Thunder enhanced speed, and Voodoo ... he can save people when they shouldn't be able to be saved."

Rose gasped, her gaze darting to the man sitting by the fire. "That's why I'm still alive. Thank you."

Voodoo nodded his acceptance of her thanks.

"I don't get it. If you knew where my brother worked, why didn't you just stay there and kill him when he came?" Rose asked.

"We waited, but he never did come. No one did. Cameras must have alerted them to our escape and massacre. They abandoned the facility," he replied.

"You still could have gone after him," Rose insisted. "You were free."

"Back then, we didn't know your brother's name, he just called himself Doctor. We didn't know who was safe to approach in the military and who was involved, so when no one showed up at the facility after two weeks, we just disappeared. Eventually, we approached Eagle Oswald of Prey Security, and now we work for him. It's because of Prey's resources that we eventually managed to get your brother's name."

"So why not go after him?" Rose asked.

"Because we can't find him. Wherever he is, he has money backing him to keep himself hidden. He knows that if we ever find him, we'll kill him, and we're not easily stopped. He knows what'll happen if we ever get to him."

"I've heard of Prey Security, but I thought they had more integrity than to come after an innocent person for someone else's crimes," Rose said.

"Little ladybug, Prey doesn't know we took you. We will do whatever it takes to get to your brother, including betraying our boss, a man who has given us everything we needed to survive these last six years."

"Including using me. Making me once again suffer at my brother's hands, even if it's through you."

~

December 28th
    10:11 P.M.

Why was she always the pawn?

Unwanted by her parents, unwanted by her brother, manipulated into becoming the person she was through torture and neglect, and now punished because her brother was a psychopath with delusions of grandeur.

For once in her life, she just wanted to be Rose. Wanted to matter just because she was herself, a human being, deserving of love and affection. Never had she wanted to be her parents and Ridge's little scientist robot, existing only to serve their goals. Neither did she want to be used by Steel and his team to get their revenge.

When did she get to just be herself and live her own life?

"You were all we had," Dragon said with a shrug, like her very existence was inconsequential.

Anger sparking, she glared at him. "If anything, I should be the one who gets to use you to seek revenge on my brother. After all, you said you only met him ten years ago, back then I would have been thirteen, Ridge had been raising me for nine years already. I've done almost double your time suffering at his hands."

The large hands massaging her feet stilled for a moment, and she got the feeling Steel didn't like hearing that he and his team weren't the only ones who had been victims of her brother. Dragon, on the other hand, merely narrowed his eyes at her.

"How do we know you weren't in on everything your brother has done?" he demanded.

That was a ridiculous enough question that it absolutely earned the eye roll of all eye rolls. "Yeah, I hear the military employs a whole lot of thirteen-year-olds. Honestly, I can't believe you were all stupid enough to think a man like Ridge cares about anybody other than himself, and anything other than his own goals."

"We were desperate," Steel said like that explained away everything.

But it didn't. It didn't explain away the fact that she'd been kidnapped, locked up in a windowless cell with no furniture and no toilet except for a hole in the floor. Been starved and dehydrated, tortured with hot and cold, whipped, and then almost buried alive. Okay, the last had been instigated by herself, but of course she was going to try to escape when they were holding her prisoner.

Trailing a finger along the bandages circling her wrist, she looked Steel dead in the eye. "Oh, you were desperate. Guess that makes it okay then. You want revenge on my brother for doing what he did to you, which granted, is totally messed up, and I have no arguments with you that you deserve it, but going after me only makes you the same as him."

Steel winced, and she felt the tension in the room rise several notches. It probably wasn't wise to taunt her captors, but honestly, Rose found she'd reached the end of her rope, and apparently, what she found there was a complete lack of care about anything, including what happened to her.

"Just because you might not have been in on it when you were thirteen doesn't mean you aren't now," Dragon said defiantly.

"Clinging to that to make yourself feel better?"

"We have no proof you weren't working with him," Dragon said.

"And using editing romance novels as a cover?" she asked, laughing at the absurdity of it all. "Look, I'd love to say I'm shocked to find out what my brother did, but the truth is I'm not. Ridge has always been psycho, and he's always wanted to find out if he could manipulate DNA. When you find my brother, you can kill him. I don't care. Actually, that's a lie, I do care. I know I'd sleep easier knowing he's dead. But using me to get to him won't work."

"You're his sister," Dragon insisted.

"And you're his creations. Using yourself as bait would work better."

"We talked about that, but he'll know it's a trap," Steel explained.

"He would have known using me was a trap, too."

"But we were hoping he would have risked it to save you."

"Then you hoped wrong. Why would Ridge care about saving me when he spent almost a decade and a half abusing me?" Rose wasn't ashamed to admit that she'd been abused. She understood she'd done nothing wrong, nothing deserving of what her brother had done. She also understood why other kids who had been abused internalized it and blamed themselves.

It was just different for her because her brother always talked about molding her into his creation. He might not have altered her DNA, but he had still played with her head in his attempts to create a protégé.

"That's why you were so good at withstanding what we did," Steel said softly, and she wondered if he realized he'd stopped massaging her feet and was now gently caressing them.

Hardening herself against the soft touches, she just shrugged. "Starving me, locking me out in the snow without proper clothes, making me sleep in a room that was hotter than the air you were pumping into that cell, whippings, canings, beatings, those were all things I knew how to deal with before I even knew what the word torture was. Ridge's favorite was locking me in an old well. There was a cover, so it was completely pitch black, and the bottom was mud, urine, feces, and a little water. I can handle whatever you throw at me."

Although she jutted her chin out, daring them to disagree, daring them to do their worst, she wasn't prepared for the horrified looks on the faces of the men in the room. Even Dragon looked queasy over what she'd just told them.

Of course, she'd always known what her brother had done to her was sick and twisted, but it had just been normal for her as a kid. Part of her life as much as schoolwork and chores. Seeing the horror on the faces of the men who had abducted her with the express purpose of inflicting pain on her, somehow made her childhood abuse seem that much worse.

Spurred on by her righteous anger, Rose shoved down the blanket, ignoring Steel's protests, and lifted her hips enough to wriggle down her pajama bottoms, exposing the lines of scars up her thighs.

"I didn't get my ability to do first aid through altered DNA. My brother made me learn to put in stitches by practicing on myself. I learned to run fast by being forced to run laps in the middle of the night. I had to start over if I tripped or was pushed so hard that I threw up. I strengthened my muscles with chores that were too hard for a little girl to do alone, but I knew I had no choice so I figured it out."

Shivering even though her body had mostly warmed back up, Rose was breathing hard as she tugged her pajama bottoms back into place. She tucked the blanket around herself again, using it as a shield of sorts even though the thin material offered no protection from anything but the cold.

"There is nothing you can do that will break me, and nothing that will get Ridge to care enough to risk his own life for mine." Taking a deep breath, she said the words fearlessly, even though she didn't want them to be true. "So you may as well just kill me and get it over and done with."

With a growl, Steel reached out and grabbed her, hauling her into his lap. Around her, displeased grunts echoed from the others, and when she looked around at all of them, she was totally confused as to why they cared so much about killing her all of a sudden.

"How many times do I have to say you aren't dying, little ladybug?" Steel demanded.

Bracing the palm of her good hand on his chest, she balanced her hand with the cast awkwardly beside it and tried to ignore the fact that with her legs spread over his thick thighs, her center was pressed directly against the bulge in his pants. "I don't believe you," she said simply. "I don't think your buddy Dragon buys that I was abused by my brother, and he wants to kill me. I heard him say it after you got me out of the basement."

"Dragon is an idiot who messed up with the woman he likes because of our plan to go after you," Steel explained, and since Dragon didn't disagree, she assumed that was true.

"Using me won't work," she reminded them.

"We get that now."

"You won't let me go."

"Can't," Steel corrected. "Someone broke into your house. If we send you back home, your brother will have you picked up and taken to him. My guess is he'll try to torture you for information on us, see if you know where we took you."

Yep, that sounded like what her brother would do.

But where did that leave her?

"I was going to take you home," Steel told her, one of his large hands hesitating before palming her cheek. "When you did your impressive little gymnastics trick, I was cooking you dinner. I was going to lace it with sedatives, wait until you passed out, then we were taking you home."

"I want to believe that," Rose said softly, finding that it was true, she desperately wanted there to be at least one person in her life who she could depend on and trust. "But I still don't know where that leaves me now. You say you don't want to kill me, but you also say that you won't take me home and let me go back to my life. Which means the only other option is that you intend to keep me here as your prisoner indefinitely."

CHAPTER

Twelve

December 28th
10:23 P.M.

Steel liked the idea of the little ladybug forced to stay there, his sweet, strong, crazy little captive, far too much to be considered normal.

Of its own accord, his thumb drifted to the crease of her lips, then dragged along her bottom lip hard enough that desire flared in the forest green eyes staring back at him. His little ladybug didn't even seem to know how to process touch that didn't cause her at least a bite of pain.

It made him want to rediscover a part of his old self that would have worshipped her body with gentle caresses and featherlight touches. Now he wasn't sure that part of him still existed.

Maybe it was a good thing his little ladybug responded more to pain.

"Not indefinitely," he told her.

Those words had her gaze widening. "You're going to let me go?"

He really had become a monster because Steel wanted so badly to tell her no. That he was going to keep her forever. That she was his now, and he was never going to let her go.

Swallowing down the possessiveness that threatened to choke him, he forced his head to nod. "I have a deal for you."

Suspicion had her brows darting down to form a V. "A deal? Why does that sound suspiciously like yes, I'm going to let you go, but ha-ha I was only joking. I'm going to keep you here forever?"

The little ladybug had a pessimistic streak a mile wide, and he chuckled, surprised at how easy little snippets of laughter had snuck into his life these last several days. "Not forever," he assured her.

"But ..."

"But until we get your brother." They'd gone about this all wrong. If they hadn't jumped all in to something without properly thinking through the consequences because they were so hellbent on getting their revenge, they would have started with this. Now they had to work hard to gain Rose's trust, but if they'd gone to her in the beginning, he wouldn't have added more scars to her already battle-worn body and soul.

Those pretty eyes of hers widened again. "You want me to help you kill my brother?"

"If it's too much for you, then we wouldn't ask you to be involved in the actual killing," Voodoo rushed to add. The medic had taken a particular liking to Rose. He was almost as protective of her as Steel himself had become, which was probably why Dragon appeared to have given up on his let's just kill Rose and be done with it plan. If he tried, he'd be going up against all five of them.

Protectiveness aside, Voodoo didn't really get what made Rose tick, though.

Steel might not understand it all either, but he knew one thing for certain. There was nothing and no one that this woman, straddling his thighs, would ever back down from, and she would slit her brother's neck without a second thought or a moment of regret.

Rose laughed, loud and hard. He could tell by the small wince that the drugs Voodoo had dripping into her through her IV were doing a reasonable job of masking her pain levels without completely eliminating them. But she didn't seem to care, her laughter was so rich and free that he felt like an idiot just sitting there and staring at her in awe.

How many chances had life given her to laugh like that?

And why did he feel such a strong need to ensure that from now on, that was all life gave her?

"I think what my little ladybug is telling you is she's all in for participating in killing her brother," Steel drawled.

Shooting him a half-hearted scowl, Rose muttered, "I'm not yours."

"If you say so." The smirk he gave her was specifically designed to get her all riled up. The last thing he wanted was her slipping away from him again, into a pit of despair and hopelessness.

His little ladybug should never suffer again.

Not for a single second.

"You are impossible," she snapped, but again she didn't seem all that angry about it.

"Yep," he agreed. He was also hers, but he doubted she would appreciate that declaration.

"You really want to help us kill your brother?" Thunder asked, a thread of doubt in his voice.

"How long have you hated Ridge?" she asked, twisting slightly so she could look over her shoulder at the rest of his team.

"A decade," Thunder replied.

"I've hated him for double that. Even before our parents died, he used to hurt me. They did too. They're psychos, my whole family. Every single one of them. Apparently, I am too." she muttered that last part under her breath, but since she was perched on his lap, he caught the words.

For the last ten years, all Steel could focus on was finding Dr. Gardner and forcing the man to undo what had been done to them. Turn them from monsters back into human beings.

Maybe he'd been looking at things wrong this whole time.

Maybe he wasn't a monster, just a little bit psycho, too. After all, he had developed feelings for the little ladybug, so it was obvious that Ridge Gardner hadn't really been able to remove empathy from his brain. It still existed, it had just twisted into something else.

Maybe a little bit psycho wasn't all that bad after all.

"I'm sorry you went through that, Rose," Steel told her, sweeping his palms down her arms and then back up again.

Surprise widened her eyes as she turned to look back at him, the sound of her real name coming from his lips instead of the nickname catching her by surprise, although he sensed there was more to it than that.

Ever since she'd escaped her brother's hell, she'd isolated herself from the world, much the same way he and his team had. There had probably never been anyone to tell her they were sorry for her suffering. Likely never even been another person she'd shared that with.

Why would she?

Life had shown her nobody cared.

But he cared, and it was just now that he realized how lucky he and his team had been to go to Eagle Oswald and be accepted without question into the Prey family.

The betrayal of their boss sat heavily inside him, and Steel knew he needed to tell Eagle what they'd done, assure him that they would make it right, and hope that the man didn't kick them all to the curb.

For now, though, he kept his focus on Rose, who shifted uncomfortably. Her shrug was too forced, and he wasn't fooled by her act of nonchalance. "It was all I knew," she said, like it didn't bother her, but he knew it did. How could it not?

"You'll get your vengeance, little ladybug," he vowed, praying she agreed to help him, because if she didn't, he wasn't sure what his next move would be. Calling Prey, possibly, and having Rose put in protective custody with them. She'd probably fight it, definitely hate it, but as long as she lived, he was okay with that.

"If I help you," she said.

"If you help us," he agreed.

As he watched, he could practically see the calculations running through her mind as she tried to decide if this was her best move. In reality, it was her only move, and she knew it. She just had to come to terms with it.

"I accept," she finally said, and Steel let out a breath of relief. "Nothing would make me happier than making Ridge pay for everything he ever did to me. But ..." she drew the word out and shot him a sweet smile. "I have a condition of my own."

Huffing a chuckle, his hands shifted on her shoulders until his fingers stroked the back of her neck, and his thumbs lightly pressed against the pulse points in the hollow of her throat. "What's your condition, little ladybug?"

"I won't go back to the basement. If I'm helping you, I deserve better accommodations than a concrete cell with no furniture and a hole in the floor for a toilet."

He heard every word she didn't speak as clearly as the ones she did. If they put her back in the basement, she'd never trust them and only keep looking for a way to escape. They'd cleared away the rest of the rubble, and some of the cells furthest from the stairs were technically usable, but Steel had no intention of putting his little ladybug back in a cell.

"You get the room you were in while you were unconscious," he assured her.

"Okay," she agreed, and from her tone it was clear she thought he'd been going to fight her on her condition. Little ladybug had no clue what she did to him. The way she'd shifted something vital inside him with her brazen strength and determination.

"But."

"Of course, there's a but," she cut him off.

"For now, I have to keep you locked in the room," he told her. Steel didn't feel good about it, but he also knew Rose didn't trust him yet, and she certainly didn't trust his team. The chances of her taking an opportunity to run were still high, and he couldn't let her escape and run right back home into danger.

"Of course," she said with a sigh. "Still a prisoner. Always a prisoner."

The weariness to her words ate away at him, and he knew whatever tiny bit of trust they'd built had just shattered.

Warring with his need to protect Rose and his desire to gain the precious gift of her trust was going to make working with the little ladybug one hell of a ride.

～

December 29th
    1:24 P.M.

With a yawn, Rose stretched and blinked open her eyes.

The first thing to register was the sunlight streaming through the window, the second was the pain in her body.

It felt worse today, blanketing her with a heaviness that weighed her down and made her want to curl up under the covers and play pretend all day long. Pretend she hadn't been kidnapped, wasn't being held hostage, didn't feel like every bone in her body, along with every inch of skin, had been bruised.

But hiding never helped.

Certainly didn't fix anything.

Truth was, she was not only lucky to be alive, but lucky that Steel and his team were willing to let her go after they got what they wanted.

It wasn't that she was grateful to them for that, not exactly anyway. After all, they'd abducted her, tortured her, and were now using her for their own gain. They didn't care about her, and letting her go was the bare minimum they could do after what they'd put her through. She still hated every single one of them with a passion, only ...

Why did that feel like a lie?

"Stupid Steel messing with my head for his own amusement," she muttered as she gathered all her strength and pushed back the covers, kicking them off her until she lay there, panting, in the same pajamas she'd been wearing for days.

Annoyed that she could feel anything for Steel when he was doing all of this to her, Rose dragged up another round of energy, even though she was feeling seriously depleted, and managed to push herself up into a sitting position. The IV in her arm was gone, even though it had been there when she was brought to her room late last night.

Knowing someone had been in there when she was vulnerable in sleep made her feel nauseous, and she absolutely hated that she hadn't woken up when they entered her room. It was Voodoo, she knew that, just as she knew he wasn't going to hurt her. Steel would have been with him because the man was infuriatingly possessive of her, even though he had to know she hated him.

It irritated her even more to know that having Steel accompany anyone else who came near her made her feel safer. Steel wasn't a good man. He'd brought her here with the purpose of inflicting pain on her, and more than that, she knew he wanted to continue inflicting pain. Spanking her, and wrapping his hands around her neck as he thrust inside her virgin hole.

That her body heated, and her insides clenched at the thought had her growling at herself.

"Get it together. He's crazy and dangerous. He might be possessive of you, but he doesn't really care about you. If he did, you wouldn't be here. Try to remember that and stop getting all horny for him, it's embarrassing, and you should be ashamed of yourself," she snapped at her body as she swung her legs over the side of the bed.

Because she knew there was more than likely a camera hidden somewhere in the room, she looked around, trying to see if she could spot it.

Unable to find where it was hidden, Rose still assumed it was somewhere and called out, "Hope you heard all of that, Steel. I hate you and I hate what you're doing to my body."

Feeling more out of control than she had in a long time, Rose pushed slowly to her feet. The dizziness was a little better than she'd expected, even if the throbbing throughout her body got worse with the movement.

After agreeing to help Steel and the others with the revenge plan and getting them to agree to let her at least stay in a bedroom, Steel and Voodoo brought her up here. Voodoo had added more painkillers and antibiotics to her IV, and she remembered climbing under the covers.

The second her head hit the pillow, she'd been unable to hold her eyes open, and she'd immediately passed out. She wasn't sure if it was all her or if there had been some sedatives in the IV, but in the end it didn't matter. Sleep was what she'd needed the most, especially after that run through the snowy woods, and she felt better for it this morning.

Or afternoon.

Whatever time of day it was.

When she was sure her legs were going to hold her, Rose padded across the floor toward the window. Her bare feet stung a little with each step, and she was sure she'd scratched them up last night.

Running hadn't been her best plan, but she hadn't been thinking clearly. All she'd known was that she needed to get out. With a slightly clearer head, now she could acknowledge that she should have lulled them into a false sense of security and then made her move.

If she'd done that, would they have ever told her the truth?

Would they have offered the deal that she could work with them to earn her freedom?

"Oh well, too late to second-guess yourself now, what's done is done," she reminded herself as she stepped up to the window. Not only did she want to try to figure out the time of day, but she needed the connection to the outdoors, even if it was only looking at it through glass.

Opening the window and drinking in the fresh air would be better, but she had no doubt that after her little escape attempt, Steel would have made sure that all access points to the room were locked, window included.

Other than a circle of lawn that appeared, at least from her vantage point, to go the entire way around the house, all she could see were trees. It was likely miles from the closest road, the closest house, and much as she hated to admit it, right now she didn't have the stamina for that kind of journey.

What's the point anyway?

They have special skills.

Enhanced hearing, sight, smell, strength, and speed. Even if you got out of the house, they'll only come after you, find you, catch you, and bring you back.

Battling off a wave of helplessness, Rose pressed her fingertips to the cool glass, needing desperately to do something to stave off the claustrophobia. While of course it wasn't as bad as when she'd been buried alive under the rubble after she brought the ceiling down, it still coursed through her veins, making her twitchy and nervous.

Steel said they didn't want to kill her, and she assumed working with her meant not physically hurting her. Regardless, they *were* hurting her. She didn't know the rules there, didn't know what to expect, and that amped up her anxiety. With Ridge, she always knew what to expect, how far to push, and while she'd push these guys, taunt them at every step, she wanted to learn the rules of engagement.

Letting her forehead fall to rest against the window, she stood there for several minutes, drawing in slow, measured breaths, focusing on the beauty just out of reach outside. The way the sun shimmered against the fresh snow made it appear that someone had dumped a ton of glitter from above. The contrast between the dark branches of the deciduous trees and the green evergreen fir trees made the forest look magical, especially with the snow resting on tree limbs.

Usually, the sight of snow made her groan internally because it just reminded her of all the childhood chores she'd had to perform in the snow without proper winter attire. But today all she wanted was to be out there, feeling the sting of the cold against her skin, breathing in lungfuls of chilly air.

From the sun's position high in the sky, she knew it had to be around the middle of the day, which meant she'd slept for more than twelve hours straight. It was enough to have her feeling better, but not enough for her to figure anything out.

What if it takes months to find Ridge?

Years?

Are they going to keep you locked in a bedroom all that time?

The panic she'd just beaten back came shoving forward again.

There was nothing for her to do to keep it at bay. She had nothing, just this room with its pretty matching furniture. There was no computer, no phone, not even a book to read or a board game to play. She had no clothing other than her pajamas, she couldn't even go and take a shower or a bath because she had nothing to wrap around her cast and nothing to wash herself with either.

She had nothing. The only thing in the world she owned was the clothes on her back.

For someone who had spent her entire life being busy, or withstanding a punishment she knew would come to an end within days at the most, the prospect of spending potentially years locked in this one room with nothing to occupy her mind was enough to almost drive her crazy.

But what choice did she have?

It was endure this like she'd endured every other torturous ordeal life had thrown at her or break, and no matter what, she wasn't going to shatter.

Not for her brother.

Not for Steel.

Not for anyone.

CHAPTER
Thirteen

December 29th
2:39 P.M.

There was no use putting it off any longer.

It had to be done, so Steel knew he may as well just do it.

Picking up his cell phone, he dialled Eagle's number and then waited.

Less than two seconds later, his boss picked up. "Steel."

Something in the way Eagle said his name had him on edge. Was it possible that his boss knew what they'd done?

No.

How could he?

They did have some cameras scattered throughout the property, but he was pretty sure that Prey didn't have access to them. Then again, Prey was Prey, and the Oswald siblings were resourceful and determined. Oldest sister and second oldest sibling, Raven, was a computer genius who had learned from the best of the best, and Eagle's wife, Olivia, was also an expert on computers.

Maybe it *was* possible that Eagle knew they had abducted Ridge Gardner's sister.

"We need to talk," Steel said. This wasn't going to be pleasant, and he was prepared to be told that they needed to pack up and leave the house immediately. Of course, he wouldn't have done this without talking to his team first, so they all knew he was calling their boss to confess and were prepared to accept any consequences Eagle decided on.

They'd made their choices, and whatever happened next was on them, not Eagle.

"I'd say we do," Eagle agreed. Although there was a sharpness in Eagle's voice, there was a relaxed quality, too, and while Steel was usually good at reading people he couldn't get a read on his boss.

There was one thing he was pretty certain of, though.

"You know." A statement, not a question, because it was the only reason he could think of that Eagle would sound the way he did. If he was wrong, he would have told his boss anyway. Keeping this from Eagle after everything the man had done for them had always felt wrong. He'd just shoved away the guilt because he'd been so focused on getting one step closer to revenge on Dr. Gardner.

"I do."

"How?"

"You really think Olivia and Raven didn't get me access to the cameras in your house?" Eagle sounded amused now. "My wonderful wife and sister set up a program that only alerts me when the facial recognition software picks up someone new. This is the first time that's happened, since we added the Charleston Holloway family to the program while they were staying with you. Imagine my surprise when I get an alert last night and open the camera feed to see a young woman running out your front door."

"If you know, why aren't you here already?" There was only one person outside of him and his team who knew the location of this mansion, and it was Eagle himself. When they'd been flying members of the Charleston Holloway family in and out, they had everyone wear a blindfold from the moment they stepped on the plane until the moment they got to the front door.

Why had Eagle not sent a team straight there if he knew they'd abducted someone?

"I was coming, I can assure you of that. Even if the facial recognition software hadn't pinged the woman as Rose Gardner. I had already called Alpha Team, and had them preparing to head out, but then I saw you bring Rose back inside. You took care of her, warmed her up, set up an IV, sat with her, touched her, calmed her. I saw the way you looked at her, Steel, and I know that look."

"What look?" His obsession with Rose was confusing. He knew he was developing feelings, but he had no idea what to do with them, how to process them, or how he was supposed to make them work in any meaningful way when Rose hated him, and rightfully so.

"Same look I had on my face as I had Olivia dragged down to one of the holding cells in Prey's basement," Eagle replied. "Can I assume that your enemy's little sister has been residing in the cells you built in your basement?"

They had never told Eagle about the renovations they'd performed once they moved in, but now that he knew the man had access to the mansion's cameras, he wasn't surprised that their boss knew.

Scrubbing a hand down his face, this conversation wasn't going at all the way he'd expected. It was both a blessing and a curse not to have to break the news that they'd gone rogue, but he wasn't sure what Eagle intended to do about it.

"She was, but the feisty little thing managed to pull the ceiling down on herself."

Eagle's rich laugh came down the line. "I'm impressed. Tell her she has a job at Prey if she wants one, and she can teach everyone else how she managed that."

"We moved her up to one of the bedrooms, and despite my telling her several times to stop moving because she was causing herself more pain, she decided to try to escape." No one's pain had ever affected him the way his little ladybug's did. Rose hated him calling her his, but the thing was, he was pretty sure she already owned more of him than he realized yet.

"How long have you had her?"

"Since Christmas Eve."

"And what are your plans with her?"

"Someone broke into her place after we sent her brother a video of ..." He trailed off, not wanting to say out loud that he'd had an innocent woman tortured to the man he respected and who had helped give him and his team a purpose as well as a home. "It's not safe for her to leave. Her brother tortured her as well, her entire childhood. She agreed to help us get to him, and then after that, we told her she'd be free to leave."

"I'm not stupid, Steel," Eagle said, his voice losing the relaxed edge, becoming hard and focused, and he knew, despite the fact that Eagle hadn't immediately fired him, or sent a team out there to kill him, his boss was disappointed in them and angry at their choices. "You tortured the poor woman and sent a video of it to her brother. I won't say I don't understand the whys, but that doesn't make it okay."

"It was supposed to be easy," he said softly.

"Of course, it wasn't going to be easy. Rose is innocent, and you knew it despite whatever nonsense you cooked up in your heads to excuse it."

"We no longer have consciences. Using her should have been easy for us."

"No, Steel. This idea you all have of being monsters is just repeating what you were told. I'm not denying that Ridge Gardner messed with your ability to process emotions, that he disrupted what should be a natural process. But that doesn't make you monsters, and it never did. Do you think that if I believed for a second you were incapable of feeling emotion, that you were a monster, that I would allow you around my wife and children?"

While he and his team had spent some time around Prey, and they always made an effort to appear as human as possible around the kids, he didn't agree with what his boss had just said.

"Luna specifically loves what she calls the whizzy flying rides you give her," Eagle said, his tone softening again as he spoke about his five-year-old daughter.

The whizzy flying rides were nothing more than holding the child's hands and spinning in circles, a simple thing he'd done merely to try to prove to everyone he wasn't entirely a monster, and because the bossy little girl demanded them any time he saw her. The child was every bit her father's daughter, and he knew Eagle would burn the world to the ground for Luna, his two-year-old son Apollo, and his wife.

For any one of his siblings, their partners, and his nieces and nephews.

For any member of any one of his teams, their partners, or children.

For him and the men on his team.

Guilt hit him hard, and he was overcome with a need to make things right. "We shouldn't have gone after Rose."

"You shouldn't have," Eagle agreed.

"He told us often that we were his perfect killing machines."

"He's a liar. One who deserves to die. One who I already promised to help you deal with. I got you a name, you should have trusted me to find out where he was."

"We were desperate."

"I understand that, but I don't want you going rogue again."

"You're not firing us?"

Not killing us?

"Don't be ridiculous. But I won't pretend I'm not disappointed and angry about what you did. Rose deserves better. Do I need to send in a team to extract her?"

They both knew if he did, that Delta Team could kill them all without blinking. But they both also knew that they wouldn't. Prey was filled with good men and women who put their lives on the line every day to save innocents and make the world a safer place. Killing any of them, especially when they would be trying to rescue an innocent woman being held captive, would truly make them the monsters they believed themselves to be.

"No. She's safe with us even if she doesn't believe it."

"Then make her believe it," Eagle said like it was that simple. "Don't waste an opportunity for a future because you believe the lies you were told in the past."

With that, his boss ended the call, leaving Steel sitting there, staring at his cell phone, wondering how Eagle could have more faith in his humanity than he did.

~

December 29th
   3:42 P.M.

Sometimes boredom could be as bad as overstimulation.

As a child, Rose had experience with both. Since she was home-schooled, she was expected to learn at double or triple the rate that children typically would in a regular school. Her brother expected perfect grades from her and created his own program for her to study, a combination of what their parents had used with him, and his own tweaks based on his experience. Most of her day was taken up with that schoolwork and her chores. There was barely time for her to catch her breath, and she usually collapsed into sleep at the end of the day, not even bothered by the hard wooden bed she slept on.

Then there were the days when Ridge flew into a rage and locked her in a closet, or the basement, or the dreaded well. On those days, there was nothing to do but count down the seconds until it was over.

Rarely did her brother keep her locked up for more than a handful of days at the most. He needed her to do the chores, and he wanted to believe she could be trained and molded into the perfect protégé. Someone who would work with him and carry on their parents' legacy.

If Rose hadn't faked being bad at biology and chemistry, she doubted she would have escaped him.

But she had, and in the end, she'd wound up a prisoner anyway.

And now she was dying with boredom as she paced around her room getting more irritated with each step.

She could handle the pain. It was annoying, and it made her want to curl up in a ball and hide from the world, but it was familiar and that made it bearable. Some dizziness lingered, but she wasn't sure if it was the head injury or the fact that no one had brought her any food since she was locked in there last night.

Maybe they weren't really going to work with her. Maybe they'd just wanted to lull her into a false sense of security, but were really planning on leaving her to slowly starve to death.

Rose was just contemplating throwing herself at the first person to step through the door, assuming someone would—and if they didn't, she'd break the glass in the window and jump and pray for the best—when the doorknob jiggled.

A moment later, it swung open, and Steel stepped in, a stack of bags and boxes in his arms.

She might have gone with her plan, attacking the only way she could, even though she knew it wouldn't have the desired effect, wouldn't even if she wasn't covered head to foot in bruises, if nothing else, it would have made her feel better. But Steel didn't close the door behind him, and he shot her a smile as he walked to the bed and began setting things down.

He knew he'd left the door open, there was no way he couldn't. Maybe he just wasn't worried about her trying to escape again because he knew he and his team could take her, or maybe he was trying to build trust.

Part of her hoped it was the latter, but that was a thought she ruthlessly squashed. The only chance Steel and the others had at breaking her was if she allowed herself to fall for the mind games. They were working with her to get what they wanted, not to be nice to her.

"Didn't know what you like so I got some of everything," Steel said. There was a note to his voice that hadn't been there before, only she didn't know what to make of it.

"Some of what?" she asked, eyeing the bags with a hint of curiosity.

"Everything," he repeated, looking over his shoulder and shooting her a wide smile.

When he did that ... damn, he was one good-looking man. Terrifying sure, but so handsome it almost hurt to look at him.

"We didn't look through your closet when we—"

"Kidnapped me," she helpfully supplied, giving him her sweetest smile, which made him chuckle.

"Not going to let me live that one down, are you, little ladybug?"

"Would you if you were me?"

"No." The smile slid off his face, and Rose regretted making the comment, true though it was.

They might be making nice with her because they had found a new use for her, but the facts were, they were still holding her prisoner, even if her cell was nicer now, with a huge comfortable bed, a bathroom, and a big picture window. If the door was kept permanently locked, it was a prison cell, and she needed to make sure she remembered that.

Still, Steel appeared to be making an effort, so she should, too.

Stepping up to the bed, she poked one of the bags a little to glance inside. "Clothes?"

"Pretty sure I guessed your size right, but I don't know if you're a dresses and boots, or jeans and sweater kind of girl."

"I can be either," she admitted the small truth, not to try to make Steel see her as a real person and be more willing to let her go, she knew he wasn't going to change his mind, but because she couldn't figure out how she felt about this man.

She hated him, yes, absolutely, for everything he'd done to her. But he set her body alight in ways she hadn't experienced, had never wanted to experience, and there was some strange sense of security in his obsession.

"Then you have something to wear no matter how you're feeling."

"I'm sure my bedroom will be pleased to see me dressed up with nowhere to go," she shot back with an eye roll.

Something that might have been as close to guilt as this man was capable of feeling flickered in his dark eyes. "Rose—"

"It's fine," she quickly cut him off. She was already having trouble keeping him squarely in the captor role, she didn't need him to say anything to make it even harder. "What else did you get?"

"Snacks. Again, I didn't know what you liked, so I got some of everything."

Rifling through the bags he indicated, she found potato chips, popcorn, and a whole array of different types of candy. Locating some M&Ms, Rose pulled them out, finding they were the peanut ones she loved and quickly ripped open the packet.

"Mmm," she moaned as the sweet taste exploded on her tongue. "These are my favorite." Her stomach growled loudly, and she might have been embarrassed, only it was Steel's fault she was starving so she saw no reason to hide it.

"Uh, yeah, about that, sorry, I should have brought you lunch earlier, only I had an important phone call to make, and you were still asleep when I brought up breakfast."

It helped a tiny bit to know he'd brought her breakfast, and she hadn't woken up until at least lunch time. Much as she'd love to ask about the phone call, Rose merely shrugged. "Would have been nice if the room came with food, but at least I have a bed and a toilet."

"The room does come with food," he growled.

"If you say so."

"I do say so." Reaching over for one of the bags, he picked it up, stuck his hand inside, and brought it out with two freshly wrapped sandwiches. "I made us lunch."

"You made them?" she asked dubiously, not bothering to reach for one. "Last time you said you made me something, you also mentioned adding drugs to it to knock me out. I think I'll pass." Her stomach grumbled loudly again as she said it, and the huge man standing before her growled again.

"Do you have to be stubborn all the time?"

"Yes."

"I said I added the sedatives to the food because I was intending to take you home."

"Yet I'm still here," she reminded him.

"To keep you safe. Would you just eat the sandwich?" Unwrapping it, he took a big bite, then handed it over to her. "There. See? No sedatives."

Since she really was pretty hungry, Rose reached out a trembling hand and took the sandwich he offered, hoping he wasn't going to point out the way her hand shook. Thankfully, he didn't, just strolled across the room and sat down on the chaise lounge, opening up his own sandwich and beginning to eat it.

Because she wasn't ready to believe Steel when he said the room came with meals, Rose nibbled slowly at her lunch, making the most of it, just in case it was days before she was given more to eat. Even though they didn't know one another, he'd managed to make it pretty much the way she would for herself. A slice of turkey, tomato, cheese, and lettuce. Simple yet delicious, and perfect for her stomach when she hadn't eaten much these last several days.

"There are toiletries there too," Steel told her. "Shampoo, condition, body wash, girly stuff."

"Girly stuff?" For some reason, the idea of him knowing about *girly stuff* because he had a girlfriend or wife made her irrationally jealous. Which was crazy. Steel wasn't hers, and despite him constantly claiming her, she wasn't his either.

It was fine if he had a girlfriend.

Fine if he had a wife.

Totally a-okay if he had a daughter.

"Had a sister." He grunted. "Before."

"Before my brother?" Now she felt bad about her attitude. Honestly, she had no idea what came over her when it came to this man.

"She was a lot older than me, helped raise me when our mom got sick. She died in a car accident about six months before I signed up for your brother's program. I was always glad she never saw what happened to me. She'd have been so disappointed to see the monster I've become."

"You're not a monster," Rose told him, taking a tentative step toward the lounge where he was sitting. She could hate him for what he'd done to her, but she could also understand what had driven him to do it.

He'd also given her gentle touches last night, protected her against Dragon, who wanted her dead, and obviously spent a lot of time buying her clothes, toiletries, and snacks. Whatever else Steel was, he wasn't a monster, of that she was sure.

"You're the second person to tell me that today," Steel mused.

"But you don't believe it."

"I'm not sure," he said slowly, and it felt like the most honest thing he'd ever said to her.

Dropping down to sit beside him, they ate in silence, and it wasn't uncomfortable. In fact, maybe it was actually comfortable, and she had no idea how to feel about that.

CHAPTER
Fourteen

December 30th
   11:53 A.M.

"For her?"

The grunted words had Steel freezing halfway up the stairs. Dragon was watching him from the foyer, shoulder propped up on the door to one of the many living rooms the large Gothic mansion had, watching him with an inscrutable expression.

Over the last thirty-six or so hours, ever since they'd told Rose everything and asked for her help, Dragon had stopped mentioning killing her. It wasn't that Steel thought the man had had a change of heart, it was just because Dragon knew it was pointless. They weren't going to kill Rose, so he had to accept it and make the best of it.

Deep down, Dragon didn't really want to kill Rose anyway. Killing her would only prove Cassandra right for walking away. The man was just frustrated and confused about his feelings for the woman, since they had all believed themselves incapable of forming those kinds of connections.

Steel was every bit as confused by his feelings for Rose, but Eagle had told him he wasn't a monster, and the little ladybug had agreed. If she could still see him as human, even though she hated him, and he had zero doubts that she did in fact despise him, then maybe the damage Ridge Gardner had done to them didn't run as deeply as they'd always believed.

As they'd always feared.

It was easier to accept that you had been turned into a killing machine, a monster, than it was to hope you hadn't only to find out you were wrong.

They'd all taken the easy road these last six years. They'd accepted that their ability to feel empathy was gone, their consciences effectively removed. They'd never fought against the notion, never tried to see if it was wrong. They kept themselves sequestered here, just the six of them unless they were on an op for Prey, and didn't make any attempts to let anyone get close.

Now something had changed for him. It wasn't like he suddenly believed he was completely normal, but Steel couldn't deny he had developed feelings for his little ladybug. Obsession yes, attraction absolutely, but there was more to it than that. Protectiveness, a desire to know everything there was to know about her, even a gentleness he hadn't thought he was capable of.

"Yeah, for her," he replied.

"You really like her."

"I do."

"Even though she hates you, us, for what we did to her."

"Yes."

"You're prepared to fight to earn her forgiveness."

"I am." The words surprised him even though they were true. He just hadn't thought about it like that before. But a glance at what he held in his hands told him that he really did want to earn Rose's forgiveness. Or at least try.

For a long moment, Dragon was quiet. "Then don't give up like I did."

With that, the other man turned and disappeared into the room behind him, leaving Steel staring after him. As much as he wanted to tell Dragon not to give up on Cassandra, to take the time to accept that he had feelings for the woman and then do something about it, he also knew that until Dragon got to that place on his own, it was pointless.

Hurrying up the stairs and down several hallways to get to the room where Rose was staying, he unlocked the door, deciding they were doing away with that. Rose wasn't going to run, not yet anyway, and if he wanted to keep it that way, he had to show her that she really was there because it wasn't safe for her to go home, and not because she was a prisoner.

"Hey," he said, feeling uncharacteristically awkward as he opened the door and found her sitting on the floor by the window playing cards. He'd already brought her breakfast this morning, so it wasn't the first time he had seen her today, but every time he laid eyes on her it was like a punch to the gut.

No amount of developing an obsession for his pretty little captive was going to change the facts that Dr. Gardner *had* messed with their emotions and their ability to process them normally. Maybe it wasn't to the extent they'd always feared, but he knew he was never going to be the same as other men. There would always be a hardness, a coldness, a need for roughness as a release for his anger. Was that something Rose would be able to accept?

Was he kidding himself here?

The small smile she offered told him things weren't completely hopeless, but there was a restlessness in her gaze, and he knew he couldn't keep her locked up forever. His little ladybug had lived most of her life as her brother's prisoner, now he was doing the same thing to her.

If he kept it up indefinitely, he was going to crush her spirit, and that wasn't acceptable.

"Hey," she replied, curiosity in her gaze as she eyed what he held in his hand. Still, she didn't ask about it, stubborn little thing that she was.

"Want to walk the grounds?"

For a second, pure need flared in her eyes, but she quickly tamped it down and gave a nonchalant shrug. "Thought I was to be kept in here until you found a use for me."

That stubborn streak of hers had him chuckling. It was plain to see she wanted out of this room, was losing her mind locked in there, but she was going to pretend otherwise just so she didn't give him any edge.

"Come on, little ladybug, I packed us lunch." He held up the picnic basket that he'd made for them. He'd bought it the other day when he was ordering things for Rose. Steel had no idea what had possessed him to do it, he wasn't the kind of guy who packed picnic lunches to eat in the garden, and yet ... apparently, he was.

"Well ..." She drew out the word, but he saw the tension in her muscles, how hard she was fighting against jumping up and running out of the room.

"Now, little ladybug." He injected just enough order into his tone to make her automatically jump to her feet, and he knew from the flare of arousal in her forest green eyes that part of her liked submitting to him.

"Fine." She huffed, but she basically bounced across the room to join him.

Together they left the room, heading downstairs, and when they stepped outside, Rose paused to drag in a huge lungful of air. He could tell by the way she winced that her cracked lungs protested the deep breath, but she didn't seem to care, repeating the process several times over.

"Coat," he ordered, grabbing the one he'd left hanging just inside the front door and thrusting it into her hands.

"Yes, *Dad*," she muttered under her breath as she shrugged into it.

"Gloves." She rolled her eyes but stood still while he slipped the mittens onto her hands. It was a tight fit over the cast on her left hand, but it went on, and it would offer her protection from the cold.

"You take such good care of your prisoners," she taunted, but there was amusement in her eyes as she watched him.

"Brat," he said with a smirk, enjoying every second of her bratty behavior. "Scarf next."

As he wrapped the woolen material around her neck, he let his knuckles brush across her skin, bumping the hollow of her neck where her pulse fluttered wildly. Rose sucked in a breath at the contact, and it felt like every drop of blood in his body flooded south.

With her sufficiently wrapped up against the cold, he guided her off the porch. As soon as the thin winter sunlight hit her face, Rose tilted it up, closing her eyes as she just stood there, taking more deep breaths.

Watching her enjoy the simple pleasure of the sun on her skin had him so hard, he had to palm himself to try to shift his jeans to a more comfortable position. As though somehow sensing the movement, Rose opened her eyes, her tongue darting out to sweep along her bottom lips as her gaze locked on his hand.

"Let's go," he barked at her. If they stayed there a single second longer, he was going to have her naked and spread out before him, and she wasn't ready for that yet. Whatever else he'd done to her, he wasn't going to take her without her wanting it as badly as he did. When she was ready to beg to feel him fill her up, then he'd have his dark way with her.

Snatching her hand, he started tugging her along with him as they headed for the trees. "Holding hands, really?" she asked. "I'm not going to run."

"Too bad, I enjoy the chase."

"I'm not four, I really don't need to hold your hand." Although she said the words, she made no move to attempt to tug her hand out of his hold. Not that he would have let her.

"Keep being a brat, little ladybug. See where that gets you. Don't forget you already have one punishment coming when you're healed."

"You're not really going to spank me," she scoffed, not sounding altogether certain of that.

"Oh, little ladybug, you have no idea of the things I'm going to do to you."

Half expecting her to tell him she wasn't going to do anything with him, she didn't. Just stared up at him with wide eyes, filled with desire and arousal. Rose was strong and tough, and ruining her was going to be a lot of fun.

∼

December 30th
5:58 P.M.

. . .

She should have told him that she had no intention of playing whatever game it was Steel was trying to get her to engage in. There had certainly been more than enough opportunities for her to do it as they'd wandered the gardens. At every turn, he seemed to make more innuendos, and every time the words telling him to stop seemed to clog in her throat.

Instead, Rose kept being a brat, taunting him, egging him on, playing the exact game she had no right to participate in.

Truth was, she didn't know the rules, didn't know how serious Steel was. If he was just messing with her or if he really would put her over his knee and spank her until she was begging him for more.

The thought that she would like that seemed so preposterous. Yet Rose couldn't deny that every time he threatened it, she got wet.

It would have been embarrassing, and yet it was like Steel knew exactly what he was doing to her with his threats, and he loved every second of it.

Aside from their banter, the afternoon in the garden had been sweet. He'd packed food for them, sandwiches and brownies, along with a thermos of steaming hot tea. He'd packed a tarp for them to sit on as well as some blankets, so they didn't get wet sitting on the cold wintery ground. He fussed like a mother hen, making sure her coat was buttoned up even when she got warm from walking, adjusting her scarf whenever it slipped a little and didn't completely cover her skin.

He'd even roared obscenities into the silent woods when he'd realized he'd forgotten to give her a beanie to wear, and pulled one out of the picnic basket hard enough she was sure he would have ripped the thin material. But when he tugged it onto her head, he was almost impossibly gentle.

For a while, she'd almost been able to pretend that he wasn't her captor, that she wasn't a prisoner, that they were just two people strolling through the forest. They didn't talk a whole lot, Steel seemed more comfortable with the silence, and honestly, she was too.

When it had started to get dark and he told her it was time to head back to the house, her spirit started to drop. This had been a perfect afternoon, but now it was back to reality. She'd be taken back to her room, locked in, left there until he decided she was allowed out for respite, for a breath of fresh air.

A pet.

That's what she felt like. One he'd realized he had to walk if he didn't want it to go crazy and start destroying things.

Only she wasn't a pet, she was a real person, and she didn't want to spend twenty or so hours a day locked up in a single room.

Her mind searched for a reason not to be locked up again, one that didn't sound as desperate as she felt. As a kid, when she lived with Ridge, it had been easier to accept being his prisoner because she honestly hadn't known any better. That had been her entire life, all she'd ever known.

But now she'd had a taste of freedom.

Five years of being able to make all her own choices, do whatever she wanted when she wanted, and going back to being a prisoner again was a whole lot harder than she'd thought it would be.

"Can I cook dinner?" she blurted out as she trudged up the porch steps. The Gothic mansion was stunning. It looked like something out of a movie set, and yet to her it may as well have been plain concrete walls. A prison was still a prison even if it was a beautiful one.

"Cook dinner?"

"For everyone," she added. It was a bit of a lame excuse, but at least it would buy her a couple of hours, depending on what she cooked. "I swear I won't add any poison to it or anything."

"Brat." He chuckled as his hand came lightly down on her backside. It wasn't hard enough to hurt, the welts there were healing well, but the jolt was enough to bring her body closer to his, and she found he'd shifted so he was in front of her, meaning she was bumped up against him.

The bulge in his pants pressed into her stomach, and she kept expecting him to shove her to her knees, unzip himself, and force her to take him in her mouth or her hands. After all, she was his prisoner, and it was more than obvious that he was attracted to her.

But he'd never once done that.

Usually, he just palmed himself, shifting the extremely impressive bulge a little, and then continued like he wasn't hard as a rock. Didn't guys hurt when they were hard like that, but didn't do anything about it? Or if they didn't hurt, then at least they got uncomfortable?

She was certainly uncomfortable.

Rose kept having to squeeze her legs together because there was a throbbing between them that made her want to slip her fingers there to do something about it. She'd never done that before, didn't even know what to do really. Well she knew the basics because obviously she edited romance novels for a living, but she'd never had any practical experience.

Never wanted to.

Until now anyway.

This crazy, dangerous man, who she hated even though she was finding that maybe she didn't, had her body so confused it didn't even know what it wanted anymore.

Or maybe the problem was that her body knew exactly what it wanted, but her head didn't.

"You can cook us dinner," Steel agreed as his large hand grasped her elbow and he guided her inside.

For a man she knew had super-human strength, he touched her with great care and gentleness. If he wanted, he could snap her in two. There would be nothing she could do to stop it, but he didn't.

In the foyer, he began to undress her, removing her beanie, then sliding the mittens off her hands. "You know I can do that myself," she reminded him when he began to unwind the scarf from around her neck.

"Mmhmm," he said, his voice low, almost seductive, and she knew it was no accident that his fingertips skimmed her pulse points as often as he could.

"And believe it or not, I do know how to unbutton a coat," she added when he brushed away her hands as she tried to do it.

"You have a broken arm."

"But I'm not helpless."

"No," he agreed. "Not helpless, little ladybug."

His words weighed on her as he led her through the house. They were simple words, but they felt like they had a whole lot of meaning behind them. She got that she wasn't what they'd expected when they'd decided to kidnap Ridge's sister, but she didn't really know what Steel saw when he looked at her.

"Have fun?" Blade asked, looking up from his laptop as they entered the kitchen.

"The grounds are gorgeous," she replied, because she wasn't ready to admit to anyone, not even herself, that she had enjoyed having Steel at her side as they wandered the gardens.

"Little ladybug is going to cook dinner," Steel announced.

"Oh?" Thunder looked surprised as he strolled into the room.

"You'd rather lock me back in my pretty little prison?" she asked, arching a brow at him. At least he had the grace to look slightly chastised.

"We've never had a ..."

"Prisoner," she supplied for Thunder with a sweet smile.

"Brat," Steel murmured from behind her, his breath warm against her ear as he leaned in to whisper the word. "But Thunder is right. We haven't done this before. But you're wrong, little ladybug, you're not our prisoner. You're a guest and you should be treated as such, so I won't lock you in your room. Don't make me regret that." His hand brushed across her backside as he spoke, and she knew he meant there would be another punishment added to the list if she made an attempt at running.

Only she didn't think she would.

They were right that it wasn't safe to go back home now if Ridge had sent his people to her house. This was probably the safest place she could be, even if these men had abducted and tortured her.

Which absolutely said something about her crazy life, her crazy family, and her crazy self.

"You're really okay with her wandering the house freely?" Lion asked as he and Voodoo joined them in the kitchen.

"I am, but I'll take responsibility for her if the rest of you aren't," Steel said.

A shiver hit her system at the possessiveness in his words. The man scared her on so many levels, and the fact that he had enhanced strength was at the bottom of that list. For her entire life, she'd had to be a mini grown-up, always in control, handling anything life gave her, studying and chores beyond her years, pain and suffering most people would never endure.

She never had a chance to let go, let someone else take the reins.

But Steel's dominance made her want to submit, to let go of the tight control she kept on her life and herself and let him take over.

Which terrified her.

What if he turned out not to be trustworthy? What if she gave him power over her and he abused it? What if she allowed herself to let him in and he used that to destroy her?

CHAPTER
Fifteen

December 31st
   2:16 P.M.

It was the last day of the year.

Tomorrow should be like any other day. Steel had never cared before that a new year was starting, it had always just felt like more of the same. Especially these last ten years. It wasn't like they went and watched the fireworks somewhere. There was no family celebration or hanging out with friends. They were each other's family and friends.

So New Year's Day had always been just another day, except for this year.

This year felt different.

Bigger.

Like it was not just the start of something new, but the start of something bigger.

It was more than finally having a name for the doctor who had messed with their bodies and stolen their lives from them in the process. It was more than having a way to finally get to him, to get the revenge they'd been dreaming about for a decade.

"You going to just stand there staring at me, or do you have something to say?" Rose demanded, looking up from the book she was reading.

"Brat," he murmured as he stalked into the room.

Even though it had been his idea to stop locking Rose in her room, to do something to try to earn her trust, he hadn't slept a wink the previous night, worried that she would try to make a run for it when she thought they were all sleeping. Just because she knew that she'd be caught, between the cameras and their enhanced skills, she didn't stand a chance at getting out of this mansion undetected, it didn't mean she wasn't desperate enough to try.

But she hadn't tried.

And in fact, when she'd come down to the kitchen this morning, she'd looked stronger and more rested than he'd seen her. Bruises still mottled her skin, and she still wore a cast, and he knew from the stiff way she moved that she was still in pain. But the dark circles under her eyes had receded, and she was fresh and clean from a shower, dressed in clothes he'd bought for her.

It wasn't quite as good as seeing her in his clothes, but that primal caveman side of him liked seeing her in things he'd provided for her.

"You really must want to be punished," he told her as he stopped before the chair she was curled up in and drew himself up to his full height.

"I don't think you have any intention of following through," she informed him with one of those sweet smiles he knew was designed to egg him on. "You keep mentioning punishments, but so far, you have yet to deliver any."

Her sassy little voice made him laugh. "Don't think it's a punishment if you want it, little ladybug."

"Never said anything about wanting it," she said primly, making him laugh again. Ruining her was going to be sweeter than any smile she beamed at him. "Now, were you leering at me from the doorway for a reason, or was it just to be creepy?"

Snapping his hands around her wrists, careful to keep his hold on her broken one gentle, Steel had her out of her chair and flush against his body before she could blink. Holding her so her feet were off the floor, and she had no choice but to let them hang there or wrap them around his waist, he was pleased when she chose the latter.

"Appreciating the view, not leering, little ladybug," he told her as his hand came down on her backside, harder than he'd done the day before, making her whole body jolt forward, rocking her center across the bulge in his pants.

Instead of crying out at what wouldn't have been more than a slight sting, or telling him to stop, Rose moaned, and arousal sprang to life in her deep green eyes. Bringing his hand down again, he drove them both crazy as the friction was enough to remind them of what they weren't ready to do yet.

A third spank was all he knew he could handle before he stripped her naked and had his fun with her, so he set her back on her feet, leaving her dazed and breathing hard.

"Actually, I did have a reason for watching you from the door," he said.

"Oh?"

"It's snowing, so we can't go outside, but I wanted to know if you wanted to hang out." Damn, he felt like a teenager all over again, asking Rose if she wanted to spend time with him, but he craved her company more than he craved air to breathe, so he shoved aside those feelings he'd thought he'd long since outgrown.

"Show me something you used to enjoy from before. Before my brother messed with your head and your body, back when you were just a regular guy," Rose blurted out.

Not what he'd been expecting her to say, but since she hadn't told him to get lost, he could work with it. An idea immediately popped into his head, something he could share with Rose that he'd never shared with anyone else, not any of his friends or girlfriends before, and not his team.

"You know most people tell the other person where they're going before they storm out of a room," Rose called after him as he strode for the door.

"Most people follow when they've just asked someone to share with them," he shot back with a smirk.

"Except you never actually said you would share anything with me, you just turned and walked away," Rose grumbled, but she came to trail after him as he headed out of the library and down to the office.

They had a main office they used for plotting their revenge. The walls were covered in dozens of photos, piles of paperwork were stored on a desk, and they had a huge conference table where they'd set themselves up when they worked. That room was too busy for what he had planned, too hard, and cold, a reminder of why he'd brought Rose here and that she could leave when they all had what they wanted. Ridge Gardner dead.

So he went to the smaller office, which was rarely used, but it had what he needed, although he could tell Rose had no idea what he was up to when he went to a filing cabinet and opened it.

"Perfect," he said when he found what he'd been looking for and spun around to see Rose staring at him with a furrowed brow.

"Paper?"

"For origami."

"Origami? That's what you wanted to show me?"

"I learned from my grandmother when I was a boy. Her first husband was Japanese, but they were married for only a year before he tragically died in a house fire, saving two little neighbor children."

"Did they live? The children?"

"They did. He was the love of my grandmother's life, although I know she loved my grandfather, too. They only had one son, and they lost him too soon as well. My dad died when I was too young to remember him. My sister was ten years older than me, so she helped my mom raise me, especially after my mom got sick. They're all gone now."

"I'm sorry, Steel, I know it sucks not to have a family, but at least you got to enjoy them while you had them," Rose said softly.

He knew he'd been lucky to have a family that loved him and cared about him. Rose hadn't had that at all. She'd been raised by a psychopath who got off on inflicting pain on her.

No more.

No one would ever hurt her again.

She was his now, and he protected what was his.

"Want to learn how to make a rose?"

She chuckled but nodded. "I'd love to. I've never done origami before. Ridge didn't believe in anything that wasn't studying and work."

"We can learn more after this if you want, but origami takes a lot of practice to get right."

"Lucky I'm a patient girl then."

"Lucky," he agreed with a chuckle. "We'll do it together."

Grabbing stacks of paper, he headed through to the dining room so they could spread out at the table. Once they were both seated with a piece of square red paper in front of them, he started giving instructions.

It had been a long time since he'd done origami, and he was definitely out of practice, but as he talked Rose through it, everything began to come back to him. Roses had been his grandmother's favorite because they were the first thing her husband had ever made for her, and they'd been the first thing she'd taught him, even though there were simpler ideas to start with.

His grandmother always told him that anything worth doing wasn't just worth doing well, it was worth jumping all in with.

Was that what he was willing to do with his Rose?

Jump all in and not let the fear of failure hold him back?

She didn't lose her temper as she struggled to get the folds correct. The cast made it even harder, and her first attempt looked more like a mangled piece of paper than an actual rose. But she didn't give up, just had him write out the instructions so she could work on it over and over again.

Each try was a little better, a little cleaner, a little more rose-looking, and when she finally held up one that was very clearly a flower, she beamed at him in delight as she held it proudly.

"I did it," she said excitedly.

"Never doubted you would." While she'd been repeating the flower over and over again, he'd been working on his own creation. A dozen red roses with stems.

When he held them up, Rose's eyes filled with tears, and his heart felt like it stuttered to a stop inside his chest.

Did she hate them?

Did she feel uncomfortable that he'd made them for her?

Surely, she had to know that he was attracted to her, that he was borderline obsessed with her, that he wanted to own every inch of her mind, heart, body, and soul, and give her the scraps he had left of his.

"You made them for me?" she asked as fat little teardrops trailed silvery lines down her cheeks.

"Don't know who else is in the room that I might be giving them to, little ladybug," he said carefully, uncertain how to tread in unexplored terrain like this.

"I'd say they're the nicest gift anyone has ever given to me, but that wouldn't be true, because really, it's the only gift anyone has ever given to me," she said softly, allowing him a precious glimpse at the pain she hid so well. Pain he would do anything to rip out of her soul and destroy.

Instead, he reached over, palmed her cheek, and brushed the pad of his thumb across her bottom lip. "First," he corrected. "First gift anyone has ever given you."

～

December 31st
    11:02 P.M.

"Still in here."

The voice startled Rose since she'd been deep in concentration, and she set the piece of paper she was working on down because she didn't want to do anything to mess it up. She had no idea what time it was or how long she'd there. She and Steel had worked on origami all afternoon, and he'd all but had to yank the paper out of her hands to get her to go to dinner.

Straight after, she'd come back into the dining room and gotten back to work. Rose knew she could be a bit obsessive when she latched her attention onto something, but she'd quickly found something calming about the smooth folds of paper that soothed out her jangled emotions.

It wasn't easy, that was for sure, but she didn't care. If something was too easy, she quickly lost interest. It was the challenge of mastering a new skill that drew her in. Despite how complex origami could be, she was enjoying repeating the same folds over and over, watching as each attempt at a new creation improved with each try.

Steel had even let her use his laptop earlier to go online and look up origami ideas that she wanted to try out. Even though she knew someone was likely monitoring her every move to make sure she didn't try to contact anyone, Rose had appreciated the gesture of trust, and depressing as it was to admit, she didn't even have anyone she could contact.

So instead, she'd focused on the task at hand and quickly settled on flowers, there were so many different ones, some easier than others, and she had a whole garden's worth spread all over the table in an array of bright and pastel colors.

Growing their own food had been part of living on a remote, off-grid farm, but Rose had always wanted to have flower gardens. Her brother told her that it was frivolous and in the time it would take her to tend it, she could be learning something or growing something they could actually use, so when she'd moved into her own home, she'd quickly transformed the garden into a flower paradise.

"It's addictive," she told Steel as he strode over and picked up a flower she'd just finished.

"This is your best yet," he praised.

Her skin flushed, and she hated that she even cared that he complimented her. She did care, though. Compliments weren't part of her life as a child. Ridge believed that no one was perfect—well, no one except him—and that you could always improve. So even if she did something well, he always managed to find something that she could have done better.

"It's a tulip."

"I can see that. I made you this."

When he placed a ladybug in her hand, Rose couldn't help but laugh. "Thank you. It's adorable. Maybe I'll have to move on to garden insects when I finish mastering flowers. I bet there are some gorgeous butterfly and dragonfly ideas I could try out, maybe some cute little bumble bees, too."

"Later, though. It's after eleven, I thought you might like to watch some fireworks."

"Fireworks? I didn't think your place was close enough to any city that might be setting them off." She wasn't really hinting for information on where they were, she had just assumed that the mansion had to be remote because the guys were hiding from her brother, so Ridge couldn't get his claws back into his creations.

"It's not. Thunder decided to make his own, and Dragon has been itching for a chance to let out some of his aggression, so he's helping."

"Do you guys set off fireworks every New Year's Eve?" she asked as she pushed away from the table and stretched out the kinks in her back from spending so long bent over the table.

"No. Never. This will be the first."

Straightening, she looked over at Steel. "Because of me?"

"Mmhmm." He nodded, and in a rare moment of vulnerability, dropped his guard a little to show the uncertainty he was feeling. It helped to know he was as confused about the weird tension brewing between them as she was.

For once, she didn't want to be a brat, she wanted to feel something real rather than the shields she kept up to protect herself. "I like fireworks," she said softly.

The answering smile Steel gave her made her heart soar. It was well worth the small amount it cost her to give Steel something genuine. She was so tired of shields, of fear, and wanted to be able to figure out who the real Rose Gardner was. The one who just existed, who wasn't molded, who wasn't hiding, who didn't have to always be the tough girl because she had no one to count on to watch her back.

"I have the perfect place to watch them."

Nodding, Rose didn't fight it when his large hand claimed hers, and she followed him willingly through the house and up the stairs. They didn't stop on the second floor, which was where her room was, they took another flight, and then another, up to the top floor.

Steel led her down a few more halls and then opened a door, and they stepped into what had to be his bedroom. The dark wooden floorboards complemented the black walls. There was an enormous bed against one wall, its frame made of black metal. There was an antique roll top desk in a corner, shelves in another, an open door led to a bathroom, and she assumed a walk-in closet of some sort since there were no wardrobes visible in the room. On the opposite wall to the one with the door they'd just walked through were French doors that opened out onto a balcony.

That was where Steel led her.

They stepped through them, and it was almost like stepping into another world. The space was large, with an intricate metal railing at the end. Two sides were part of the roof, making it feel like this little area had been carved out. There was a huge blanket spread out on the ground, and pillows had been piled about. Fairy lights were strung up, and the sky had cleared from the earlier snow, making the little lights seem like an extension of the stars.

She didn't need to ask to know he'd set this up just for her.

It was without a doubt the nicest thing anyone had ever done for her, and that it was her captor who had done it was all sorts of twisted.

Only he wasn't really her captor anymore. She might be in his house, but Rose was fairly certain that if she demanded that he let her leave, he'd take her to Prey and let her have some say in how she was protected from her brother.

But she hadn't done that because something kept drawing her to Steel. He awakened parts of her she hadn't allowed herself to acknowledge. When your entire life had been about just surviving each day, it was hard to turn that off.

Hard to let go.

Without giving herself time to second-guess herself, to consider all the ways this was a stupid thing to do, how other people might view her, or what they'd think of her. Rose didn't even give herself time to figure out what she'd think of herself, she just acted.

Throwing herself into Steel's arms, she trusted him to catch her, and crushed her lips to his. His large hands circled her hips, holding her against him as she kissed him like she was a drowning woman and he was the only source of air to be found.

"Little ladybug," he murmured against her lips.

"Thank you," she whispered back before he could reject her. She was pretty certain he wouldn't, but not positive.

"You do crazy things to me," he admitted. "Things I didn't even know were possible."

"You do the same to me. I never thought I would want a man to touch me, but I crave yours."

"Did your brother—"

"No," she quickly cut him off. "Ridge never touched me like that. Not sexually. But I've never acknowledged that side of myself. I thought it was because maybe I just wasn't made to like it, but I was wrong. It was because I was afraid. Afraid to let go, afraid because no one has ever been there to catch me before, afraid because I'm always in control and I don't know what it looks like to release that hold."

The thing was, she felt ready.

This whole ordeal had been a wake-up call. She'd fought for her independence, to have a life of her own, but she was wasting it.

No more.

Rose was done hiding, even from herself.

"Take control," she whispered, nipping at Steel's bottom lip.

"You don't know what you're asking for, little ladybug."

"Actually, I think I do," she corrected him. He'd brought her here, tortured her, wrapped his hands around her neck, chased her, threatened to spank her, protected her from his team, shopped for her, cooked for her, shared his past with her, made her origami roses and a sweet little ladybug. "Let me lose control for a little while. I need to."

The admission was hard to make because it could be so easily used against her, but somehow, Rose knew Steel wouldn't do that.

A growl was the only warning she got before he'd taken them both down to the ground. Flipping her onto her stomach so she was lying across his legs, he shifted one of his so it pinned her own legs in place.

A curl of cold air caressed her skin as Steel yanked down her jeans and panties enough to bare her backside to the cold night. An answering curl of desire swept through her stomach.

"I warned you, didn't I, little ladybug," he said as his fingers traced circles on her bottom, around the healing welts. When she didn't answer, his palm cracked down against her skin, making her yelp, then immediately soothed over the stinging spot. "Answer me, little ladybug.

I warned you, didn't I? What would happen if you caused yourself more pain?"

"Yes," she squeaked, her body haywire with the warring desires. Part of her wanted to tell him to stop, that she didn't want more pain, but the other part was excited by this. Pain was what she knew, what she understood. Maybe she needed it woven into her pleasure.

"How many do you think is an appropriate punishment?"

"Umm ... three?"

His chuckle filled the night. "Three? I don't think so, little ladybug. Three is for wimps, and you're the strongest woman I've ever met. I think ten sounds more appropriate."

"Ten?" There was no way she could handle ten. "I can't—"

"You can," he contradicted as his hand came down again, a little harder this time. "Your body craves this, doesn't it, little ladybug?" Nudging her legs apart a little while keeping them trapped under his, he ran a finger along her center, where her body was weeping for him. "So wet," he murmured as he coated his fingers with more of her wetness and spread it over her stinging skin before cracking his palm against her backside once more.

That was three, and he repeated the process, running his fingers through her wetness, teasing her entrance, bumping against her bud, before smearing the evidence of her arousal over her bottom. Before each smack of his hand, he did that, and by the time he reached nine, her backside was throbbing, tears streaked her cheeks, and she was so turned on that if he didn't give her something more soon she was going to combust.

"One more, little ladybug, you took your punishment so well," he praised as his hand connected with her skin one last time.

As soon as he delivered that final one, he shifted her in his arms, lifting her up to cradle her against him, her legs still tangled in her jeans, straddling his, his arms locked around her as he caught her tears on his tongue.

"So strong," he murmured. "So brave, so perfect. You let go so beautifully and took your punishment like such a good girl."

"Please," she whimpered, grinding her wet center against his bulge, the stinging on her backside spurring her on, filled with a desperation unlike anything else she'd felt before. "I need more."

CHAPTER Sixteen

December 31st
11:28 P.M.

"Please," Rose whimpered, desperately grinding her wet center against his rock-hard length. "I need more."

Steel wanted to give her more.

Wanted to give her everything.

But he had to be sure.

Was this really what she wanted or was she caught up in the moment?

There was no doubt that she was turned on. Her body had been weeping for him as he'd given her ten spanks for her bratty behavior, but that wasn't an open invitation for sex.

"Be sure, little ladybug," he warned. The last thing he wanted was to be something she regretted when the New Year rang in.

In answer, she reached between them and grabbed his length, squeezing hard enough that he groaned and somehow managed to get even harder.

"You need to start that punishment over again, my bratty little ladybug?"

Sticking out her bottom lip at him in a pout, he took that as an invitation to suck it between his lip, nipping gently at it, then devouring her mouth in a fiery kiss. It wasn't enough. He needed more. Needed to taste her.

Trusting Rose to tell him if it was too much, or if she changed her mind, he palmed the back of her head, then flipped her backward so she was lying flat on her back. Grabbing a few of the pillows, he placed them behind her head, propping her up so she could watch everything he did to her, then he ripped her jeans the rest of the way down her legs and tossed them aside.

"Can't wait to taste you, little ladybug," he told her as he lay on his stomach between her spread legs, his massive shoulders keeping her legs apart even if she wanted to close them, and from the needy, breathy little moans she gave, he doubted that she did.

"You should know I've never ... not just this ... anything ..."

"I got that," he assured her. She was a virgin. It had been a long time since he'd been with a virgin. Before Dr. Gardner and the experiments, he'd preferred women with more experience, but right now, he couldn't wait to ruin this gorgeous woman spread out before him. Break her in all the best ways as he took every one of her firsts, and then put her back together again.

"And that's ... okay?"

"I would want to devour you if you'd been with a thousand men or none at all. But I am grateful I don't have to go and hunt down every man who got to touch you before I did and cut off their hands."

Her gasp at his words turned into a moan as his tongue licked along her center. There might have been no men for Rose, but there had been no women for him since his body had been changed, and as he drank in her sweet taste, it felt almost like his first time all over again.

When the clock struck midnight and they entered the new year, he was going to be buried deep inside her. But Rose wasn't just a virgin, she was tiny as well, and he was huge. He needed to make sure she was well prepared so he didn't hurt her too much when he finally sank inside her tight, wet heat.

Several orgasms should do the trick.

Fingers tangling in his hair, she gripped him tight enough that his scalp stung as he feasted on her. Alternating between long, slow, languid licks across her center, then teasing her entrance, before moving to suck hard on her bundle of nerves, flicking the tight nub with his tongue, it didn't take long until she was begging and pleading, then screaming his name as she came.

It wasn't enough. Steel was pretty sure he was already obsessed with the sound of his girl coming, and it was only round one.

"Steel, I can't," she said as she tried to push him away, his mouth closing over her bud again.

"You can and you will," he told her. "You wanted me to take over so you could let go, so let go, little ladybug."

Holding both her wrists in one of his hands, he held them against her stomach, pinning her in place, and with his shoulders holding her legs spread wide, she was helpless to do anything but take every drop of pleasure he gave her.

This time, he used his mouth and his fingers. The sound of awe as he slipped that first one inside her would forever be etched in his mind. It didn't take him long to find out how she liked it, and he kept his mouth sealed around her bundle of nerves, suckling hard and swirling the tip of his tongue around it, as he pumped his fingers in and out. With each thrust, he made sure to brush the pad of his fingers over that special spot inside her, and soon she was writhing beneath him.

When he had her stretched with three fingers inside her, he scraped his teeth across her bud, and she screamed his name as her internal muscles clamped around his fingers as she came.

It wasn't nearly enough.

Not letting up, he added a fourth finger, and she cried out, but he just sucked harder on her bundle of nerves. Her hips bucked, as much because she was riding out the orgasm as to dislodge him from her overly sensitive body, but since she didn't tell him to stop, he kept going, shoving her toward a third orgasm as he relentlessly thrust his fingers in and out, and lashed her bundle of nerves with his tongue.

Orgasm number three came with a sob, and she bucked against him as pleasure tore through her system.

Steel was so hard it hurt, but as he finally released her and stood to shove down his pants, and looked at his flushed, shaking, gorgeous girl, he knew he'd rather be painfully hard every second for the rest of his life if it meant getting to share moments like this with her.

"I have to go find a condom," he said, stooping so he could brush a finger over her cheek to catch her tears.

"No, we don't need one," she said, her slender fingers curling around his wrist. "I haven't ever been with anyone as you know, but I take birth control to help regulate my periods."

"Haven't been with anyone in a decade," he told her, and even before that, he'd never gone in bare.

"Then it's fine."

"You sure?" Although he'd love nothing more than to sink into her with nothing between them, Steel wasn't sure she understood what a gift and a privilege she was offering him.

"Positive."

That was all he needed to hear. Stretching out above her, Steel lined up and thrust inside her in a single move. Rose cried out, her fingernails clawing at his back, and he held still, giving her body time to adjust. In the end, the difference in their size meant there was no good way to do that.

When she began to relax around him, he moved, rocking his hips at first, then when she moaned as the sting of pain morphed into pleasure, he thrust harder, faster. Needing to own her, possess her, ruin her for any other men.

"Mine," he growled as one of his hands circled her neck, squeezing just hard enough that she knew he was serious.

"So bossy," she sassed as her ankles hooked around his hips, bringing his next thrust deeper.

"Say it," he ordered, going still and making her whine a protest.

"Steel," she groaned.

"Say it. Say you're mine."

"We only just met, and everything is crazy, and—"

"Say it," he ordered again, tightening his hold on her neck. If this woman thought he was ever letting her go, she was crazy. If she left there once her brother was dead, he would follow her. He'd find a way to wear her down, to earn her trust and forgiveness, to be worthy of her heart and her soul, but he couldn't let her go.

Thrusting hard into her, he released his hold on her neck and instead found her greedy little bundle of nerves, working it until he knew she was close and then stopping.

"Steel," she whined, grabbing at his hand and trying to make him go back to what he'd been doing.

"Tell me you're mine," he insisted, giving a single swipe over her bud and making her moan.

"Yours, I'm yours, just please don't stop," she begged.

"Told you you'd beg for me, little ladybug," he said smugly as he resumed playing with her bud and thrusting into her until she came with a scream.

Only then did he allow his own orgasm to crash over him, consuming him in fiery pleasure right as midnight struck and the fireworks went off behind them.

With aftershocks still rippling through his system, Steel hooked an arm around Rose's waist, grabbed the blanket, and stood, keeping himself buried inside her. Balancing her on the railing, he tucked the blanket around them and rested his cheek on her head as they both watched the explosion of colors lighting up the night sky.

"You can't take it back," he warned the object of his obsession, his little ladybug, his Rose. "You can't take it back."

~

January 1st
8:57 A.M.

Waking up to an empty bed was not how Rose wanted to start her day.

Or her year.

Sex with Steel had been crazy and impulsive, possibly one of the stupidest things she'd ever done, and yet somehow it had also been right.

They'd watched the fireworks on the balcony, Steel's hard length growing softer still nestled inside her, the blanket tucked around them, his body heat more than enough to keep her warm.

Then, when her eyes had started to grow heavy, he'd carried her inside, somewhat reluctantly allowed himself to slip out of her, then laid her down in his bed. She'd half expected him to clean her up first, that's what the heroes in the romance novels she edited always did for the heroines after mind-blowing sex, although she had no idea if real men did that in real life.

Rose shouldn't have expected it of Steel, though. His possessive, obsessive self wanted her to fall asleep still covered in the evidence of what they'd shared. He probably thought of it as marking her in some caveman kind of way. Crazy man.

What she had expected, though, was to wake up with him still beside her.

He'd been there all night. Even in sleep, she'd been aware of his huge body wrapped around hers like the protective shield she'd always longed for. But now he was gone, and she found it absolutely sucked to wake up alone after sex, especially when it was your first time.

Doubts crept in as she threw back the covers and headed toward Steel's bathroom. He was the crazy one who wouldn't let her come until she agreed that she was his, so where the hell was he?

Cranky and sore, Rose quickly washed between her legs, then did her business and threw her clothes back on. Doing a walk of shame she was sure was captured by a camera even if she didn't run into anyone, she made her way back to her room, where she showered and dressed.

Then she pasted on a look of disinterest and sauntered downstairs to the kitchen. At least they hadn't gone back to locking her in her room. That was some small saving grace, although it did little to ease her bad mood as she heard voices and saw that everyone else was gathered around the kitchen table when she walked in.

"We left you some pancakes," Voodoo told her like he was her big brother, and she rolled her eyes at him.

"Yay," she drawled.

"There's coffee too," Lion added with a snicker, and she threw him a glare.

Irritated though she was, Rose did help herself to a cup of coffee and a couple of pancakes. Someone had even apparently noticed that strawberries were her favorite fruit because there were some already cut up sitting in a bowl in the fridge.

If that was Steel and he thought he could ditch her in bed and make it up to her with fruit, he was sorely mistaken.

Still simmering in her bad mood, she dropped down into a chair at the table. Annoyingly, the only one free was next to Steel, and she glared at him as he leaned in and pressed his nose to the spot where her neck met her shoulder.

"You took a shower," he said, somewhat accusingly.

"Yeah, so what?"

"You don't smell like me anymore. Like us."

Okay, guess they weren't keeping the fact that they'd had sex a secret from the rest of his team. That was something she supposed.

"Maybe if you were worried about that, you wouldn't have left me to wake up alone in your bed." She huffed, aware she sounded slightly petulant, but not caring in the least. If he didn't want her to be annoyed about it, he shouldn't have done it.

"That's what has you all snarky this morning, little ladybug?" Steel asked, touching a kiss to where she was sure her pulse was pounding in the hollow of her neck. No matter how angry she was with him, her body was ready to go for round two.

Not that he'd be getting a round two after this unless he had an extremely good explanation for making her wake up alone and doubt herself, her body, and him.

"He didn't leave you by choice," Blade piped up.

"We woke him when we found more footage of someone breaking into your place," Thunder added.

"I can assure you he wasn't happy about the interruption," Dragon said with a grunt, and when she looked at him, she could see he had a black eye.

"Did you hit him for making you leave me in bed to wake up alone?" she asked Steel. She had to admit that was a pretty good excuse.

"Does that make you feel better, little ladybug?" Steel asked, amusement dancing in his dark eyes.

"A little," she admitted, making the guys laugh, even Dragon cracked a smile.

"Bloodthirsty little thing," Blade said, and she got the impression that was intended as a compliment, so she merely nodded and started eating her pancake.

"So, Ridge had more people search my house? You know that doesn't mean he cares about me, right?" The last thing she needed was her brother messing things up when she had a plan to help these guys get what they wanted. What happened after that was still up in the air as far as she was concerned, despite Steel's claim that she'd told him she was his and she couldn't take it back.

"We know," Steel assured her.

"But it means he thought we would have cut you loose by now," Lion said. "Probably thought he could get some intel out of you."

"I don't know anything to tell him anyway. I mean, I know what he did, but he won't care about that. He'll just want to know where to find you, and all I could tell him is that you're somewhere remote in the forest. Not like that would narrow it down any." Even if she did have a location, she wouldn't give it to her brother. She had more reason to want him dead than any of the men sitting around the table eating breakfast.

"Or he thinks we killed her," Dragon said. The words were said so calmly that Rose shivered despite knowing Dragon wasn't going to be allowed to kill her. "Relax," the man snapped at Steel, who had stiffened. "I said I wouldn't hurt her, and I won't. You were right, I was taking out my anger at losing Cassandra over what we planned to do with Rose on Rose. I'm not a threat to you," he said, turning to face her, and she nodded, believing him.

"My brother doesn't care if I'm dead or alive, and he won't ever make a deal to save my life, but ..." she trailed off as a plan began to form in her mind.

"But what?" Steel asked.

"I was just thinking, what if we played it like I managed to escape from you guys. He thinks you're over here torturing me to try to get him to agree to a meeting to hand me over. But my brother always underestimates me. Despite his ego, he never even figured out that I was only pretending to suck at biology and chemistry because I never wanted to work with him."

"Wait, you know what he's been doing? I mean, not that he was doing it, but the basics behind it," Thunder asked.

Rose shrugged. "If I got some of his notes, or samples of blood or something, I could maybe figure it out. I only know he's interested in those subjects, but I never knew what he was working on specifically. When he thought I was no use to him he let me go, but now if he thinks I hold a use again, his interest would start back up."

"Are you suggesting that we use you as bait, little ladybug?" Steel asked, voice low and menacing.

Frowning at him, she nodded. "Isn't that why I'm still here? To help you get my brother?"

"Help, not play bait," Steel informed her.

"You're being ridiculous. You literally brought me here to use as bait. I'm just agreeing it could work, only not quite the way you originally intended. Ridge won't make a trade, me for him. But he does believe you've been torturing me, and he doesn't think I'm strong enough to survive that, so he'll never believe that I convinced you I'm useless and that we ended up agreeing to work together."

Sometimes an overinflated ego was all you needed to bring someone down.

Add in an opponent who was always underestimated, and she believed this could work.

"I'll pretend that I escaped, got to a phone, called him for help. I know his old number, might not still work but maybe it will. He uses encrypted phones so I don't know if you can track him, but I'm positive he'll come to pick me up, thinking he can use that to find out where you guys are hiding. Then he'll come to you, because he thinks he'll win. Ridge will never play a game where he thinks he's going to be the loser. Then all you'll need to do is put a tracker or something on me, wait until he has me, then swoop in and kill him."

CHAPTER
Seventeen

January 1st
    9:37 A.M.

Of course, there had been times in Steel's life when he'd been scared.

Not just childish fears when he was small, but as an adult too. When he was going through his rigorous special forces training, there had been times he'd been afraid he wasn't going to make it. His first op had been full of fears and uncertainties, if he had what it took to survive in that world. Then, in those hours and days after the experimental drugs were in his system, and he started feeling uncontrollable rage, followed by suicidal thoughts.

But none of that compared to the fear of sending Rose back to the man who had already spent most of her life torturing her.

"No," he said simply.

"No, what?" Rose asked, her nose doing that adorable little confused scrunching thing.

"I don't like that plan."

"I don't get you. You're being ridiculous."

"You said that already," he drawled, consumed with the need to drag her into his arms and reaffirm the fact that she was there, safe and sound, not in any danger.

Since his team already knew that he was obsessed with the little ladybug, and that they'd spent the beginning of the New Year with him buried deep inside her, Steel saw no reason not to do exactly that.

Squeaking as he hauled her out of her chair and onto his lap, Rose's hands clutched at his shoulders. Before she could ask anything, he crushed his mouth to hers, taking her lips in a bruising kiss. She might be right, they might have brought her here to do exactly what Rose was suggesting, but things had changed.

Grabbing one of her breasts, he kneaded it firmly, making her moan, but it wasn't enough, he needed more, wanted to hear her scream his name. Claiming her backside, he began to rock her against his hard length, straining against his jeans, desperate to come out to play.

"Steel, we can't," she said, panting when he tore his mouth from hers.

"Look around you, little ladybug."

When she glanced over her shoulder, she saw that the guys had taken their breakfasts and left the room. There was no point in reminding her that wherever they were in the house, Blade would hear her come, that Dragon would smell her arousal, she wasn't used to living in a home with people like them, but she'd get used to it.

She had to. Because he wasn't letting her go.

Needing to remind her of that, he rocked his hips up into her as she ground her center against him, making another moan tumble from her lips.

As much as he hated the very thought of Rose anywhere near her brother, he knew she was right. This was the best way to draw Ridge out, and once they knew where the cowardly scientist was hiding, they could finally kill him.

"Strip," he said as he lifted Rose and set her on her feet beside him.

"We can't, the others—"

"Know better than to come in here right now," he assured her.

Although her cheeks heated, Rose quickly began removing her clothes. Watching her every move, desperate for glimpses of petal soft skin, Steel stood and crossed the room, pulling out a burner phone from the stash they kept in case they had need of them. Then he returned to his chair, set the burner phone on the table, unzipped himself, and let his rock-hard length spring free.

"You want to do this, then we do it like this."

Her pretty pink blush turned bright red, but she eyed his length with a hunger he knew she wouldn't be able to deny. "I can't call my brother with you inside me," she said with an embarrassed giggle.

"Then you won't be calling him at all." As far as he was concerned, it was as simple as that.

"But he'll know I'm having sex."

"Only way he'll know is if you let him."

"But—"

"No buts, little ladybug. That man tried to destroy you, tried to turn you into a monster in his own image, but you didn't let him. He tortured you, bruised your skin, damaged your mind, yet you stand before him now strong and beautiful, brave and determined. I want you to remember when you talk to him that you don't belong to him anymore, he has no power over you. You're mine."

"Actually, I'm my own, I belong to myself." She huffed, but she drifted closer nonetheless.

"Mine," he growled. Reaching for her, he picked her up and held her just above him, so his tip nestled against her entrance. "You told me you were mine, and I told you that you couldn't take it back."

"And what exactly do I get out of this?"

"Me," Steel replied. It wasn't enough. If he could, he'd give her the entire world, but all he had to offer her was the broken pieces of his body, mind, and soul.

"You." She said the word softly, almost reverently, and he sat there waiting for her to tell him that it wasn't enough, that she deserved more. But then she gifted him one of those precious smiles of hers and framed his face, her fingers curling into his short hair. "Mine."

That was all he needed to hear. Steel guided her down to take him inside her, and she moaned, her head falling back as he stretched her. If there was a way for him to physically mark her as his, he'd do it in a heartbeat. He'd tattoo her name on his forehead if she wanted him to, so everybody would know who owned him.

"What do I say?" she asked as he pressed the phone into her hands.

"Whatever you think he'll believe. You can do this, little ladybug, I have faith in you."

Something soft filled her eyes, but they quickly rolled back in her head when he took one of her pebbled little nipples into his mouth, and she moaned, her chest thrusting forward seeking more.

More he was happy to give her. He wanted his woman drowning in pleasure, erasing the pain of the past a little each time she remembered how her body was supposed to be touched. Maybe he wouldn't be so good at the touchy-feely kind of stuff, but he would burn the world to the ground for her, tear down hell itself, and give her more pleasure than she could handle.

Her gaze was locked on him as she dialed a number she must have known from childhood, because they didn't have a number for her brother.

Feasting on one of her breasts, he kept a bruising grip on her hip as he continued to rock his hips, thrusting into her, while the fingers of his other hand found her bud and played with it.

"R-Ridge," she gasped a second later.

Since he could only hear her side of the conversation, he focused on what he was doing, reminding his girl that her brother had no power over her anymore. That the years of pain were going to be replaced with endless years of pleasure. Steel might not be able to give her the world, but he could give her unyielding devotion.

"I-I found a phone, and I took it and ran," Rose said.

There was a ragged edge to her voice that he hadn't heard before, and he had to force the growl that wanted to break free and destroy anything that hurt her. Instead, he moved to her other breast, lavishing attention on it as he worked her bundle of nerves with tight circles.

"I wasn't sure if you still had this number," Rose continued. "They took me because of you. They thought I knew where you were, thought that you would be willing to do a trade to get me back safely."

The sound of laughter echoed through the phone, and since he couldn't wrap his hands around Ridge Gardner's neck and snap it, Steel scraped his teeth over her hard little nipple, drawing a moan from Rose's lips as her internal muscles began to flutter around him.

"Th-they beat me, burned me, whipped me," she mumbled into the phone. "I only escaped because they thought I was too weak to do anything. I know we don't … don't have much of a relationship … I know you don't love me … but I'm scared and … I didn't have anyone else to call."

A single tear slipped free, and he knew that was the truth. The damage her brother had inflicted on her psyche had Rose feeling unworthy of love and isolating herself. Same way he and his team did.

But she was worthy of everything, and he never wanted her to doubt that again.

Catching the tear on the tip of his tongue, Steel touched a kiss to the corner of her mouth, before moving back to suckle on one of her breasts.

"Will you … will you come for me?"

There was pain in her tone, and he knew it was because if this situation was real that she really would doubt if her brother would bother coming for her.

"I'm in the forest somewhere. I need to put more distance between me and them." She paused, listened for a moment. "No. I'm not turning the location features on yet. If I do it while I'm too close to them, I don't trust you to come for me. You'll leave me and try to find them. I heard bits and pieces of them talking when they thought I was unconscious. I know what you did to them, why you want them back, and why they want to kill you. Once you come for me, I'll show you the way back to where they're hiding."

That was his smart girl.

"Please, Ridge, come for me."

Her brother must have told her he would because she tossed the phone onto the table like she couldn't bear touching it a second longer.

"Make me come, now," she ordered, clutching at his shoulders and meeting him thrust for thrust. There was a desperation to her, and he knew she was already close, teetering on the edge.

Sinking his teeth into her breast, he shoved her into the orgasm her body craved, and quickly followed her over the edge, when she screamed and her internal muscles clamped around him.

The marks on her breast felt like a claim, but they would fade. Steel wondered if Rose would be willing to get his teeth marks tattooed on her breast as a permanent reminder of who she belonged to. He was already going to get a rose with a ladybug sitting on one of its petals tattooed over his heart, because for better or worse, he belonged to Rose Gardner now.

～

January 1st
   9:50 A.M.

That had to be the craziest thing she'd ever done.

Making a call to her brother, who she hated, pretending to have escaped her kidnappers, while one of her captors had sex with her.

Only Steel wasn't her captor anymore, he was …

Honestly, Rose didn't even know how to put into words what she felt for the man. There was still a lingering layer of hatred because he'd brought her here against her will and used her like a pawn, like an object with no thoughts, feelings, or needs. But there was more than that. There was attraction, plenty of that, and also something more genuine. Not affection, she didn't know him well enough for that, and she hadn't moved enough past the hate, but it was something softer, warmer.

Telling Steel she belonged to him was stupid, and telling him he was hers was stupider still, and yet Rose didn't have it in her to regret her reckless words.

One thing she was certain of was that Steel had offered every bruised and damaged piece of his soul to her, and she knew it was a gift he hadn't ever intended to offer another person.

Steel's tongue lapped across the teeth marks he'd left in her skin, and as she watched his dark dead against her porcelain complexion, warmth bloomed inside her. Crazy and twisted though it was, this was more tenderness than anyone else had ever shown her.

"I want my teeth marks tattooed right here," Steel informed her as he lifted his head.

The absurdity of the statement made her laugh, but it was the fact that she didn't hate the idea of wearing Steel's mark on her body that told her just how deep the man had managed to drag her in a short space of time.

"We'll see," she said, aiming for noncommittal, but from the smirk he gave her, she knew she'd given away some of her interest in the idea.

"Would stay inside you forever if I could," he murmured, pressing his face into the curve of her neck and breathing deeply.

Before she could echo that plan, because having him inside her was like having a missing piece of herself returned, he'd lifted her off him and set her on the floor beside him. That was probably for the best. If he knew how deeply he affected her, he'd become even more obsessive and possessive than he already was.

"Guess I'd better go and clean up," she said, moving toward her clothes.

A hand snapped out to circle her wrist, stopping her, and Steel growled, low and deep.

"Did you just growl at me?" she demanded.

"You are not going off to meet with another man without my cum still on your body. I want everyone to know who you belong to."

"I believe we've had this conversation already. I belong to myself, and it's not *some other man,* it's my *brother,*" she reminded him.

"You're not washing it off," Steel snarled, yanking her closer so his other hand could go between her legs, his fingers pressing inside her, scooping up more evidence of what they'd just done and smearing it all over the inside of her thighs.

"You are crazy," she said, but her voice had gotten husky, and a fresh wave of desire sparked to life inside her.

"Crazy for you," he agreed, and she knew arguing about this topic was completely pointless. Still, going to see her brother like this wasn't any crazier than calling him while Steel was buried deep inside her.

But his words did stir an echo of concern. "We, ah, might have a problem."

"Problem?" Steel's dark eyes scanned the room searching for something he could destroy, only this wasn't something that could be fixed like that.

"I might have mentioned to Ridge that you guys had beaten me and burned me as well as whipped me. I had to say something," she rushed to add when Steel's gaze darkened. "After all, he thinks you abducted me to use as bait, he's going to think you did more to me than what you showed him on the camera."

"Good thing you pulled the ceiling down on yourself then, you're still covered in bruises."

"Old bruises. He's going to expect something fresher, and you're still going to have to burn me."

The howl that echoed through the room made her shiver, but not in fear. If he'd done that a week ago, she would have been terrified of him, although she would have done her best not to let it show. But now the sound just reminded her that this man was obsessed with her in a way that afforded her the protection she'd always craved.

"Is it safe to come in?" Voodoo asked from the hall.

"Yes," she called out, only to have Steel snarl and snatch her off her feet, setting her back on his lap and wrapping his arms around her.

"No," he growled.

"They've seen me naked already," she reminded him. While Rose was no exhibitionist, she was pragmatic, and if they were going to hit and burn her like they needed to in order to make her story believable, then they were going to need access to her body anyway.

"Look at her, and I'll tear your eyes right out," Steel told his team with a deadly calm as they entered the room.

"Did you speak to him?" Blade asked her, ignoring Steel's threat.

"Yeah. I told him that I escaped, but that I wouldn't turn on the location features on the phone until I was further away from you guys because I didn't trust him to come for me first if he thought he could just get to you." Running her hands soothingly over Steel's pecs, she added, "I may have also mentioned that you'd hit and burned me."

"So now we have to make good on that," Thunder said, and she nodded.

"Maybe one of you guys could do it, so Steel doesn't have to."

Another growl from her grumbly guy, and his hands dug into her hips hard enough that he was going to leave bruises.

"Don't think that's going to work," Lion said with a chuckle.

"Why?"

"Because Steel will kill us if we touch you," Dragon said simply.

"No he won't," she quickly assured him, but when Steel didn't say anything, she turned to look at him. "You wouldn't kill your team, would you?"

"I absolutely would."

"But they're your team, your family."

"And you're mine," Steel said simply. "You shouldn't have told him that we'd hurt you." One of his large hands lifted from her hip to circle her throat, squeezing just hard enough that it made it a little difficult to breathe without cutting off her air supply.

"You know I had no other choice," she whispered.

"I'll never forgive myself for this."

That was the only warning she got before the hand on her neck was gone, curled into a fist and slammed into her face hard enough that she would have been knocked to the floor if Steel wasn't still gripping her hip with bruising force.

"Get her pajamas, the ones she was wearing when we took her," Steel ordered someone, as he leaned in and feathered his lips across hers.

"You have to do this," she reminded him, ignoring the throbbing in her face and the sensations that the room was spinning around them. "It's the only way to convince Ridge this is real. The only way to protect me when he finds me."

Which was the only reason Steel was doing it, she knew that.

If Ridge found her and believed she'd lied and was working with the men he wanted back, he wouldn't keep her alive to torture information out of her, he'd simply kill her and be done with it.

"I'm sorry, little ladybug." Steel's voice was tortured as he shifted his hold on her so her back was now pressed against his chest. One of his arms banded across her chest, just beneath her breasts, pinning her in place with her arms by her sides. His other hand circled her ankle, and he bent her leg up so he could switch hands, leaving him one hand free. "This is how I'd do it if I was really torturing you."

Making a concerted effort not to look directly at her naked body, Voodoo handed Steel a lighter, and Rose shivered as she realized Steel intended to burn the soles of her feet. It was a good idea, because it would have made it harder for her to run if they really were holding her hostage, but it was going to hurt like hell.

"Focus on me," Steel ordered, his teeth digging into her neck and then immediately soothing her skin with his tongue, as he held the small flame close to her skin, searing her flesh and making her flinch.

No matter how much this sucked, it was worth it. Once her brother was dead, had paid in blood for his crimes against her and Steel and his team, then they'd be free.

Free to explore this messed-up thing they had brewing between them.

Free to maybe find the love and acceptance she'd always craved.

CHAPTER
Eighteen

January 1st
   10:42 P.M.

A week ago, Steel would have laughed in the person's face if they told him he would be cradling a woman so tenderly in his arms.

Now holding Rose close to his chest felt like the most natural thing in the world.

But it didn't ease the knot of nausea sitting heavily in his gut.

After he'd burned the soles of Rose's feet, he'd harshly shoved her off his lap, depositing her on the table in front of him, then stormed down the hall to the closest bathroom where the contents of his stomach had quickly evacuated themselves.

Hurting people had never been something he enjoyed. When he enlisted in the military, it was something he was prepared to do, knowing it came with the job. After Dr. Gardner had messed with his DNA, it was something he did without conscious thought. It didn't negatively affect him in any way, and he never felt an ounce of guilt or remorse after he and his team had tortured someone for intel or ended the lives of those who didn't deserve to live.

Even when they'd taken Rose, knowing she was innocent, he hadn't expected to feel a drop of regret for what they planned to do with her. She had been deemed a necessary sacrifice, and all six of them had been good with that, their eyes fixed so firmly on their revenge that they'd been blinded to anything else.

Then Rose's defiant attitude changed everything.

It jarred him out of his single-minded objective, made him see her as a real person and not an object of value to achieving his goals. Her bravery and determination, her sass and strength, made him aware of things he hadn't thought possible.

For a decade, he had believed himself to be a monster incapable of loving another person, not safe to be around, and a danger to humanity. Knowing he'd thrown up because he'd laid his hands on a woman who was firmly lodged in his heart told him the truth.

He'd never been a monster.

Always been capable of connecting with people, even if his conscience had been badly damaged by the experimental drugs he'd been given.

If he wasn't still capable of normal human emotion, he wouldn't have been down on his knees vomiting, his stomach painfully cramping, because he'd hurt the woman who owned him.

In the end, it had been Rose's small hands stroking his back that had him looking over his shoulder. The look in her eyes, the understanding, the acceptance, had almost been enough to bring him to tears.

Instead, he'd shoved to his feet, yanking her into his arms and holding her tight while he washed out his mouth, then he'd shoved her up against the wall and taken her hard and fast. His bruising pace must have hurt her, but she'd clung to him, her nails digging into his skin as she screamed out her release loud enough that Blade would have heard no matter where he was in the house, even if he didn't have enhanced hearing.

To keep them all safe, Rose included, Voodoo had given her a sedative before they left the mansion. The plan was to get to Rose as soon as her brother was with her, but in case anything happened to delay them, he couldn't allow her to have intel that could potentially be tortured out of her.

His girl was strong, but she was still human, and it was better for her if she didn't know where she'd been kept for the last week.

That was changing afterward though.

Rose was his, and he had no intention of letting her go even if he had to lock her back up in his room until she agreed to stay with him. The mansion would be her home, and she would learn its location.

None of them had spoken on the drive to the private airfield.

No one had spoken as they loaded onto the small private jet.

Neither had anyone said a word when they landed a few states over and piled into a rented SUV.

It was almost time to drop Rose off, and Steel found it increasingly difficult to be okay with the idea of leaving her behind.

How was he supposed to drop her off alone and unconscious in the woods, knowing her brother was going to come for her?

She'd wake up groggy and in pain, no idea where she was, and call her brother to come and get her. She was walking straight into the lion's den, and she was doing it in large part for him.

"Rose can do this," Thunder said softly, shifting in the driver's seat to look at him as he stopped the car deep in the forest.

That wasn't even a question. Of course she could. Steel believed there wasn't a thing on this earth the woman cradled in his arms couldn't do.

But that didn't erase the darkening bruise around her eye or clean away the blood that had dried and crusted around the split in her cheekbone. Knowing he'd been the one to put those marks on her body filled him with a shame he hadn't thought himself capable of.

"She knew you had to do it," Lion said quietly from beside him.

Again, Steel knew that, and it was only Rose's words that hitting her was the only way to protect her that had him doing it, before that, he had been adamant that no one was putting any other bruises on her gorgeous body.

"She's doing this willingly," Blade added.

Finally tearing his gaze away from Rose's sleeping face, he met the worried gazes of his teammates. "We kidnapped her, held her captive, she wasn't in a position to consent to anything," he reminded them. That was the truth of the matter. Rose may have said the words, might have told them she'd work with them and play bait, but what else was she supposed to say?

They'd held her freedom over her head and coerced her compliance.

Maybe he really was a monster after all.

"Too late to back out now," Dragon reminded him, although not unkindly, and he knew his friend was right.

Rose had called her brother. He'd already hit her, they'd already put her on a plane and flown her to a remote mountain range. What else was there to do? He damn sure hadn't hit his little ladybug, burned her, just to back out and have it been for nothing.

With a nod, he indicated Voodoo should open his door, and once the man had climbed out, Steel slid across the back seat with Rose still in his arms. The temperature drop was immediately noticeable once he was no longer in the vehicle, and he knew the thin—now dirty and tattered thanks to them making the material look like it had survived an escape— pajamas were no match for the cold.

"How long until she wakes up?" he asked as he scanned the area, looking for a somewhat protected spot to lay Rose down. If she stayed out there unconscious for too long, then hypothermia would claim her. At least awake and moving she stood a chance against it.

"I'll give her a shot of adrenaline before we go," Voodoo assured him. "She should wake up quickly."

"And she has a tracker on her?" Although he already knew the answer, he needed the reassurance of hearing it spoken out loud.

"Eight of them," Blade replied, shrugging when Steel quirked an eyebrow at him. "Maybe a little overboard, but we need to be able to find her. This way, if they check her for trackers, they'll find one and think they're done. Even if they're suspicious and find another, they're not going to keep checking long enough to find them all."

They would have to pray Blade was right.

The tracker leading them to Rose was the only thing that would save her life.

Reluctantly, Steel carried her over to a small bush and set Rose down beneath it. Voodoo picked up her wrist to check her pulse before uncapping a syringe and pulling Rose's pajama top down enough to inject it into her bicep.

Knowing he had to go, because if he was there when Rose woke up there was no way in hell he would be able to leave her behind, Steel leaned down and pressed his lips to Rose's forehead.

"You'd better come back to me, little ladybug," he murmured.

Getting attached to their captive should never have been an option, but looking back, he knew it had been destined to happen the moment she opened her eyes in her bed, and he looked down into those deep forest green depths.

Now he needed her to survive, needed her to come back to him, needed her to submit to him and give him every inch of herself. He wanted to soothe all her old hurts, erase all her past pain, and give her the freedom to live her life however she wanted with an army at her back that would kill anyone who ever looked at her wrong.

To do that, she had to survive the man who had left deep scars on her soul.

With a last look, Steel shoved to his feet and walked away without a backward glance, knowing he was leaving his heart, his soul, and his sanity behind, lying unconscious on the forest floor.

~

January 2nd
    12:04 A.M.

Rose woke to the lingering feel of Steel's lips on her forehead and the faint hum of an engine.

Alone.

That was the first word that ran through her mind. She'd known she was doing this alone, it had been her idea, and at her insistence that she was dumped out there, but still there was a pang in her chest at the knowledge that Steel had just left her behind.

Which was perhaps the craziest thing she'd ever felt.

Or maybe just the next progression in a line of crazy things over the last week.

The man had inserted himself inside her mind, that was for sure. He was a dangerous man, his enhanced strength aside, and one who she knew would kill without hesitation. He'd also been okay with taking her, an innocent woman, and abusing her to get what he wanted.

Yet something about his possessiveness, his claims, the pain in his eyes when she went to him in the bathroom after he'd burned the bottoms of her feet, called out to all the broken pieces of her.

They'd been broken by the same person. Was it possible that together they could help each other put their pieces back together?

Could their darkness bond them, tie them together, or would it destroying them?

There was no way to know the answers to those questions unless she threw herself all in to this crazy ... whatever the hell it was between them, and she was terrified to do that.

Growing up as she had, Rose had always been aware that the thing that could destroy her wasn't pain, wasn't loneliness, wasn't torture and suffering, it was the opposite. It was allowing someone to make her feel accepted, wanted, and adored, then losing it, that was the only thing that would break her beyond repair.

Now, Steel leaving her out there, to go after her brother alone, made her feel just that exact way. Despite the pain he'd inflicted on her, he'd also been kind and gentle, sweet even, which seemed a weird way to describe the man who could easily crush her if he wanted to.

"He's not really gone," she reminded herself as the foggy feeling from the sedatives she'd been given receded. While she hadn't liked the idea of being drugged while they transported her out there, wherever there was, Rose had agreed it was their safest move. That way, her brother couldn't torture the guys' location out of her.

Unconscious left her completely vulnerable to Steel and his team, but then again, she figured with their combined enhanced skills they were basically unstoppable anyway, and if they'd wanted her dead, she'd be dead already.

"Steel is out there, he's watching over you the best way he can, you are not alone."

The pep talk did little to erase the feelings of abandonment, but she did know that the words she'd spoken aloud were true. The guys had placed numerous trackers on her, both in her clothes, on her skin, and even a couple under her skin. They wanted to be thorough because they all agreed that Ridge would check her for trackers once she got to him.

While she moved through the forest, called her brother, and waited for him to come to her, the guys would be following her every move.

"See? Not alone. Not alone at all."

Shivering as the cold seeped into her, Rose found the burner phone lying beside her and scooped it up. If she didn't call Ridge soon and get up and moving, she was going to freeze to death.

Ignoring the pounding in her head from the drugs, she rolled herself over onto her stomach and pushed up onto her hands and knees, angling her weight so it was balanced on her good arm, not her broken one. For a moment she paused there, swaying from side to side, bone weary and wondering how she was going to stand, let alone move, let alone handle coming face to face with her brother again after five years.

But she didn't have a choice.

This was her chance to help Steel and his team take down Ridge once and for all. Her brother was an even worse human being than she'd ever given him credit for. The way he'd played God with people's lives, altering their DNA, trying to create his own super soldiers, it was despicable, especially since he hadn't been honest with the people whose lives he was playing with.

Gathering stores of strength she'd almost depleted these last several days, somehow Rose managed to find a little more, and grabbed onto the bush she'd been set beneath to use it for leverage to push to her feet.

Immediately, she wished she hadn't.

The pain from the raw burns on the soles of her feet was severe. It felt like she was standing on a mat of burning knives. While the ground was cold not burning, and there were sticks littering it and not knives, it wasn't really that big a difference. She'd be lucky if the wounds didn't become infected, with all this debris getting into them.

Plus, she was going to have to walk on them, run even.

Gritting her teeth, she decided she may as well get it over with. Standing there anticipating the pain as she started taking steps was only going to make it worse, not better.

Because she knew that the guys wouldn't be all that far away, and she wasn't quite sure just how Blade's enhanced hearing worked, and how far away he could hear things, and how loud they had to be before they registered, Rose resisted crying out as she took that first step.

It was every bit as agonizing as she'd expected it to be, but somehow, she managed to clamp her teeth together and bear it. If Blade could hear even a whimper from wherever he and the others were, he'd tell Steel, and she had a feeling that her big, super-strong guy would throw in the towel and come and get her.

The thought made her smile, and she took advantage of the momentary high to start running. When Ridge came for her, she had to look like she'd been running through the woods for hours on end. The guys had helped by removing the cast on her arm, and taking out the stitches that Voodoo had put into the wounds she'd gotten when the ceiling fell in.

She knew she had to make her brother believe that she had escaped men still intent on torturing her, or he'd kill her in a heartbeat.

Big brother was a dangerous man. More dangerous than Steel and his team. They might believe they were monsters, but her brother really was one. Maybe Ridge's experiments had damaged their abilities to empathize and created a gap in their consciences, but they weren't monsters. Not at all. They were damaged men, sure, but they weren't destroyed by Ridge's games.

Her brother, on the other hand, had never had a conscience, never learned to empathize, and there was no way he could learn now.

If she messed this up, she was dead.

It was as simple as that.

When she couldn't run another step, Rose leaned against the nearest tree, dragging in a few ragged breaths and cursing her cracked ribs for making it so painful.

With shaking fingers, she dialed her brother's number and waited.

After a single ring, he picked up.

"What took you so long to call back?" Ridge snapped in that arrogant tone she remembered so well from her childhood.

"I ... passed out," she lied, which wasn't really a lie if you thought about it, most of the time since her last call until now she had been unconscious.

"You're wasting my time," Ridge complained, not an ounce of

sympathy for his poor, abducted, and tortured sister, who had collapsed from exhaustion. Not that she'd expected any. Psycho that he was.

"A-are you coming for m-me?" she asked, still breathing hard from the exertion of running. Now that she'd stopped moving, her body temperature was dropping and she was beginning to shiver. Was there a chance Ridge would just leave her out there to die?

Okay, so she wouldn't really die, Steel wouldn't let that happen, but her brother didn't know that.

"Of course I'm coming," Ridge replied, sounding annoyed. "I've been looking for those men for the last seven years. I created them, and I own them, they're going to pay for costing me seven years' worth of progress."

No way, psycho brother of mine, they're going to kill you like the cockroach that you are, and the world will be a better place for it.

"Did you turn on the location services?" Ridge asked impatiently.

"I'll do it now." Fiddling with the phone, she switched the services back on and sent out a silent signal to her brother, giving him her location, drawing him into their trap.

"Okay, I have you. I already have a team prepared, so we're leaving now. Don't move from the location you're in right now. If you do, I'll know, and I won't be happy about it."

"What should I do if they find me? If I hear them coming, should I run? Hide?"

Ridge laughed, a cold, inhuman sound. "You won't hear them coming. They're too highly skilled to make such a simple mistake."

After that, he was gone, leaving her smiling at the phone. "You won't hear them coming either, big brother. Your arrogance is going to cost you your life. You're about to lose your power, and it's going to be a beautiful thing to behold. Enjoy your last free moments on earth because once you get here, you're going to wish for death the same way you used to make me wish you'd just kill me and get it over with."

CHAPTER

Nineteen

January 2nd
   2:38 A.M.

"She's okay."

Steel tensed at the words, spoken softly by Lion, who was sitting beside him in the back of their SUV.

It wasn't the first time one of the guys had said that to him in the last couple of hours since they'd left Rose alone and unconscious on the rough forest ground.

Hell, it wasn't even the tenth time one of them had said it.

So far, he had yet to respond. What was the point? They all knew that Rose wasn't okay. There hadn't even been time for her to recover from what they'd inflicted on her, plus the ceiling falling on her. Now she had new wounds, including a gash on her cheek from where he'd hit her that would leave behind a scar.

One he would look at every day for the rest of their lives and be reminded that he was the one who had caused it.

Then there were her feet, and the fact that it was cold enough out that he wouldn't be surprised if it started snowing soon. How the hell was she in any way okay?

"She's—"

"Don't say it," he snarled at Thunder, cutting the man off before he could offer the same platitude that did absolutely nothing to quell the fear pounding inside him.

"Try to think of this as just a regular op," Blade suggested.

"It is a regular op," Steel spoke without thinking.

"Lie," Dragon said, twisting in the front passenger seat to look at him. The man's violet eyes were unyielding, daring him to disagree, to argue the point.

"We all know Rose is important to you," Voodoo spoke gently, and since he wasn't used to his team being so careful with his feelings, it left him floundering, spinning wildly out of control with nothing solid to ground him.

In the space of just days, Rose had given him something he didn't think he'd ever have.

Something he didn't feel he deserved.

"Not like you've put in much effort to hiding the fact that you're obsessed with her," Lion added.

"We all heard you have sex with her," Thunder said.

"Vividly." Blade winced and gave an exaggerated shudder, causing the tiniest crack in the tension that threatened to break him.

"Obsessed doesn't even come close to communicating how I feel about her," he admitted. It was hard saying those words to anyone who wasn't Rose.

Rose didn't get it. Not really. She had her own trauma with her brother that was every bit as dark and painful as what he and his team shared with Dr. Gardner. But it wasn't the same.

She was an innocent. She hadn't done anything to deserve the hell her brother had put her through. They, on the other hand, had willingly signed up for the project, intrigued and excited by the idea of having their natural abilities enhanced to make them superior soldiers.

Even when things started to go wrong, Steel had been the one to convince his team to keep pushing through. His faith in the scientist had been complete, and because of that, he hadn't caught on to the fact that Dr. Gardner was a psychopath with delusions of grandeur. That the man cared only about playing God, and that as far as he was concerned, Steel and his team and the other men in the project were all just guinea pigs to be used and tossed away if they failed.

It was because of him that his team had been forced to give up their lives, walk away from their families, hide out in their home, locked away from the rest of the world.

How could he be okay with finding happiness and peace when his teammates' lives were still in tatters?

"It's okay to fall for her, you're not doing anything wrong," Thunder told him.

Only it felt like he was.

"We all know it's true," Lion continued. "You caught feelings for our pretty little captive."

Hearing his friend comment on Rose's beauty flipped a switch inside him, and he growled as he wrapped a hand around his teammate's neck. Lion just grinned at him and arched a brow, daring him to disagree that it wasn't just an obsession, it ran so much deeper than that.

With a huff, he released his hold on Lion's neck and instead dragged a hand down his face. He and his teammates might be family, brothers in every sense of the word except for their DNA, but they didn't sit around and discuss their feelings. They didn't even admit to having feelings.

For the last decade, Steel would have sworn the only feeling he was capable of was anger.

Until Rose.

His little ladybug changed everything.

"You've been a good leader, Steel," Voodoo said, his tone going earnest. "You've kept us together, kept us sane, kept us alive and safe. Going to Prey was your idea, and without that decision, chances are that Dr. Gardner might have found us long before now. You kept us going when it felt like we were never going to get a lead on the name of the scientist who tortured us. You were even prepared to follow through on hurting Rose, even after you realized something in her called out to something in you. You did that for us. Because you're our leader and you think it's your job to always put us first."

"But things change, and we're not first anymore," Blade said, no reproach in his tone. "Now your little ladybug is number one, and none of us fault you for that. You'll always be our team's leader, but if we finally kill Dr. Gardner and everyone else involved in his project, then you deserve a chance at happiness. Real happiness."

"We've all lost a lot," Lion said with a wince, and they all knew that the man had lost the most of all of them when their lives were upended by Dr. Gardner. "But if you get a chance at happiness, you grab hold of it with both hands and refuse to let it go."

"You're all giving me your blessing to find a way to make it work with Rose?" It sounded like they were, but it was a big ask. For the last decade, they'd been all each other had, and Steel didn't know how to have a future where he didn't see his team every single day.

"Do you really need it?" Thunder asked.

"Yeah, I think I actually do," he admitted. He'd already told Rose she was his, that he was never letting her go, and he'd meant every word of it, but at the back of his mind had been doubts about how he was supposed to go about making that work. While he had no problem forcing Rose to stay with him until she wanted to stay on her own, a part of him wanted her to choose him. Wanted her to stay because she couldn't stand to be away from him, and not because he'd become just another person to strip her of her choices.

"You have it," Dragon said, and that the words came from the man who had wanted to take out his anger at losing Cassandra on Rose meant everything.

Nodding his acceptance of his team's welcoming Rose into their family, Steel felt emotion clog his throat. Rose seemed to like him, although he had no idea why, but how much of it was real, and how much of it was survival?

They'd told her she had to earn her freedom by helping them, then he'd claimed her, told her she was his, and he was never letting her go. If he were in Rose's position, he would have said or done whatever it took to make it through another day.

"Hey," Dragon barked, and Steel looked over at him. "She likes you. I've been watching her. The way she looks at you ... you give her something she's been craving that no one else has ever provided."

"I abducted her."

"Yet she let you have sex with her, several times," Blade reminded him.

"I had her tortured, starved, and whipped."

"And still she agreed to help us," Thunder said.

"I forced her to tell me she was mine, told her I wasn't letting her go."

"When you left the room after burning her feet, she went after you, no hesitation," Voodoo said.

"I think love is this crazy thing that never makes sense, no matter how much you want it to," Dragon admitted softly. They all knew the man regretted choosing vengeance over Cassandra, but he was too stubborn to admit it and make a new choice instead.

"Much as I hate to break up our emotional bonding session, we got company," Blade announced, his head cocked to the side as he'd obviously heard something.

Shoving aside everything else, it would all be there to deal with and unpack later. For now, the only thing that mattered was getting their hands on Ridge Gardner and punishing him for everything he'd put them all through.

Then there would be time to figure out how a man like him could ever earn the love of a woman like Rose. As much as he craved her submission, as much as he wanted to own every inch of her, Steel equally needed her love.

He might be a monster, but if he was, he was Rose's monster.

January 2nd
3:03 A.M.

The cold had her so numb she couldn't even feel the pain in her throbbing feet anymore.

"At least that's something," Rose muttered, clenching her teeth together to try to stop them chattering.

Since Ridge had demanded that she not move from the spot where she'd been when she called him, she'd lost her ability to keep her body temperature up. Sure, she was doing jumping jacks, running on the spot, anything she could think of to stop herself getting hypothermic, but with her burned feet, cracked ribs, and all her bruises, it was painful. At least when she'd been running through the forest, it gave a purpose, so she didn't have as much time to think about the pain.

With her hair a tangled mess, her pajamas filthy and torn, and her skin dirty and scratched up, she looked like a disheveled mess who had been running for her life.

If she didn't know that Ridge would absolutely punish her for moving from this spot, for "wasting his time and making it harder for him to find her," she absolutely would have kept running and let him track her to the phone's location. But Ridge would freak out, act like he was doing her this massive favor coming after her, even though he had been perfectly content to allow her to be killed at Steel and his team's hands.

Still, even knowing the risks, she ached to run anyway. She was too cold and only getting colder. The clouds above her were thickening, and she wouldn't be surprised if it started to snow soon.

How was she supposed to survive that?

All she was wearing were thin flannelette pajamas, no underwear, no socks or shoes, no beanie, gloves, or scarf, no coat, nothing at all to protect her from the elements. She supposed she could always call Steel if it got too bad. He'd made her memorize his phone number, but if she did that, she risked ruining everything.

"You can do. It's only cold. You've survived it before, you can do it again."

The problem was that when she was a kid, Ridge hadn't really wanted to kill her, he wanted to turn her into his mini-me, and when he realized that wasn't happening, he at least wanted to use her as his slave to do all the housework and chores. Likewise, Steel hadn't really wanted her dead when he'd had her locked in the underground cell and pumped freezing air into the room.

Both of those things had been done to her in an attempt to break her spirit. But the weather didn't care about her spirit. It wasn't just trying to shatter her into pieces that could then be reassembled in her tormentor's image. It would just freeze her to death because it was simply doing what it did.

A slight rumble in the distance caught her attention, and Rose's head snapped up. She'd been lying on the ground, curled up in a ball, trying to conserve as much heat as she could manage, but now she shifted her stiff muscles and forced herself to stand.

In addition to the quiet hum of an engine, she could just make out lights dancing through the trees.

Ridge was coming.

It had been five years since she'd laid eyes on her brother, and she could have gone a lifetime without seeing him again.

"This is for a good cause," she reminded herself. "In just minutes, Ridge is going to be the one begging for mercy, and no one is going to show him any."

Watching as the lights came closer, the engine louder, Rose soon saw there wasn't just one vehicle, but five of them. Her brother must be worried that the guys were out there somewhere, hunting her, and he was being led into a trap.

Still, his ego had brought him here anyway. He wanted Steel and the others back, and he knew this was his best chance at getting to them, so he was prepared to risk it. She had no doubt that each one of those vehicles was filled with as many men as there was space for, but honestly, Ridge could have brought with him an entire army and he still wasn't going to win.

By the time the vehicles pulled to a stop before her, Rose shook so badly she ached. Her muscles protested the constant sharp movements, but there was no way for her to stop them no matter how badly she wanted to.

A man dressed all in black was the first to step out of one of the vehicles. He carried in his hands an M16, and he scanned the area, paying no attention to her.

Next out was her brother and following him were more men in black who piled out of the other cars, but Rose's attention was locked on the man before her. They looked like siblings, both had the same pale skin and smattering of freckles, both had the same red hair and deep forest green eyes. But that was where their similarities ended.

Her brother was a psychopath, lacking the ability to feel any empathy toward another living being. He was cruel because it amused him, and he believed himself to be superior to everyone he encountered. He was an evil man, and while maybe she had some issues thanks to her messed-up family, she would only ever hurt another person to save herself, never for fun.

"You're a mess," he sneered as he looked her over, probably annoyed he'd have to put her dirty self in his pristine car, which no doubt had smooth leather seats in his favorite shade of dark blue. Her brother was nothing if not predictable.

"Gee, I'm so sorry that I'm filthy because I was abducted because someone hates you and decided to use me to get to you," she snapped, hating the chattering of her teeth took the heat out of her words. As a child, she never would have spoken back to her brother like that. Instead, she'd given him silence when he yelled and screamed at her, punished and tortured her, because she knew he hated her stoic silence.

Now she wasn't a child, nor was she powerless. She wanted the rage she felt for him to be known.

"Ungrateful wench. Always have been," Ridge snapped.

"Wench? Are you a thirteenth-century nobleman?"

Irritation all but sparking off him, her brother nodded at the only other person not dressed all in black and holding a weapon. The other man was a little younger than her brother, but older than she was, maybe more the same age as Steel and his team. Giving her a look like he was almost afraid to get too close to her, Rose actually relaxed at the thought. At least this man wasn't going to get a kick out of hurting her.

"Strip," Ridge ordered. "I won't take a chance that they put a tracker in your clothes in case you escaped."

It was more the cold than the fact that she would have to get naked in front of two dozen men that had her stomach dropping. The material of her pajamas might be thin and no match for the cold, but at least it was something.

Knowing arguing was pointless, her shaking fingers struggled to undo the buttons, but she got them undone and shrugged out of her pajama top, then the bottoms, leaving her fully exposed to the elements.

Ridge's nose curled up as his gaze skimmed her body, then settled on the bite mark on her breast. "They bit you. Animals. That's all they are, no better than an animal. Check her for trackers."

Fury lit a fire inside her at the insult to Steel. It was Ridge's fault that his DNA had been altered, that he had been forced to give up his life, that he battled rage he managed to keep contained enough to function, and suicidal thoughts. If anyone there was no better than an animal, it would be her brother, only concerned with himself and his own wants, needs, and desires. Hell, a lot of animals showed more compassion to others than her own brother was capable of.

The timid man stepped up, giving her an almost apologetic look as he ran a wand over her. It set off as it passed over her head, picking up on the tracker behind her ear. Leaning in, the man ran his fingers over her skin, and she had to fight not to sigh and lean into the minimal warmth.

"Here, she has one taped behind her ear," timid man called out.

"I didn't know," she hurried to assure her brother, unsure if Ridge would blame her.

"Of course you didn't. You were never smart enough to know much of anything."

The insult slid easily off her. Rose knew she was smart, smart enough to have figured out her best bet at freedom was pretending she wasn't smart. Thankfully, the timid man seemed in a hurry to get this over with, because he didn't re-check to make sure there were no other trackers close to the one he'd found, and therefore missed the one injected just under her skin a mere inch from the one taped on.

Buzzing again when it reached her feet, timid man stooped and ran a finger over her ankle, coming away with another of the trackers. That still left four, and one for sure he'd already missed. Peeling off the tracker on her ankle, he didn't find the one injected under her skin close by, and when he stood, Rose let out a sigh of relief.

She was safe.

Even if her brother managed to take her away before the guys got there, they'd be able to follow her every move.

It was over, or at least close enough. The wheels were in motion, and Ridge wouldn't be getting away with his crimes against nature, free to keep playing with innocent people's lives.

No sooner had she had the thought than there was a blur of movement that captured everyone's attention.

Whoa.

She'd known Thunder had super speed, but she'd never seen it in action before.

Pandemonium broke out around them. Weapons fired, there were shouts of surprise and then pain as Steel and the others moved in and began to kill off Ridge's men. Timid man shrieked like a little girl, and Rose actually rolled her eyes at him, then startled when her brother grabbed her and shoved her into the car he'd climbed out of only minutes ago.

"You led them to me," Ridge hissed as he shoved her over the console into the passenger seat and climbed in behind her.

"Your problem was always underestimating me," she told her brother as he flung the car into drive and sped off. "Every time I survived one of your torturous games, you acted surprised, every time I achieved something, you acted surprised. Hell, you seem surprised that I can handle life at all. But they're coming for you, and they're going to make you pay for what you did to them. There's nothing you can do to stop it from happening. Your creations are going to destroy you, and I'm going to help, and love every second of it."

CHAPTER

Twenty

Thanks to the enhanced skills Dr. Gardner had given them, Steel and his team didn't even need to set up a surveillance system. They'd parked themselves the maximum distance away from Rose that they could while Blade could still hear her, and Dragon could still smell her.

Then all they'd had to do was wait.

As soon as Blade announced that he could hear approaching vehicles, they'd adjusted their position so they wouldn't be spotted, and then Lion had shimmied himself up a tree so he could put his enhanced vision to good use.

Before they were even close enough to be detected, they knew that five vehicles had driven up on Rose's position. Five men dressed in full tactical gear were in four of the vehicles, which made for twenty opponents. Another three in gear were in the remaining vehicle, and then the doctor himself and what was clearly one of the scientist's minions.

Twenty-three to six, Steel liked those odds.

He had no doubt that the men Dr. Gardner had brought with him were highly trained, but he was also confident that they weren't super soldiers. If the mad scientist had already created another working team, he would have sent them out after Delta Team long before now.

So whoever the unlucky teams were that accompanied the doctor, they didn't stand a chance. Steel wouldn't have felt regret for killing them either way, since they were a threat to his little ladybug, but the fact that they had to know what the scientist was up to and were willingly backing him meant they were just as evil as far as Steel was concerned.

They deserved to die.

"Uh, Steel, man, don't lose it," Lion called down from up in the tree where he was perched.

There was no way he wasn't going to lose it when Lion sounded tentative and concerned. A growl rumbled through his chest because there was only one thing Lion would be worried about.

"What did he do to her?" Steel demanded.

"He made her strip," Lion replied.

Red rage clouded his vision. Whatever Dr. Gardner had done to mess with their ability to feel normal human emotions had amplified their anger. Just because he and the rest of his team had learned how to control it over the last ten years didn't mean it wasn't still there.

A constant companion.

Simmering under the surface, waiting for something to set it off.

The words his brother had just spoken were enough to do that.

"He's worried about trackers," Blade added, head cocked to the side.

"She complied without fighting it, and he's sending his lackey in to wave a wand over her," Lion continued.

Beside him, Thunder tensed, ready to spring into action if they needed to get someone to Rose immediately. The man could close out the distance between them and Rose and the others in less than a minute, which should be enough time to prevent anything disastrous from happening.

Steel hoped.

Prayed.

"They found the one behind her ear," Lion continued his commentary.

They all tensed as they waited to see if her brother would locate the secondary one hidden just an inch away.

"He didn't," Lion answered the unasked question. "Guy is moving the wand down her body."

In his mind, Steel could picture Rose's bruised body on display to all the men surrounding her. Her delicate skin exposed to temperatures that could easily kill her. She'd be shaking, even though he knew she wanted to look tough in front of her brother, there was no way her system wouldn't be doing everything it could to warm her up.

Unless she'd already slipped too deep into hypothermia, where it now lacked the ability to even attempt to regulate her body temperature.

No.

Lion said she was standing and complying with her brother's commands. She wasn't lost to hypothermia yet.

"Found the one on her ankle," Lion told them. Then a moment later, "But just the stick on one. She still has four trackers on her."

Their plan was to take out whoever had come with Dr. Gardner here and now, and then knock Ridge himself out and return with him to their mansion, where they could lock him up in the basement and have their fun with him before killing him. The trackers were insurance in case Rose's brother had done a snatch and grab.

That wasn't what they thought Ridge would do, because he believed Rose to be close to the location where they'd taken her when they kidnapped her, but since this was his woman's life on the line, he wasn't taking any chances.

"Let's go," he said to the others. They'd given Dr. Gardner enough time to believe that if they were tracking Rose, they would have already launched their attack, but he didn't want to give the man too much time. The last thing he wanted was Rose alone with her brother for any reason.

His little ladybug was as tough as they came, but her brother was a damn psychopath who got off on hurting her. The man was never going to lay a hand on Rose again. It was time for her to be the one to inflict a little damage.

As soon as Lion's feet hit the ground, they were all off, moving as one, a tight-knit group that may as well share one mind when they were on an op. While the rest of them didn't have Thunder's enhanced speed, they worked out for hours a day, every day, so they were fast and strong and well prepared to take on a measly twenty-three-man army.

Letting Thunder make his impressive entrance as a distraction, Steel adjusted his hold on his weapon, not wanting the fury raging inside him to control him and have him break it. While he wanted to kill each and every one of these men with his bare hands as a punishment for daring to threaten his girl with their presence, they had to go with speed and efficiency.

Like they'd known it would, the blur of movement as Thunder rushed through the gathered group threw it into chaos.

Weapons fired, and people shouted as he and his team began to make quick work of picking off the guards one by one. Knowing his team could handle taking out all of them, Steel focused instead on Rose.

When it all boiled down to it, he would sacrifice anything to protect her.

Including his own revenge.

The thought slammed into him like a ton of bricks. It was true, he realized as he staggered slightly in his single-minded need to get to Rose, protect what was his. If he had to make a choice between vengeance and Rose's life, he would choose his little ladybug every single time.

What was the point of killing his enemy, the man who had destroyed his life, if it cost him the only shot at a future he was ever going to have?

"You led them to me," Dr. Gardner hissed at Rose as he grabbed her and threw her into the closest vehicle.

Whatever answer she sassed back at him, and Steel was one hundred percent certain his little ladybug had something to say to the brother she despised, was lost to him as the car sped off.

His howl of rage at Rose being taken away from him drew the attention of the closest armed men, and they quickly turned their weapons on him.

Something feral came over him, a primitive part of his brain that Dr. Gardner had been trying to find and exploit, and he gave into it. It demanded that anything that presented itself as a threat to him going after his girl be destroyed.

Tossing his weapon aside, Steel launched himself at the closest man.

Unprepared for his strength, the man dropped as Steel connected with him. Using every inch of enhanced strength the deranged doctor, who had just cowardly fled the scene of what he knew was going to be a slaughter had given him, Steel snapped the spine of the man pinned helplessly beneath him.

Picking up the body, he threw it at two men who were trying to fire at him, but also trying not to hit their colleague.

All three of them went down, and before the two still alive could manage to get out from under the weight pinning them down, Steel was there. He grabbed one man's skull between his hands and crushed it like it was nothing in a move reminiscent of Jason Voorhees from the Friday the 13th franchise.

The remaining man fumbled for his weapon, fear evident in his eyes, even as acceptance filtered in. Before the man could pick up his weapon and aim, Steel slammed his foot down on his face, crushing his skull like he'd just done to the other man's.

Silence filled the area.

No more screams, no more weapons fired.

Not even the roar of the engine from the car cowardly Dr. Gardner had fled in, with Rose as his hostage, was still audible.

The only ones still standing were him and his team. You didn't create a special ops unit of monsters and expect to be able to control them. Or at least you didn't if you were smart.

"He took her," he snarled at his team.

"That way," Blade said, pointing to the east.

Dragon held a tablet in his hand and nodded. "I've got her on the screen. Hold it together, we're going to get her back, and then we're going to make her brother wish he'd never been born."

With a nod, Steel moved toward the closest vehicle and jumped in. Thunder might be able to chase the car on foot, but the rest of them wouldn't be able to keep up with a moving vehicle, and he needed his girl back in his arms, needed to find a way to convince her to want to be his.

~

January 2nd
   3:18 A.M.

At her taunt, Ridge snarled and snapped out a hand, wrapping it around her arm and tugging her forward.

The move would have hurt regardless, but the wrist he grabbed was her broken wrist. His fingers tightened, and Rose would have sworn she could feel the bones shifting inside her as he dragged her half across the seat so she was almost sprawled in his lap.

"You make nice with the little monsters, sister?" Ridge sneered.

Shoving the pain out of her mind so she could focus, she met her brother's gaze squarely. "Call them monsters all you want, they're better men than you'll ever be."

Ridge laughed. "Make no mistake about it, little sister, they are monsters. I created them. I found a way to shut down their consciences. The last time I saw them, they were nothing more than animals, barely able to control themselves, consumed with anger."

"Of course, they were angry, you were holding them prisoner."

"I was studying them," Ridge corrected, like his word choice made any difference to what he'd done.

Holding people captive in a cell so they couldn't leave and controlling every aspect of their lives was one hundred percent holding them prisoner, no matter how her brother wanted to dress it up to pretend he was merely playing at science.

"You're delusional if you think any one of them can care for you." Ridge scoffed. "They aren't capable of it. I saw it myself, you lived it, they whipped you raw."

Rose wasn't arguing that point.

That was exactly what Steel and the others had done to her. But then Steel had forced her to take the sedatives, and he and Voodoo had patched her up. The same thing they'd done after she pulled the ceiling down on top of herself. Her memories were hazy, but she'd heard the genuine fear in Steel's voice as he told her she wasn't allowed to die, and he'd ordered Dragon not to kill her.

She wasn't deluding herself into thinking Steel was a normal guy, or that he was ever going to be one. Her brother had messed with his DNA, and that was never going to change, but he wasn't really a monster.

The monster in all of this was Ridge himself.

"Do you have any idea the time and money they've cost me?" Ridge ranted, his gaze darting between her and the forest around them as the car picked up speed. "Because they got free, I lost my funding to keep working with the military. That cost me access to the kind of subjects I needed."

"You didn't stop, though," she said, confident nothing would stop her brother once he became fixated on something. Ridge and Steel had that in common.

"Of course, I didn't stop. But none of my other subjects can withstand the anger. It either leads them to kill the others, or they wind up suicidal and end their own lives. I need those men back, I need to see what made them different, how they withstood the changes."

"They didn't just withstand them. They thrived. They live productive lives working for the best private security company in the world. They built their own little family unit, and yes, they hurt me, yes, they used me, but then they realized it was wrong and they started to … accept me." That was the best way she could describe how things had changed between her and Delta Team. They might not be the kind of men to tell her they were sorry, and to tell her she could be one of them, but she was there, they'd trusted her to help them with their quest for vengeance, which spoke louder than any words ever could.

"Stupid little Rose, always so desperate for love and affection," Ridge mocked. "They're not sorry they hurt you, they just found a better way of using you. Playing nice to get you to agree to play bait for them."

Maybe she would have believed that if it were true, but Steel had been adamantly against the idea. He hadn't wanted to risk her safety, he'd just known it was the best course of action. She'd had to talk him into it, and the fact that he'd been on his knees throwing up after burning the soles of her feet told her everything she needed to know.

If Steel was a monster, she didn't care, because he was her monster. It was the craziest thing in the world to even consider any sort of future with the man who had been her captor, but he gave her everything she needed, everything she craved, everything she'd thought she would never get.

Threatening to spank her for causing herself more pain made her feel seen and cared for, while also giving in to her need for pain.

They had so much to learn about one another, but the thing was, she actually *wanted* to learn everything there was to know about her crazy captor. Steel dominated her in a way she needed someone to take over and let her mind check out for a while, and yet he tucked a blanket around her so she wasn't cold, or massaged her feet to warm them, and cooked her homemade meals. He was possessive and jealous and obsessive, but he had a softer side he believed had been eliminated by her brother's overzealous games. She wanted to help him realize it still existed.

And she needed someone to help her find her own softer side, which had been buried under layers of trauma so deep she had no idea how to go about finding it.

"You can believe whatever you want, but it doesn't mean they aren't coming for me," she told her brother.

"Coming for me," Ridge corrected with all the arrogance she would have expected from him. He truly seemed to believe that the entire world revolved around him. He was the sun and everyone else was the planets. Whatever he wanted was all that mattered, and nothing that happened didn't involve him.

"For both of us." Rose wouldn't pretend that Steel and his team didn't want her brother dead, they absolutely did, and since he'd tried to run, they'd be coming after him so they could get their vengeance. But she also knew Steel would go to the ends of the earth for her.

"Stupid little girl. Get it through your head, they're just using you. They cannot empathize with you or feel guilt over what they did to you. They tricked you like the stupid child you are, and if they use you to get to me, they'll only kill you without remorse because you're a loose end they don't care about. I don't understand how someone related to me can be so stupid, and—"

"And I don't understand why someone related to me is such a

psychopath," Rose snapped as she reached out from her position and yanked on the wheel as hard as she could.

The guys were coming after her, she knew they were despite Ridge's rant, and she wanted to make sure Ridge wasn't able to get them too far away. She wanted this over now. Listening to her brother demean her while acting like he was the smartest person to have ever existed was too much.

Ridge howled in annoyance and tried to wrangle control of the steering wheel back. To do that, he had to release his grip on her broken arm, and since the limb was already screaming in agony, Rose thought she may as well go for it.

Latching her good hand onto the wheel, she let her body drop forward, down into the recess in front of the driver's seat. Tangled with Ridge's legs though she was, she pressed her bad arm onto the gas pedal, making the car jerk forward.

"What the hell are you doing?" Ridge snarled, trying to make a grab for her.

Using her body to push him out of the way, Rose pressed down further on the gas pedal, making the car's speed dramatically pick up.

"You're going to kill us both," Ridge screamed.

"I'd rather kill us both and be done with it than let you go on experimenting on people like you're a god. You're no god, Ridge Gardner, you're just a plain old flesh and blood human, with a large slice of demon thrown in," she screamed back, pressing all the way down on the gas pedal as her hand still on the wheel yanked hard to the left.

As far as she was concerned, taking out her brother was the best thing she could ever do with her life, and would have the added bonus of infuriating him to know the little sister he placed zero value on had been the one to end his life. For the first time ever, she had something worth living for, but Steel would still find the peace he'd craved in knowing that the man who had played with his DNA was dead, even if she died along with Ridge.

They fought over the steering wheel, and Rose never let up on the gas pedal.

Not until the car plowed into something, sending pain rippling through her entire body, did a deadly quiet, calm, blackness descend on her mind as she fell into unconsciousness.

CHAPTER
Twenty-One

January 2nd
   3:27 A.M.

It had been mere minutes since Rose was snatched from his sight, but to Steel it felt like a lifetime.

He knew better than most how much pain you could inflict on another human being in a short amount of time. Anyone on his team could have someone howling in seconds, and that was without needing to resort to a gunshot or knife wound.

There had been more than enough time for Dr. Gardner to have his little sister screaming in agony. The only thing that had him holding onto any semblance of a shred of control was the fact that Blade hadn't alerted him to any cries of pain from Rose.

Would his friend lie to him?

To keep him sane, yes. But still, he trusted that the man he considered a brother would let him know if Rose was suffering in any way.

Thunder was driving them through the forest like a madman, as though his enhanced speed extended to driving a vehicle. Despite their speed, the man was navigating with an expertise that could have gotten him a job as a racecar driver.

Ridge hadn't gotten much of a head start, a minute or two at the most, so Steel was tense, expecting to see the other vehicle at any second. He wasn't sure how things would play out. Dr. Gardner didn't seem like the kind of guy who would rather end his own life than be captured, he was too arrogant for that. But nor did he seem like the kind of man who would give up even if the facts were that he was outnumbered and outgunned.

Using Rose as a bargaining chip was the most likely scenario, because the scientist had surely figured out by now that Rose was working against him, that she'd teamed up with them. While Steel knew that Dr. Gardner considered he and his team nothing more than monsters, carefully created killing machines without consciences, he was starting to accept that he was so much more than that.

He was pretty sure, if it came down to it, he would let the doctor go to save Rose's life.

More than that, he was pretty sure his team would agree with that decision because they all accepted that Rose was his.

Beside him, Blade suddenly stiffened, and Steel quickly followed. If the man had heard something, it wasn't good news.

Likewise, Dragon's head went up, his nose sniffing as he obviously caught a whiff of something he wasn't pleased with.

"What?" he growled.

"Sounded like a car crash," Blade replied, shooting him a worried glance.

"Smelled like it too," Dragon added.

"Thunder—"

"Go faster, I know," Thunder said, cutting him off and sending the car careening forward as it picked up more speed.

Less than two minutes later, he saw it.

The vehicle Ridge had thrown Rose into and taken off in was leaning precariously against a tree at the top of what he was sure as hell hoping wasn't a very steep decline.

Out of the vehicle before it even stopped moving, Steel rushed toward the other car. He had no idea if Ridge Gardner was armed, but even if he was, the man had to be injured, there was no way he was going to just open fire on them. Probably didn't even know how to shoot a gun, after all, Dr. Gardner designated all tasks he deemed beneath him to other people.

"Careful," Lion warned as his team moved at his back. "We don't know how unsteady the car's position is."

"One wrong move and we could send it down there," Voodoo added, moving cautiously to the edge of the drop.

"How far?" Steel asked.

"Thirty feet give or take," Voodoo replied.

The way the car was balanced would make getting a good grip on it difficult, but not impossible. All he had to do was find the best way to get a hold of it, and then he could lift it back up so it had all four wheels firmly on solid ground.

Before he could decide on the best spot to grab onto, a startled squawk came from inside the vehicle, and it swayed a little. The sound was distinctly feminine, but the windows of the car were tinted so dark that he couldn't get a clear picture of what was happening inside.

At least he knew Rose was still in the vehicle and not lying dead at the bottom of the cliff.

"I only see one person in there," Lion told him.

Another moan came from the vehicle, and it wobbled a little more. It had been stopped by a dead tree trunk that had fallen sideways, landing partially over the edge. Some of the tree's roots were still buried in the ground, but he had no doubts that a dead tree could only hold up the weight of a car for a short time.

They had to get Rose out of that car, or that car pulled back away from the edge.

"Door's partially open on this side," Thunder called out, standing on the driver's side of the car.

Moving so he could get the same line of sight, Steel got as close to the vehicle as he dared but was careful not to bump the car in any way. He had the strength to lift it and move it safely away from the cliff, but to do that, he needed a good hold, and until he could find one, he wasn't going to risk sending Rose over the edge.

"Little ladybug?" he called out. According to Lion, only one person was in there, and the voice he'd heard belonged to a woman, he was sure of it.

Maybe Rose had been trying to make a break for it when the car crashed, and that's why the driver's side door was open. Dr. Gardner had fled in a rush, so it made sense he hadn't buckled himself in. If the door had been open when the car crashed, he might have been thrown out of the vehicle.

While the doctor didn't deserve a quick death after everything he'd done to Rose, to him and his team, and to who knew how many other innocent men and women, Steel cared more about the man being dead than him suffering first.

"S-Steel?" Rose's weak voice called out. She sounded woozy and out of it. Chances were she'd hit her head and been knocked unconscious.

"You need to get her out," Blade said softly from beside him. "That tree is going to give at any second, and when it falls, it's taking the car and Rose down with it."

"Right here, little ladybug," he assured her, while nodding at Blade to let him know he understood the stakes.

He hadn't lost Rose yet, but he could at any second.

"My head hurts," she moaned softly, and he swore. He needed her focused and able to assist in her own rescue.

Even though he knew he could lift that car, it meant nothing if he tried to grab it and couldn't get a hold. All he'd do was end Rose's life instead of saving it.

Shifting slightly so he could get a better view, Steel could just make out the huddled form of Rose's body, crammed in the space between the driver's seat and the front of the car. How she'd ended up there he had no idea, and right now it didn't really matter.

"I know it does," he soothed, or tried to, although he wasn't sure he sounded calming in the least. "The car is balanced over the edge of a cliff."

"So it's not just my head that makes it feel like the world is moving beneath me," Rose groaned.

"No, it's not. The world is really moving beneath you. We have to get you out. Do you think you can move closer to the door so I can try to reach you?"

A pained moan sounded from Rose, and he felt his entire body tense at the sound. She was in pain, and he couldn't make it better. Couldn't even order her to stay still because he needed her out of that car.

"I ... don't think so," she murmured, defeat coating her words. "I feel ... heavy."

"Concussion," Voodoo murmured from beside him.

If Rose couldn't get herself to the door so he could try to reach her, he had no choice but to risk getting a hold on the car.

"It's going to go at any second," Blade warned as the car shuddered, making Rose cry out.

"Steel?" her panicked voice called for him, and while it soothed the roughness inside him to know that when she was scared his girl wanted him, it also amped up his fear. He was seconds away from losing her for good. Perched as she was in the recess at the front of the car, there was no way she could survive the fall.

"I'm here, little ladybug, and I got you," he assured her, praying he hadn't just made the last words she'd hear from him a lie.

Tearing his gaze from her shadowy form, he forced himself to take a few steps back, so he was standing right at the back of the car, his eyes scanning for a place to grab hold of. Only cars weren't made to be held onto like that, so they didn't come with handy little handholds.

The sickening crack of splintering wood filled the quiet night, and as the car tipped forward, Steel threw caution to the wind and launched himself at it.

~

January 2nd
3:36 A.M.

She was going over the edge.

That was one thing Rose was certain of. The throbbing in her head made it difficult to think, and her entire body felt too heavy to move, but she did know that the tipping of the car she was in meant only one thing.

It tipped precariously, and she rolled further into the recess at the driver's seat. When the car fell, she'd either stay where she was and get crushed to smithereens when they hit the ground, or she'd be tossed about like a ragdoll, or she'd get thrown out the open door.

Where the hell was Ridge?

He'd been there when they crashed, she knew that because they'd been fighting for control of the steering wheel. He'd been gone when she crawled back to consciousness, and she wanted to believe that it was because he'd been thrown from the vehicle and was dead now, but what if he'd survived the crash?

She had.

There was every chance her brother had, too.

If that was the case, he'd run as soon as he woke up, knowing that the men he had created were coming for him. Ridge might have been the one to play with their DNA and create them, but that didn't mean he wasn't terrified of them. He, better than anyone else, knew just what Steel and the others were capable of.

Another crack rang in her ears, and the car tilted further until it felt like she was lying on her back, and then she was falling.

Like when she'd been trying to escape her cell in the basement and managed to bring the ceiling down with her, it felt like she hung in the air, weightless, with nothing tying her down to the earth.

It would be so easy to float away, but unfortunately, there would be no flying away, the only place she was going was down.

Then, right when she was positive it was too late, that nothing could save her, the car suddenly shuddered and stopped moving.

Instead of dropping, she was suddenly moving higher.

Too tired to figure out what was going on, Rose let her eyelids flutter closed. Maybe she really was moving down, and her brain, maxed out on pain and adrenaline just didn't know what was happening.

Did it really matter?

If Ridge was dead, it was over. Steel and the others would be free to live their lives however they wanted. He didn't need her now, and honestly, she wasn't even sure what that meant for her.

When she'd been with Steel at his mansion, she'd believed in his possessiveness, believed that he meant it when he demanded that she acknowledge she was his. Hell, she'd believed it in the car when she was arguing with Ridge.

But now ...

Now she wasn't sure what would happen if Ridge were dead. If he wasn't, then she knew Steel would follow through on his threats to keep her as his prisoner until he'd used her to get what he wanted.

Maybe death wasn't so bad.

"Rose."

The insistent voice prevented her from sliding fully back into the darkness. She liked it there, it was quiet and peaceful. There was no pain, no anxiety, there was nothing but ... nothing.

After living a lifetime with someone trying to control your every move, your every thought, your every breath, being nothing was infinitely appealing.

"Come on, little ladybug, don't give up on me," Steel's insistent voice ordered, only she wasn't sure she had the power to do as he wanted.

Wasn't sure she had the power to do anything but slip off into sleep.

Beautiful, blissful sleep.

The vehicle she was in suddenly rocked, like it had been jarred, and she was tipped forward a little again. Beneath her, it felt steadier, no longer like she was hanging in the air, about to plummet to certain death.

Hands were on her, but since she knew they were Steel's, she didn't fight them. Just lay there and let him grab her and maneuver her out of the little space she was curled up in.

"She's shaking," Steel said, panic in his voice.

"Hypothermic," Voodoo said. While the healer's voice was calmer, she could sense a thread of fear in it as well.

Was he worried Steel would kill him if she died?

Surely, he had to know that Steel wouldn't actually kill any of the men he thought of as his brothers.

He couldn't be worried about her ... could he?

"Do something," Steel insisted, and she felt herself settled on his lap.

Someone must have passed him a blanket because something soft was tucked around her, and it was only then that Rose realized she really was shaking. Violently.

Even though she wasn't sure where Steel's head was at, and what he was going to do with her going forward, a part of her insisted she do something to soothe his panic. Attempting to say his name, all she managed was a moan, and the arms holding her tightened painfully.

The pain helped to ground her a little, though, clearing away some of the cobwebs.

"Fix her," Steel ordered, and the way he said it was so insistent that it amused her, and she huffed a small chuckle and managed to open her eyes.

"I don't need fixing," she rasped, her voice feeling weak just like the rest of her.

Dark eyes snapped to meet hers, and she felt rather than saw his relief. It was too dark to see much of anything, but Steel's face was right above hers, and the way a puff of warm air caressed her skin told her more than being able to see him clearly ever could.

Maybe he really had meant everything he'd said to her about wanting her. Maybe it had nothing to do with her usefulness.

That was hard for her to believe because her whole life with her brother had been all about what use she offered to him, what he could get out of her. It made sense that she would see Steel the same way, especially given the reason she'd ended up in his clutches and the deal he'd made with her.

But she wanted to be more to someone than just something they could use.

She wanted to be seen just for herself. Wanted to be with someone who would help her figure out who she actually was and what she really wanted out of life.

"Yeah, you do, little ladybug," Steel told her, but she could no longer remember what she'd said or what that meant.

"Ridge, is he ...?"

"I can't see his body," Lion replied from somewhere close by.

Before any of them could say anything else, the roar of a helicopter cut through the night, and Rose got a sinking feeling in her gut.

"Is that yours?" she asked, already knowing the answer.

"No," Steel replied, voice tight.

"Then it's Ridge's. He wasn't in the car when I woke up, he must have gotten away."

If Ridge wasn't dead, then her deal with Delta Team wasn't over. She was still their prisoner.

Now that she'd betrayed her brother, he was never going to make another arrangement with her. She would be useless to Steel and his team, which meant she was looking at spending the rest of her life as their captive.

A sob burst free, and she couldn't even remember the last time she'd cried like that.

"Rose." Sounding panicked, Steel clutched at her as though that could fix whatever was making her cry.

But it couldn't.

Nothing could.

"She's just overwhelmed. She has a concussion, let me get an IV in her," Voodoo said.

"No, she wouldn't cry because she was overwhelmed," Steel snapped. "Tell me," he ordered her. "Tell me what's wrong so I can fix it."

"I f-failed," she said through her tears. "Ridge isn't d-dead. I d-didn't fulfil our d-deal so I'm s-still your c-captive."

"No," he barked, hard enough that she hiccupped on a sob and fell silent. "You aren't my captive. If you want to leave, then you tell me and I'll call my boss and ask him to take custody of you. He'll help you work out a plan where you'll be safe from your brother but still be free to live your life. You are in charge of your own destiny, Rose. Always."

"But you said I had to stay until we got Ridge."

"That was before."

"You said I was yours."

"And you are. Always will be. But I only want you to stay if you want to stay. I want to own you, but not like that, only because it's what you want as well. Only you can choose your future, Rose. Only you are the boss of your life, little ladybug."

CHAPTER
Twenty-Two

January 3rd
   3:27 A.M.

Nine days.

That was all it had been since he and his team broke into Rose's home and snatched her from her bed, and yet it felt like a lifetime.

In those nine days, everything he thought he knew about himself had been turned on its head. He'd come to the realization that what Dr. Gardner had done to him had broken parts of himself that could never be put back together, but it hadn't broken him.

The proof of that was that he'd managed to find the strength and control to put Rose's needs before his own. Instead of forcing her to honor the deal they'd made, that she remain their prisoner until her brother was dead, he'd given her the freedom to take the reins of her own life.

"You going up to bed?" Dragon asked as Steel switched off the kitchen lights and headed for the stairs.

"Yeah," he answered wearily. He hadn't slept since Rose called Ridge, and while he could stay awake longer than forty-eight hours when needed, these last two days had been a rollercoaster ride of fear and emotion. More emotion than he'd felt in a decade, and it had caught up with him.

"We'll get him," Dragon assured him.

That Ridge had gotten away, obviously remained conscious through the crash, and fled, calling in a helicopter to come and pick him up, should mean that the op was a failure. But since he'd gotten Rose back alive, Steel was having trouble seeing it as such.

"We won't stop until we do," he agreed.

"It's going to be okay," Dragon added somewhat awkwardly. "Everything will work out the way it's supposed to."

"Maybe time you took your own advice," he told his teammate, his friend, his brother. A man he had fought alongside for almost a third of their lives, a man he trusted with his life, a man who had given in to the monster inside him instead of fighting against it.

If Dragon couldn't find the strength to put Cassandra first, he was going to lose the woman they all knew he'd fallen in love with.

Love. As Dragon nodded his acknowledgment and disappeared into the Gothic mansion's darkness, and Steel headed up to his room, the word swirled through his mind.

Did he love Rose?

Since he'd given her the freedom she craved, he had to believe that he did. The thought was terrifying because he never expected to love anyone who wasn't one of his team. Rose was different than his brothers, she'd suffered at her brother's hands, but there was a softness inside her that she fought against, beat down, because she knew softness could become weakness.

As he stepped into his room, Steel's gaze moved immediately to the bed, and the small lump curled up in the middle of it. At the sight of his little ladybug still fast asleep in his bed, wearing one of his shirts, the anxiety bubbling in his gut subsided.

By some miracle, Rose had chosen him when given a chance at freedom.

Offering her choices had been terrifying, but it was the only thing he could do. His little ladybug had lived enough of her life in a prison, she deserved the chance to fly high. He just hadn't expected her to fly right back there with him to the place he'd locked her away as though she were nothing but a tool to be used.

Only now he knew Rose was so much more than that.

She was everything.

Stripping off his sweatpants, Steel pulled back the covers enough that he could slide beneath them without lifting them off Rose. While her body temperature had returned to normal by the time they arrived back at the mansion, she'd told him she was still sensitive to cold.

There were new bruises on her body, and she had her second concussion in a week, so Steel tried to be gentle when he molded his body to hers, tucking himself around her like a protective shield.

With a small content sigh, she snuggled closer, her hair tickling his chin, her breath warm against his collarbone. That warmth spread inside him, and even though he had Rose pressed against him, it wasn't enough.

Too much distance.

He needed to be inside her, needed to meld their bodies together into one.

Slipping a hand down her body, he nudged it between her thighs and stroked a fingertip across her center. Just because he needed to be inside her didn't mean he was going to push into her without preparing her first.

Keeping his touch gentle so he didn't wake her, Steel circled her entrance, bumping a fingertip just inside before moving to her bud and working it with slow, firm strokes.

In her sleep, Rose's breathing quickened, and she shifted restlessly, her body registering what he was doing to it even as her mind kept her asleep.

When he felt her begin to grow wet, Steel withdrew his fingers, bringing them to his mouth and licking off every drop of her sweetness. Later, he'd feast on her, make her come over and over again until she was sobbing and pleading, unsure if she was asking for more or for him to stop.

But in this moment, he needed to be inside her.

Needed there to be zero distance left between them.

Rolling her onto her back, Steel shifted so his body was on top of hers, his weight balanced on his hands so he didn't hurt her. Lining himself up, he held back from sliding inside her.

Tracing his fingertips over the pulse point in her neck, he pressed a little harder, to nudge her awake.

"Mmm," Rose moaned, her lashes fluttering on her cheeks before her eyes blinked open. "Steel?"

"Need you, little ladybug. Tell me I can be inside you."

"Always," she murmured, a small smile curling up the corners of her mouth.

With a single thrust he was buried deep, and that lingering knot of unsettledness disappeared.

"You feel so good inside me," Rose murmured as he began to rock his hips.

"If I could find a way to live like this, I would." That wasn't a joke, it wasn't an exaggeration. If it was possible to live his life buried deep in Rose's body, with her permanently in his arms where he knew she was safe and he could protect her, he absolutely would. "You're mine, little ladybug. I gave you a chance to be free of me, and you chose to stay. I won't give you a second chance to leave."

"I don't want to leave." Even though he knew it cost her, she pushed her shoulders off the bed so she could press a kiss to his lips.

"I'm not a good man. Not one who deserves you. I might have learned there is more humanity left in me than I'd realized, but I also know that part of me will always be a monster."

"My monster." Rose hummed, touching another kiss to his lips.

"Yours," he readily agreed. "Always yours. I will burn the world to the ground to keep you safe. I will walk through hell, I will fight the devil himself, anything I have to do to protect you, I'll do. I'm going to be better at protecting your body, but I'll do my best to protect your heart as well."

"You already proved you can do that when you gave me a choice. My life hasn't had many, and even the ones I've had, I've made the choices that were the opposite of what I knew my brother would want me to make. I've never had the freedom that you gave me. I've never even had a chance to figure out who Rose Gardner really is."

"Mine," he told her, as he picked up the pace, thrusting into her faster, harder. Steel knew he should back off a little, knew he had to be hurting her battered body, but he could already feel her internal walls fluttering, and her cheeks were flushed with arousal as desire danced in her eyes.

"Yours," Rose agreed as she twisted her fingers into his short hair and brought his face down so she could claim his mouth in a searing kiss.

Balancing his weight on one hand, Steel moved his other to where their bodies joined and worked her bundle of nerves, circling it, rolling it between his thumb and forefinger, and when he tweaked it roughly, Rose fell apart.

Capturing her cries of release, her internal muscles clamped around him, setting off his own release. It sparked along his spine, firing out to touch every molecule of his body, and setting it alight. Pleasure consumed him, and he kept his fingers working her bud throughout their joint release to prolong it for Rose as long as he could.

When all that was left were aftershocks of pleasure, Steel rolled them so he was on his back and Rose was draped across him, his softening length still snug inside her. Since he was so much taller than her, her head tucked perfectly beneath his chin, and she nuzzled her cheek against his chest, above his heart.

"I'm glad I chose to stay with you," Rose whispered sleepily as her body grew heavy against his as she drifted off.

"So am I, little ladybug, so am I," he whispered back, but he doubted she heard his words as sleep had already claimed her.

∼

January 3rd
   9:19 A.M.

I will burn the world to the ground to keep you safe.

Why was that the best foreplay? Even now, hours later, when she thought of Steel's vow, she felt her body tingle, her blood heat.

She'd slept most of the day before away, and for the first time in well over twenty-four hours, she was starting to feel vaguely human. When they'd finally arrived back at the mansion yesterday, Steel had taken her up to his room, put her in the bath, and washed every inch of her with a tenderness that had made her eyes sting.

Then he'd dressed her in one of his shirts and tucked her into his bed. Falling asleep encased in his scent had been exactly what she needed, and she'd slept deeply and dreamlessly.

Waking with him buried deep inside her wasn't what she had expected, but it wasn't unwelcome in the least. His promises that he would protect her body and her heart had pushed her into the best orgasm of her life.

"If you keep thinking that loudly, I'm going to have you tied to the bed screaming my name until it's the only word you know," Steel's voice rumbled from beneath her, and Rose lifted her head from his chest and arched a brow at him.

"Is that supposed to be a threat?" she asked. It sounded like a wonderful way to spend the day, and she didn't even care that her body would be the one screaming when they were done, only it wouldn't be screams of pleasure it would be ones of pain. Her head still throbbed, and her broken arm had been reset and a new cast put on it. There were new bruises on top of old ones, the gash on her cheekbone that Steel had given her had been cleaned and closed as best as you could with a wound that was over a day old before it got treated.

She hurt, but she burned for this man.

It really was the craziest thing because she barely knew him, and yet at the same time, it felt like she knew him somewhere deep down in her soul. They were kindred spirits for sure, even if their lives had been very different.

Guess she had one thing to thank her brother for. Without his insane plans, she never would have met Steel. There was no way to undo their meeting, it would always be another dark spot in her mind, another time she was used and abused for someone else's purposes, but they could build something new on top of the old.

"It will be a punishment for every bit of pain you'll make yourself feel if you test me, little ladybug," Steel warned, but there was no real heat to his tone. He sounded worried about her, and that had her eyes misting over again.

Crying had never been something she did. She'd always known, understood even when she was too small to be able to express it in words, that tears excited her brother, made him hurt her more, and gave him exactly what he wanted. So, she'd learned to shut them down. They didn't fix anything, they only held the power to make things worse.

But now she felt like she was finally free. Steel's offer to let her go even though she knew it wasn't what he wanted, was all she'd needed to hear to know that staying with him was the right thing to do.

Not only did she want to help them find her brother and make him pay for everything he'd done, but she wanted to stay with Steel, get to know him better, and explore the crazy attraction that burned brightly between them.

For the first time in her life, she had something good, and she wanted to grab hold of it and refuse to let go.

"Are you crying?" Steel asked, a thread of panic in his tone. "Do I need to call Voodoo?"

The sincerity of his words made fresh tears run freely down her cheeks, but she smiled through them. No one had ever put her first before, and yet she knew that was exactly what Steel had done the day before. He and his team could have focused on Ridge, used their skills to track him from the car, and find him before he got on that helicopter.

But they hadn't done that.

They'd stayed with her and saved her life.

"Not those kinds of tears," she assured him. It was so weird because Rose had always viewed tears as a weakness, but it didn't make her feel weak to cry in front of Steel. Instead, it made her feel free because she knew he wasn't going to use those tears against her. "I'm not in pain—"

"Liar."

Huffing a chuckle, Rose gave a nod of acknowledgment. "Okay, so I *am* in pain, but that's not why I'm crying."

"Then why the tears, little ladybug?" Steel's large hand swept across her cheek, catching her falling tears, then smoothed a lock of hair behind her ear.

"Because you make me feel safe enough that I don't have to worry every second about being strong, about having it all together," she answered honestly. There had been enough lies and darkness between them already, going forward, she wanted only honesty and light. For sure she was going to want a bite of pain in the bedroom, her body still craved what it knew, but outside of that, she wanted to experience softness, gentleness, all the things she'd never had but always longed for. Steel might seem to be the most unlikely man to give her that, but she wasn't an ordinary woman, and the way he protected her with his strength meant more to her than sweet words, or candlelight dinners, or deep talks about their feelings.

"You are the strongest woman I've ever met," Steel told her. The hand that had caressed her cheek now circled the back of her neck, squeezing just hard enough to give her a twinge of pain. "But sometimes strength is realizing when you need to step back and let someone help hold you up."

What was she just thinking about how Steel might not be the master of sweet words? Guess she'd better rethink that, because he seemed to know exactly what to say to make her heart swell in her chest.

"No one's ever given me that before," she admitted. No one had ever given her anything before. Her brother had just used her, and she hadn't been brave enough to let anyone else in. Steel had barreled into her life, giving her no choice but to let him in, and she found she couldn't regret it.

"And I didn't think anyone would ever give me what you have," Steel told her, a rare moment of vulnerability in his dark eyes.

Their broken pieces were like magnets drawing them together, and the more time she spent in Steel's arms, the more it felt like they could rebuild their lives, rebuild themselves, come out stronger than anything her brother had done to either one of them.

Her stomach chose that moment to grumble loudly, breaking the moment, and reminding her she had been too nauseous to eat the day before.

"Sounds like it's time for breakfast, little ladybug," Steel said, sliding out of her as he lifted her up and off him and setting her on the bed beside him.

"I'd love a bath first," she said. She was hungry, but she couldn't seem to wash off the feel of her brother's clammy hands on her. That brought up too many memories of the past, and she wanted to be free of those shackles so she could fly free and find her future.

"If you have a bath, I'll only have to mark you all over again."

Rolling her eyes at him, she laughed. "I see we have a bit of a thing going on here. You know it's not actually good for me to walk around covered in our ... expressions of pleasure ... all the time. It could wind up giving me infections."

"Need my mark on you," he said as his fingers trailed along the healing bite mark on her breast.

Ridge had used it against Steel, calling him an animal for biting her, but she'd enjoyed the sting of his teeth breaking her skin, and she didn't hate Steel's idea of tattooing the mark onto her skin as a permanent reminder that she was his.

"If I got the tattoo, what would you get to mark you as mine?" she asked. If she was doing this, it was a two-way thing. He had to wear her mark as well.

Eyes lighting up, he leaned in and pressed a kiss to the bite mark before placing a hand over his heart. "I'm getting a rose with a ladybug tattooed right here," he told her like it was already set in stone as far as he was concerned.

Her damn eyes got misty all over again. "You really serious about that?"

His brows furrowed like he couldn't understand her need to ask the question. "Of course I am, little ladybug, I already told you that I'm yours. Now let's get you some breakfast, and then I'll give you a bath. If you're getting the tattoo, then I suppose I don't have to keep you wearing my mark."

Standing, he reached over to scoop her up. He hadn't let her walk a single step since he rescued her from the car, because he was worried about the burns on her feet causing her pain. As she curled into his arms, tucking herself against his chest, Rose knew she'd made the right choice when she agreed to come and stay with Steel.

After twenty-three years, she'd finally found a home and a family that actually cared about her.

CHAPTER
Twenty-Three

January 3rd
8:34 P.M.

"I can't believe I'm really going to do this."

Steel analyzed every inflection in Rose's voice to make sure there was nothing there he needed to be concerned about. All he could detect was excitement and a tiny thread of nervousness.

From here on out, he had decided it was his job to make sure Rose never worried about another thing, never felt fear, never wondered who she was, and never felt trapped. She was his, and he needed to make sure she never regretted her decision to stay with him rather than go to Eagle and find her own freedom.

That the freedom she wanted was there with him, still left him in disbelief.

"I can't wait to see my mark on your skin." His hand slipped up under the shirt she was wearing—one of his and he was never going to get tired of seeing her in his clothes—and ran his fingertips over her breast.

"You know we're going to have to take the shirt off to do this, right?" Rose asked, and this time he could hear the clear amusement in her tone. When he growled, she laughed. "And you can't kill your friend for touching my breast when it's the only way to get the tattoo on my skin. The tattoo that *you* wanted me to get."

"You saying you don't want it, little ladybug?" he asked as his hand dipped, trailing down her flat stomach and then slipping under the waistband of her leggings. "You're not wearing underwear," he said on a groan as he felt her bare skin as his hand slid lower until a fingertip hovered just above her needy little bud.

"No," Rose answered, as she shifted a little, trying to get his fingers where she wanted them.

Only, he had no intention of touching her until he was ready. She was his to play with, an equal to him in every other way except in the bedroom. There she was his to make come over and over again until she couldn't speak, couldn't think, could barely breathe through all the pleasure bombarding her body.

"Patience," he warned as Rose squirmed again.

"Lion is going to be here any minute to start the tattoo, you can't put your hand there and then leave me hanging," she said, her voice just shy of a whine, and he smirked.

"I can do whatever I want, you're mine, aren't you?" Touching a fingertip to her bundle of nerves, he feathered circles on it. "Maybe I'll work you right to the edge and then stop, make you sit there while Lion does the tattoo, knowing it was your own bratty fault that you weren't allowed to get off."

"You wouldn't." Her bottom lip stuck out in a pout, and Steel couldn't resist leaning in and nipping at it.

"Oh, little ladybug, I absolutely would. Or maybe I'll sink into you, get myself off, but not let you come, then make you sit on me while you get your tattoo."

Rose giggled, and the sound was so soft, and light, and free that his heart thudded hard in his chest as it swelled with emotion. "Okay, now that I know you wouldn't do. You don't want Lion to see my breast, even though he has to in order to do the tattoo, no way you're going to let him see me naked and stretched around you."

Okay, so she had him on that one. But he absolutely would teach his little brat a lesson and not let her get off.

Shoving her leggings down her legs, Steel pushed his sweatpants aside enough to free himself, then snatched Rose off the couch and onto his lap, slamming home in one thrust.

She cried out as he filled her, but her fingers clawed at his shoulders, and she was already trying to rock her hips to get some friction.

Couldn't have that.

Pinning her hands was awkward with the cast on one of them, but his hands were so much larger than her wrists, and he was able to hold them both together and against his chest. His other hand grabbed her hip, holding her still and making her pout again.

"Told you, little ladybug, you're not going to come. You're going to feel me fill you up, and then you're going to sit there with my cum dripping out of you while you get your tattoo and remind yourself that only good girls get to come."

"You're mean," she whined, and Steel just laughed.

"You have no idea, little ladybug. Playing with you is going to be fun."

Because Lion could come at any moment, and Rose was right that he didn't want anyone but him seeing her naked ever again, his grip on her hip tightened as he began to move her up and down on his length.

"Don't come," he warned Rose when he felt her internal muscles flutter around him. It wasn't much of a punishment for sassing back at him like a brat if she got exactly what she wanted.

Being inside his girl had him seconds away from finding release, especially when he didn't have to make sure they came together, and Steel adjusted his position as he picked up the pace. Thrusting his hips up into Rose as he used his grip on her hip to slide her up and down his length, he came with a growl as a powerful orgasm tore through his body with the power of a hurricane.

A split second later, he heard Rose cry out as her internal muscles clamped around his and she found an orgasm of her own.

Narrowing his eyes at his naughty little ladybug, she merely grinned back at him, looking smug. "What?" she asked, all innocently. "I can't help it that that position made me see stars. Two weeks ago, I didn't even think I was interested in sex, and now I can come without any external stimulation."

Since she seemed so pleased with herself, Steel found he couldn't be too annoyed with her. He was going to punish her later for coming though. "I hope you enjoyed that orgasm of yours, little ladybug, because once Lion finishes with your tattoo, I'm taking you up to my bed and I'm going to edge you for hours, until you're begging and pleading, promising to do anything I want as long as I let you come."

Rose shivered, and her internal muscles fluttered around him again, apparently already aroused at the thought of her punishment.

"Uh, maybe you guys should finish up in there, because I really don't want to get beaten up for doing the job Steel ordered me to do," Lion called out from just outside the door.

Lifting Rose off him, Steel set her back on the couch. "One moment," he yelled back to Lion.

Since he didn't want Rose getting an infection from constantly walking around covered in his cum, he satisfied himself with the fact that she would soon be wearing his mark anyway, and hurried to the door.

Edging it open, just enough to look out, he scanned the items Lion had with him. "You got a wet cloth or something to clean up blood?"

"I got this." Lion held up a damp towel.

"Perfect. Go get another," he ordered as he disappeared back into the room, closing the door behind him.

By the time he'd wiped Rose clean and pulled her leggings back up to cover her, then helped her get comfortable on the couch, Lion was walking into the room.

"What position is going to be most comfortable? I don't want this hurting you," he said to Rose.

"I don't think it's going to make a difference, I'm hurting from head to toe," Rose replied, sounding amused again.

"Blade," Steel bellowed. "Bring painkillers. Now."

"Do you have to scream like that?" Lion winced. "The guy could hear you if you whispered his name from anywhere in the mansion."

Steel merely shrugged. "You can hold my hand, squeeze it if you need to."

Rose's smile softened, and she reached up and ran her fingers through his hair. "I think you know I can handle the pain. How many times have we had sex since I broke my ribs? But since you seem to have a problem with me being in pain, I'll hold your hand, and you can squeeze mine if you need to."

Lion huffed a chuckle, and Blade snorted as he walked into the room, making Steel glare at both of them.

He'd already gotten his tattoo earlier that day, and Rose had snuggled beside him on the couch, her head resting on his stomach while Lion worked. The feel of her tucked close had been so perfect that he'd told Lion to take his time, drag out the moment as long as possible.

Deciding he'd do the same for his girl, after she took the painkillers with an eye roll and a smile of indulgence, he shifted her position on the couch so he could lie beside her, and then Lion got to work. Since tattooing on the breast he'd bitten would lead to infections, they'd taken a photo of the bite that Lion had then used to make a template to tattoo her other breast.

They were almost done when the living room door suddenly banged open and a very uncharacteristically panicked Dragon appeared. Blade had stuck around, and Thunder and Voodoo had appeared at some point during the tattooing process, so now all six of their heads turned to look at the man.

"It's Cassandra," Dragon told them. "She just called me. Something's wrong."

Dragon will do anything to keep Cassandra safe when she's dragged into the danger surrounding his team in the second book in the action packed and emotionally charged Prey Security: Delta Team series!

Fateful Revenge (Prey Security: Delta Team #2)

Also by Jane Blythe

Detective Parker Bell Series

A SECRET TO THE GRAVE

WINTER WONDERLAND

DEAD OR ALIVE

LITTLE GIRL LOST

FORGOTTEN

Count to Ten Series

ONE

TWO

THREE

FOUR

FIVE

SIX

BURNING SECRETS

SEVEN

EIGHT

NINE

TEN

Broken Gems Series

CRACKED SAPPHIRE

CRUSHED RUBY

FRACTURED DIAMOND

SHATTERED AMETHYST

SPLINTERED EMERALD

SALVAGING MARIGOLD

River's End Rescues Series

SOME SAVIORS CAN BREAK YOU

SOME REGRETS ARE FOREVER

SOME FEARS CAN CONTROL YOU

SOME LIES WILL HAUNT YOU

SOME QUESTIONS HAVE NO ANSWERS

SOME TRUTH CAN BE DISTORTED

SOME TRUST CAN BE REBUILT

SOME MISTAKES ARE UNFORGIVABLE

Candella Sisters' Heroes Series

LITTLE DOLLS

LITTLE HEARTS

LITTLE BALLERINA

Storybook Murders Series

NURSERY RHYME KILLER

FAIRYTALE KILLER

FABLE KILLER

IVORY'S FIGHT

PEARL'S FIGHT

LACEY'S FIGHT

OPAL'S FIGHT

Prey Security: Bravo Team Series

VICIOUS SCARS

RUTHLESS SCARS

BRUTAL SCARS

CRUEL SCARS

BURIED SCARS

WICKED SCARS

Prey Security: Athena Team Series

FIGHTING FOR SCARLETT

FIGHTING FOR LUCY

FIGHTING FOR CASSIDY

FIGHTING FOR ELLA

Prey Security: Charlie Team Series

DECEPTIVE LIES

SHADOWED LIES

TACTICAL LIES

VENGEFUL LIES

CORRUPTED LIES

TRAITOROUS LIES

Prey Security: Cyber Team Series

RESCUING NATHANIEL

RESCUING TOBIAS

RESCUING MICAH

RESCUING JOSIAH

Prey Security: Delta Team Series

PERFECT REVENGE

FATEFUL REVENGE

Christmas Romantic Suspense Series

THE DIAMOND STAR

CHRISTMAS HOSTAGE

CHRISTMAS CAPTIVE

CHRISTMAS VICTIM

YULETIDE PROTECTOR

YULETIDE GUARD

YULETIDE HERO

HOLIDAY GRIEF

HOLIDAY LOSS

HOLIDAY SORROW

Conquering Fear Series (Co-written with Amanda Siegrist)

DROWNING IN YOU

OUT OF THE DARKNESS

CLOSING IN

About the Author

USA Today bestselling author Jane Blythe writes action-packed romantic suspense and military romance featuring protective heroes and heroines who are survivors. One of Jane's most popular series includes Prey Security, part of Susan Stoker's OPERATION ALPHA world! Writing in that world alongside authors such as Janie Crouch and Riley Edwards has been a blast, and she looks forward to bringing more books to this genre, both within and outside of Stoker's world. When Jane isn't binge-reading she's counting down to Christmas and adding to her 200+ teddy bear collection!

To connect and keep up to date please visit any of the following

www.ingramcontent.com/pod-product-compliance
Lightning Source LLC
Chambersburg PA
CBHW050421260626
47156CB00003B/1108